Sam crossed t[...]
leaned over Libby, hands braced on the [...]
chair, leaning forward so she couldn't escape. He
surrounded her, hijacking her senses. Eyes as deeply
brown as the richest chocolate cake pinned her to
the seat. The fresh scent of his aftershave tickled her
nose and spun her back through time, to clandestine
embraces behind the dining hall, stolen kisses
beneath the dive raft, that last night when they had
spread a blanket beneath the moon and—

"I want to add a condition of my own."

This close, his voice seemed to vibrate through
her. She tightened her fingers on the clipboard but
refused to look away. Though when his gaze dropped
to her lips and his own mouth quirked, she had one
wild moment of wondering what kind of condition he
was going to impose.

Dear Reader,

My motto is, "I'm slow, but I always get where I'm going." This book is perfect proof.

The first seeds of Sam and Libby's story were planted back in 2001 when my husband and I took our three sons to a weekend family adventure camp. My visions of family bonding around a campfire with hot chocolate and s'mores were rudely hijacked by miserably cold nights, nonstop rain and some fellow campers who seemed to believe that the only reason the rest of us were there was to serve as backdrop for their nonstop family photos. I spent the bulk of the weekend faking a smile for the sake of my kids, while on the inside, I was far, far away, at a very different and much more enjoyable camp.

I wrote the first incarnation of this book later that year. It got some very encouraging attention, but it wasn't quite right yet.

Time went by. We added more kids to the family and I wrote other books, but Sam and Libby stayed with me. When it came time to look at their story again, it was like reconnecting with old friends—though really, is it fair that I am the only one who aged over the years?

I hope that your time with Sam and Libby is as enjoyable as it's been for me, and that they will lead you to visit my website at www.krisfletcher.com, or drop me a line—kris@krisfletcher.com. I promise to write back.

And I promise to be a lot faster at writing back than I was at writing the book.

Yours,

Kris Fletcher

A Better Father

KRIS FLETCHER

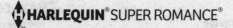

H HARLEQUIN® SUPER ROMANCE®

Recycling programs
for this product may
not exist in your area.

ISBN-13: 978-0-373-71845-0

A BETTER FATHER

Printed in U.S.A.

ABOUT THE AUTHOR

Kris Fletcher was first introduced to camping by the Girl Guides, who taught her how to tie a mean sheepshead knot, and later by her mother, who taught her how to TP a campsite. She refuses to discuss how and when these skills may have come in handy until the statute of limitations has expired. Kris grew up in southern Ontario, went to school in Nova Scotia, married a man from Maine and now lives in central New York. She shares her very messy home with her husband, an ever-changing number of their kids, and the occasional grand-hamster. Her greatest hope is that dust bunnies never develop intelligence.

Acknowledgments

I owe a giant debt of gratitude to about half the people on the planet, but especially to these folks:

The writers of *Galaxy Quest,* for that whole "Never give up. Never surrender!" thing.

The Central New York Romance Writers, for teaching me so much.

The Purples—Gayle Callen, Christine Wenger, Molly Compton Herwood and Carol Pontello Lombardo—for the brainstorming, the hand holding, the Retreats and the amazing friendship. And also for not posting those pictures to Facebook.

The ladies of the Hive and the Series Romance loop, for listening to me all these years without ever once voting me off the island.

Jessica Faust, agent extraordinaire, who has the patience of a saint and the red pen of an inquisitor. I have needed both of them over our years together, and she always, always comes through.

The wonderful ladies at Harlequin who had a hand in bringing this book to life—Kathleen Scheibling, who gave so generously of her time, insights and advocacy; Wanda Ottewell, who was willing to take a chance on a too-short manuscript by an unknown author; and Piya Campana, who has been the picture of grace and wisdom while I do the newbie dance.

And my husband, Larry, who doesn't understand this dream but loves me enough to help me chase it anyway. That's what I call hero material.

CHAPTER ONE

HIS NEW HOME.

Sam Catalano stood at the top of the hill outside the office of Camp Overlook, sparing a moment to drink in the sight that had lived in his memory for so long. Soaring pines and brilliant green maples. Red-roofed cabins circling larger brown activity buildings. The St. Lawrence River beckoned from the edge of the woods, sparkling into the horizon, a glittering blue line separating this little piece of Ontario from the States.

Unlike Sam's world—at least the way it had spun out of his control over the past few months—very little had changed at the camp in the dozen years since he last walked away. It was constant. Comforting. The last place where his life had been simple and secure. The perfect place to bring his son and start their new life.

He pulled his phone from his pocket and hit the speed dial for home, needing to hear Casey's voice again before he headed into a meeting he did not want to have. But before the call could go through he heard another sound—that of laughter bubbling out of the camp office. Slightly low, vaguely husky and achingly familiar, it brought every hair on his body to full attention.

Libby.

Oh, crap.

He'd thought he was ready to see her again. He'd done more mental prep for this meeting than he had when he played the final game in the Stanley Cup. Two minutes ago, he would have said, yeah, it would be awkward, but he wasn't about to let a little lovers' history come between him and his future.

That was before he heard her laugh. All of a sudden he was eighteen again, back here at camp, smack-dab in the middle of his first real relationship and so crazy with want that he'd actually talked himself into believing in things like forever and happily-ever-after.

He'd made Libby believe in them, too. And then he'd walked away from her.

"Hello?"

The sound of his sister's voice pulled him back to the moment, the phone, the call. Damn. Libby was messing with his mind already, and he hadn't even seen her yet.

Snap out of it, Catalano. Live the goal.

"Hey, Brynn, it's me. Just wanted to check on you and Casey before I head into the meeting. Everything okay?"

"Fine and dandy. Casey stacked four blocks by himself this morning, the damned dog made it outside every time he needed to go, and I was propositioned by both Hugh Jackman *and* George Clooney. Decisions, decisions."

"Someday my life will be as exciting as yours. Is Casey busy?"

"Right here. Um, you got a call from a social worker this morning. The one who has to do the home study."

The home study.

At the reminder of what his life had become—social workers and lawyers and court dates, all to ensure he maintained custody of his own son—his feet curled inside his shoes, digging into the soles in an instinctive fight-or-flight response. His gut contracted tight as a fist and he had to forcibly remind himself to breathe out before the black spots started dancing in front of his eyes.

"Thanks. Text me her number and I'll give her a call." He kept the words light so as not to worry Brynn. She did a good enough job of that on her own. "Let me talk to Casey."

"Hang on."

He heard Brynn telling Casey that Daddy wanted to talk to him—then the snuffling sound of the phone being passed over—then a rasping kind of noise that probably meant the phone was being dragged over clothing—then the wet breathing that made him grin every time.

"Da Da Da Da Da!"

And just like that, everything in him lit up and relaxed. His boy was safe and happy and his, still his. For the moment, at least, all was right in his world.

"Hey, squirt. Are you being a good boy for Auntie Brynn?"

"Box!"

"Yeah, I heard you were playing with your blocks. Did you knock them down and go boom?"

"Boom!"

"Way to go, bud. I have a rock for you." Sam scooped a gray-speckled stone from the side of the path, rubbing his thumb over the black band snaking across the surface. "From your new home."

"Home?"

The plaintive tone to the word made Sam's gut tighten. "Yeah, Casey. Daddy will be home tonight in time to put you to bed. I have to go now but I'll see you then, okay? Love you."

He ended the call, grinning at the picture he'd set as his phone's wallpaper, of Casey with his face painted like a pirate. His son. The child he never thought would be his, the reason he had turned his life inside out and upside down. The only goal that mattered anymore.

The reason he was about to face down the woman whose heart he had broken twelve years ago.

STANDING AT THE LONG TABLE that stretched across the back wall of the Camp Overlook office, Libby Kovak snapped the rings together on the last staff handbook binder and closed the cover with a contented sigh.

"Another check mark on your to-do list, Libby?" Myra MacLean, the camp owner, smiled as she peeked over the top of her low-riding glasses. Libby gave a quick nod and pushed the binder to join the others, lined up neatly in the middle of her center of operations.

"Other than the inevitable additions and shuffling, these are good to go."

"And you will handle those changes with your usual gracious efficiency, I am sure."

Libby pushed her hair behind her ear and laughed. "If you think I'm being gracious during the last-minute scrambles, then I should be picking up my award for Best Actress anytime now."

Myra chuckled softly before falling silent to look out the window. Libby's pulse did a hop-skip. Myra had been gazing out the window a lot the past few weeks. She'd also been laughing a lot less than usual, which was to be expected given her sister's recent diagnosis. It broke Libby's heart to see Myra hurting. She'd lost count of the times when she had walked back into the office after completing a chore on the grounds and found Myra on the phone, deep in conversations that were obviously ripping her apart, given the slowness of her responses and the way she jumped on Libby's entry.

"What is it they say about change?" Myra mused without turning from the window. "That it's the only constant in life?"

"Something like that."

Myra's nod seemed forced. "They always leave out the part about it not being easy."

Ah, damn. Things must be getting worse with Myra's sister. Having lost her own grandmother, her only family, just last year, Libby was all too familiar with the kind of pain and choices Myra must be facing.

"No," she agreed softly. "It's not easy. But somehow, we all make it through."

Myra turned back to her with a grateful smile. She gave the window another quick glance, then walked across the creaking floor to flip through the binder with something far closer to her usual spark. She scanned the pages, running her finger down the charts, tapping at the cartoons Libby had added to the material and smiling.

"I will never forget the day you showed up here and asked for a job," she said out of the blue. "There have been so many times since then when I realized that hiring you was probably the best thing I ever did for this camp."

Libby forced a smile she didn't really feel. Her own memories of that day were a lot less pleasant, not because of anything Myra had done, but because of the life twist that had forced her to go job hunting at a time when she had fully expected to be starting classes at university. The fact that she'd been nursing the rawest heartache of her life only strengthened her resolve to forget that day.

Ah, well. That was ancient history, and while, as Myra had said, it hadn't always been easy, Libby had indeed made it through. And she had landed in a pretty decent place, if she did say so herself.

She was no longer that terrified eighteen-year-old who had come begging for a job at the camp that had been the only constant in a life spent eluding landlords and bill collectors. She'd had a hell of a wake-up call, but once she had accepted the fact that the only person she could count on for protection was herself, things had turned around. Now she had her job. She had her degree, all the sweeter to her because it had taken so long. She had the town house where she and Gran had finally been able to settle, where they had planted a garden and painted the walls and where Gran had been able to let go of life secure in the knowledge that her Lillibet would be okay.

And through it all, she'd had the camp. No matter how crazy the rest of her life became, she had spent the past twelve years showing up to work at a place where the trees and the river and the rocks had been a constant reminder that if she just stood strong, even if she was scared, even if she was lonely, she would endure.

"Speaking of change," Myra began, and something in her tone made Libby look up sharply. Her heart began to thud in a yes-no, yes-no tattoo.

Because along with learning that she had only herself to rely on, Libby had learned long ago that it did no good to ignore facts out of sentiment. Her heart ached for Myra, and she would give anything to spare the woman the sorrow she was experiencing, but Libby had eyes and ears. She had seen and heard enough over the past few weeks to realize that Myra would probably be leaving the camp to care for her sister. Not right away. Hopefully not until the end of the summer, or even later than that. But Libby's gut told her that Myra was getting ready to go.

And whenever she thought of that—when she got past the way her breath seemed to seize whenever she tried to imagine the camp without Myra—she remembered the day a year ago, not long before Gran died, when Myra put an arm around her shoulder and squeezed and told her that when the time came, the camp would be hers.

Myra glanced out the window once more, then gave a

little gasp and squinted at the clock on the wall. "Goodness. It's eleven already."

Libby checked her watch. "Almost. Do you have a hot date then? There's nothing in the appointment book."

"Oh, dear." Myra's fingers fluttered to her lips and she checked the window once more. "He's early."

Libby had spent her childhood learning to read the signs that said problems were on the way, then honed that skill over years of working with kids whose main purpose at camp was pulling the most outrageous prank of the season. She could smell trouble while it was still jumping from one neuron to another, and the scent was growing stronger by the minute.

"*Who* is early?" Libby's palms grew clammy at the whiteness of Myra's cheeks. "Is something wrong?"

At that moment, footsteps sounded on the porch stairs. Myra turned from the window and sighed.

"Libby, dear, I'm afraid I owe you an apology."

SAM POCKETED THE PHONE and Casey's stone before mounting the steps to the office two at a time. He didn't know what kind of reception he was going to get when he walked across the kid-worn planks of the porch and stepped through the door, but whatever happened, he would undoubtedly deserve it.

With a quick check that his collar hadn't crept up on him, and a deep breath of the mild June air, he gave a sharp rap and opened the door.

He found himself in the middle of a knotty pine office plucked straight from his memory, right down to the unforgettable mustiness of ancient wood tickling his nose. If not for the computers perched on the pair of battered metal desks, he would have sworn the past twelve years had bypassed this room.

Two women occupied the space. Myra MacLean stood near the window with her hands clasped, a nervous smile lifting the wrinkles from her face. She always made him think of the great blue herons that nested along the banks of the river, with her long skinny legs and an even longer, skinnier neck. Three or four decades of eating Cosmo the cook's famously decadent chocolate whipped cream cake hadn't put an extra inch on Myra.

But it was the other woman who made him brace himself, the one standing in front of a table loaded with binders, shooting looks of incredulity from him to Myra.

Libby.

Her hair was a darker red than when he had first dared twist her curls around his fingers. Disbelief widened her hazel eyes and parted the lips he still tasted in occasional dreams. Sam had figured out long ago that Libby's lips were what God had in mind when He decided that people should have a mouth. The kind of lips that made a promise.

"Hello, Sam." Myra's grin faded and her cheeks flushed as she glanced toward the other woman. "I'm sure you remember Libby Kovak."

Like he could ever forget her.

Libby snapped that gorgeous mouth shut, slapping on a mask of politeness that was far too indifferent to fool anyone.

"Sam. Well." She hesitated, then moved slowly from behind the table and extended a work-worn hand. "Imagine seeing you again."

To tell the truth, he had imagined it. Many times.

He took her hand more by reflex than thought. Her palm slid into his, melded to him, and even while the rational section of his brain reminded him to *grip, shake, release,* another, more primitive part of him urged him to *grip, tug, pull closer.* This grown-up version of Libby was even more magnetic than the girl he'd left behind. Sure, he'd caught glimpses of the woman she'd become in the pictures on the camp's website, but in those shots she was usually buried in a sweatshirt, hugging a kid, or hiding behind a clipboard. In person she seemed…softer. More feminine, though maybe that was because she was wearing some floaty kind of skirt that swayed with her every movement.

In their years together, first as campers, then counselors, Sam had seen Libby in tight jeans, short shorts and a bathing suit that made his mouth go dry. On one memorable night he'd seen her clad in nothing but starlight. So how could he still be amazed at the way the simple swirl of a skirt turned her legs into an invitation?

"Libby." His voice stuck somewhere between his throat and his mouth, so he coughed and tried once more. "Hello, Libby. It's been a long time."

"Hasn't it, though?" She pulled her hand away from his.

Damn. He thought he'd let go about three or four heart-thuds ago.

"What brings you to our neck of the woods?" She shot an unreadable look at Myra as he lowered himself onto a battered orange plaid sofa. "Just passing through?"

Her *I hope* was unspoken but most definitely not unheard.

He glanced at Myra for the assist. This was her cue. But Myra avoided his gaze while seating herself at her desk, leaving him gripping the arms of the sofa and readying himself to say the words.

When Sam had first looked into the camp a couple months back, he'd been astonished to find Libby listed as the assistant director. That hadn't been her plan. Last time he saw her, she'd been days away from heading off to university, to teaching, to a life beyond the small tourist town of Comeback Cove. Even though he knew that life had thrown a curve into those plans, he had never imagined that the curve was really a circle leading her back to camp.

But once he got past the *hope she's okay* stage, it had been a no-brainer to imagine how she would react to his appearance. And once she learned the reason why he was back, well…

He shuddered.

Live the goal.

"Actually, I—"

"Oh, my goodness." Myra placed a hand to her heart, her tone far too bright to be spontaneous. "Where are my manners? Sam, would you like something to drink? Coffee, tea, hot cocoa?"

"I'm fine, thanks." Good as a drink might be, he doubted that Myra stocked whiskey in the camp office.

"Well." She folded her hands together again and risked another beseeching kind of look at Libby, who had perched on the edge of a chair as if ready to bolt at any moment. "Have you had a chance to look around, Sam? There have been many changes since you were last here."

Twelve years would do that to a place. A person, too, he thought, assessing the wary cast to Libby's posture.

"We have year-round programming now, thanks to Libby's efforts. We've added more cabins and expanded the dining hall and enclosed the craft building. Libby overhauled our curriculum and rewrote the staff and parent handbooks, and just last year she added an orienteering piece to the—"

"Myra," Libby cut in, "I'm sure Sam doesn't need to hear that. After all, he's just here for a trip down memory lane, right?" The look she leveled at him was half daring, half desperation. *"Right?"*

He could curse in six languages but as far as he could tell, none of the words were adequate for what he was feeling at that moment. He took a second to breathe, slowing his heart in preparation for the hell that was about to be unleashed, when Myra finally decided to do the right thing.

"Libby. Dear. Sam's not passing through," she said with a heavy sigh. "He's come to buy the camp."

CHAPTER TWO

YEARS AGO, Libby had gone on a space shuttle simulator ride at the fair. She would never forget the pressure during the mock liftoff, the sensation that there was an invisible elephant squashing her chest.

But compared to the impact of Myra's words, that make-believe elephant felt more like a Chihuahua. "You can't be serious." She could scarcely get the words out past the breath she was holding. The camp was hers. It was more than her job. It was her safety, her security, her *home*. It was hers, dammit, hers by virtue of the hours and the thought and the work and the love she'd poured into it over the years.

It was hers. It couldn't go to anyone else. Especially not Sam Catalano. She would not, could not let him take it away. Not from Myra, and not from her.

Sam leaned forward, earnestness practically radiating from his rounded shoulders and clasped hands. "I've never been more serious in my life."

It was a good thing she knew better than to be suckered in by his act.

"You. Really? As serious as you were about—" She clamped her mouth shut just in time, glancing at Myra. Libby had no illusions. Of course Myra knew that for one lusty summer a dozen years ago, Libby and Sam had been an item. The whole camp had known. But Myra didn't need to know that Sam had then gone on to break her heart.

Nor did she intend to give Sam the satisfaction of knowing how completely he'd turned her world inside out.

"Now, then." Myra's deceptively soft words cut into her mental meanderings. "Before you start to panic, Libby, dear—"

"I'm not panicking." Furious, lost and breathless, but absolutely not panicked. She'd dealt with worse than this in her thirty years. There would be no panic needed or allowed.

Murder, however—that was another option altogether.

Myra slipped lower in her chair and spread her hands across the stained and wrinkled desk blotter. "You know about the situation with my sister," she said softly. "Alzheimer's is…well. Esther is going to need a lot of care. Expensive care. She doesn't have many resources, and since I want to be with her anyway…" Her voice faltered. "I'm so sorry, Libby. I know this is a shock, and I meant to handle this better. It's…well…things change."

So this was why Myra had been so reflective and nostalgic. Libby remembered her fleeting thought that Myra was planning to hand the camp over to her and winced.

As if reading her mind, Myra looked at her with regret. "Please understand, Libby. I know I promised you that—"

"Don't even think of it." *And please, please don't let Sam know that he's just stolen yet another of my dreams.* She swallowed the tears clogging her throat and reached across the desk to squeeze Myra's hands, wishing she could ease their shaking with her touch. "I'm so sorry. Of course you have to do this. She's your family."

"She's all I have. Except you, of course."

Rule number one: no one else is ever going to put you first.

Myra blinked and forced a smile. "When Sam called to ask if I would ever consider selling, well, it seemed like an answer to my prayers."

Much as she wanted to believe the Almighty had listened to Myra, Libby had a hard time believing that prayers could ever be answered through a newly retired hockey player currently riding a wave of popularity due to a stint as a naughty rogue in a series of body-wash commercials.

Okay. Maybe she was overreacting. Maybe she was too raw to be rational at the moment. But Libby didn't trust Sam Catalano, and not just because he'd loved her and left her without a word of explanation. She had facts on her side. Widely reported facts, such as the string of starlets he'd dated and discarded during his NHL years. Or the undeniable fact that he had stuck with college just long enough to land a pro contract, turning his back on the degree she had fought so hard to obtain. Or the highly disconcerting fact that he'd walked away from his contract and his team the minute their season ended just last month, for nothing more substantial than *personal reasons.*

Not that she had learned any of this on her own, of course. Sam had grown up just a half hour from Comeback Cove, so the local papers always treated his every breath as headline news. But there was no denying that the man had a lousy history when it came to following through on his commitments.

Overreacting, hell. The more she thought about it, the more she felt she owed too much to Myra, had given too much of her own heart to the camp, to let someone with Sam's track record get his unreliable hands on it.

"Myra," she said softly, "I know this might feel like your only option right now, but are you sure there's no other way? Maybe if you waited a bit…"

"Prospective buyers don't grow on trees, Libby. Perhaps, if Esther didn't— Well, that's neither here nor there, is it?"

Libby closed her eyes and tried to focus all her energy as a shield against the hunk of testosterone lounging far too casually on the sofa. She longed to ask him to leave so she could talk to Myra in private. She needed a minute to breathe, to pull herself together, to quell the little voice shouting *Not fair!* and focus on saving the situation.

On the other hand, what could she lose by letting him hear her concerns? The situation couldn't possibly get any worse.

"Myra, I have to be honest. You've always said Overlook is special because everyone involved is so committed to it. Do you think that's going to stay the same with an owner who is probably planning to be here part-time, if that?"

She felt like a heel, adding to Myra's worries, but the woman needed to have all the facts before she could make an informed decision.

A frown creased Myra's forehead, but Sam was the one who spoke.

"Not part-time," he said. "Full-time. No more hockey, no more commercials, no more publicity except for charity work. As much as possible, I'm going to be Joe Average."

It must have been the trace of regret in his voice that made it impossible to believe him. Libby couldn't stop herself. She snorted.

Sam gave her a hard glance. "What?"

"Come on, Sam. Do you honestly expect anyone with half a brain to believe you can walk away from the money and the fans and the endorsement deals to live in the boonies and run a camp?"

He opened his mouth, but she rushed on before he could speak. "No. Wait. Wrong question. I do believe you can do that. After all, you've already taken the first step." She glared at him through narrowed eyes. "But for how long?"

Myra uttered a soft, "Oh, my."

"I'm here for good."

"Really."

"Yes."

No explanation. No justification. No discussion.

And there was no way she was buying it.

"Your actions have been pretty well documented around here, Sam. When you walked away from your team with no explanation, well, you were the top news for a week." She ran clammy hands over the gauzy folds of her elastic-waisted Emergency Bloat skirt and cursed whatever hand of fate that had delivered Sam Catalano and PMS on the same day. "I don't recall hearing anything that lets me believe you have what it takes to make a lasting commitment."

Myra's lips pursed. So she hadn't been aware of Sam's track record. But being the fair-to-a-fault woman she was, she immediately turned to Sam.

"Is there something I should know?" she asked quietly.

Libby held her breath.

The sudden lines around Sam's mouth and the almost-silent tap of his finger against the arm of his chair were the only indicators of whatever internal debate he might be conducting. When he nodded, it was more of a jerk than an acknowledgment.

"Yes. I'll explain." He focused on Myra. "To you. And only you."

Heat flashed through Libby, pulling her out of her chair. "Hang on. This was my question. My concern."

"But it's not your property," he said, and the impact of his quietly even words almost pushed her back down. As it was, she had to clamp her mouth tight to keep him from seeing precisely how wrong he was. He might have the money to buy the camp, but it belonged to *her*.

"Libby." Myra's hands fluttered through the air like runaway thoughts before she clasped them together and set them in her lap. She closed her eyes for a moment, sighed, then looked Libby in the eye.

"This isn't how I would prefer to handle this," she said. "You know that you are much more than an employee."

Libby forced herself to nod.

"But if this is truly something I should know, and if this is the only way Sam will disclose the information..."

"Yes." Sam stood to face Libby. He looked past her—out the window, she presumed, to the river that was always there, always wearing down the rocks—then blinked and made her the center of his focus once again.

"Yes," he said again, gentler this time, almost regretfully, but there was no mistaking the resolve beneath the word. "This is strictly between us."

By "us," Libby knew he did not mean him and her.

"Fine." She grabbed her clipboard and headed for the door. "I guess I'll step outside. Because when *I* start something, I'm willing to do whatever is needed to see it through."

TEN MINUTES LATER, Sam crossed his arms and sat back in his chair. "So there you have it."

"Oh, Sam. I'm so sorry. Although..."

"Let me guess. You can't understand why I don't want Libby to find out." He shoved his hand into his pocket and rubbed Casey's stone between his fingers. "You know there's history between us."

She didn't ask him to expand. Not out loud. The way she folded her hands in her lap and kept her gaze steady on him was question enough.

"Things didn't end well," he said at last. "All my fault. But I feel... I think she's had enough to absorb for one day. I don't want to, you know. Rub things in her face."

"You mean, because you have a child and she doesn't? You do realize that Libby spends a good deal of her life tending to other people's children."

He grinned at her undeniable point. "But it's more than that in this case. She's sunk her life into this place. Having me waltz in and take it over has to hurt. She doesn't need to know that I'm doing it because I'm building a new life with my kid, especially since she's probably out there writing her letter of resignation as we speak."

"Fair enough." Myra considered him for a moment, then nodded and leaned back in her chair. "We haven't discussed her role thus far, but to be blunt, Libby is the sole reason this camp is doing as well as it is. In fact, you're going to need her to stay on if you want to stay in compliance with our policies this summer."

He couldn't keep the laughter inside. "You're joking, right?"

"No, I'm not. Because, of the two of you, she is the one with the education and experience to meet the guidelines for the position of camp director. She might not be happy with you, Sam, but she loves this camp too much to do anything that would be detrimental to its continued operation."

"Whoa. Time-out." He made a T with his hands, then leaned forward. "Are you saying I need to keep her on for the whole summer?"

"No, not necessarily. If you can find someone else with twenty-four weeks of supervisory experience and an appropriate degree, who isn't already committed to another camp, well, then, of course you could let her go with a generous severance package. But considering it's already June, I would say you don't have much hope of that."

"I'm not trying to get rid of her." At least, not officially. "Heck, she's been here this long, she's earned the right to stay as long as she wants. But…" His words trailed away as he imagined juggling a new job, a new role as single parent, a custody suit and Libby, all at the same time.

Live the goal.

Myra's voice cut through his sudden disorientation. "I know it will be awkward, what with your history and all. But the time will pass faster than you realize. Once camp ends and the facilities are used for retreats and such, well, even you are qualified to run those."

"Gee, thanks."

"But I want your word that Libby will have a job here as long as she wants one."

Myra was absolutely right to look out for Libby's best interests. But it was obvious from the reception he'd received that Libby bore him even less goodwill than he'd anticipated. Totally deserved. Totally understandable. Totally terrifying.

"Myra, I'm not sure—"

"Your word, Samuel."

Ah, crap. She'd played the Samuel card. He sighed, knowing from long-repressed experience that once she started in with the full names, there'd be no backing down. He would just have to find a way to skate around this.

Did he want Libby to stay? No. He was juggling enough already without adding a resentful assistant to the mix. But he needed to play this carefully, to find a way to either get back in her semigood graces or have her decide on her own to leave before life could become any more complicated.

At the moment, though, he needed to move forward with his deal.

"You have my word." He extended his hand. Her gaze skittered from his palm to his face, no doubt taking his measure. He refused to blush or look away. At last she accepted his offer with a quick shake.

"Fine, then," she said. "Be a dear and call Libby in, would you, please?"

There was no logical reason why those simple words should have him worrying again, but he'd learned long ago that intuition was often a great substitute for logic. As he walked to the door and called to Libby, he did a quick mental run-through of everything he had said or done since entering the office. Nothing made him want to slap himself on the forehead, so he was probably fine.

Of course, if Myra was factoring the kid he used to be into the equation, he was doomed.

LIBBY KEPT HER HEAD HIGH and nodded to Sam as she entered the office. He answered with a mock bow. Cute.

"Sam, you left the door open. Please close it, and, Libby, sit down, dear." Myra waved toward the desk chair as if Libby hadn't sat there every working day for the past twelve years.

She perched on the edge of the seat so she was facing only Myra. "There's something I need to know," she said before Myra could begin. "I understand your position. You have to sell. But is this a done deal, or is there time to make any modifications to the agreement?"

Myra's chair creaked as she leaned back and gave Libby the shrewd look that she knew meant they were probably thinking along similar lines.

"That's interesting. We were just discussing a further condition of the sale."

"So changes can still be made." Libby gave a silent cheer. Maybe, just maybe, she could save the camp. Saving her sanity would be an added bonus.

Myra turned toward Sam, who returned her gaze for a second before transferring his attention to Libby.

"What did you have in mind?"

He sounded bored. Good. Unless he'd changed more than most humans do in a dozen years, that "couldn't care less" attitude meant he was worried.

"I think—" she began, but Myra cut her off with a raised forefinger.

"I'm so sorry, dear, but might I go first? There's something I'd like to ask of you."

"Of course. Anything." Libby grasped a handful of skirt fabric on her thigh and gave it an impatient squeeze.

"I think that the sooner I can move on, the better it will be for everyone. Nothing will be served by me doddering around here like the ghost of summers past, confusing everyone as to who is now in charge."

Libby's head swam as the implications of the sale came clear. Not only was she losing the camp, she was losing Myra. This time she didn't care if Sam saw the tears pooling in her eyes.

"It won't be right without you," she said. "I can't imagine… I don't want to think about it without you."

"I will miss you. The whole camp, of course, but especially you and…" Myra's voice faltered and she glanced out the window again. Not in the direction of the river this time, but down the hill. Toward the dining hall.

After a second she shook her head, blinked a couple of times and gave Libby a very unsteady smile. "Well. We'll adjust. Both of us. We're strong old broads, aren't we?"

"Better than life has dealt us," Libby answered, paraphrasing words Myra had said to her more than once. Myra laughed, and Libby forced herself to join in, reminding herself that moments like this would soon be gone.

An odd sound from the side of the room, something between a cough and a choke, dragged her attention back to Sam. She turned instinctively in his direction and caught him staring at her with an expression that could only be described as disbelief. Almost as if he'd seen a ghost.

As soon as she caught his eye he looked away and shook his head. A moment later he was leaning forward, focused on Myra once more. She must have felt his attention because she sighed, then returned to business.

"I want the transition to be as smooth as possible. For everyone," Myra added with a nod toward Sam. "And, Libby, dear, the fact is that the camp needs someone with your qualifications to operate by the book. So it would do my heart good if you could see your way clear to stay on here, at least through the summer."

Stay? With *him?* Dear heavens, had Myra taken complete leave of her senses? If she thought for one minute that Libby could exist anywhere in the same town—no, the same province—as the man in the corner, well, she—

Oh.

Her earlier, sketchy thoughts about adding a condition to the sale took on a clearer, tighter focus. She could work with this. She could *use* this.

"Yes," she said to Myra. "Of course I'll stay through the summer. For you." She took a deep breath, buying herself time. "But I do have a couple of requests of my own."

Myra cocked an eyebrow. Over in the corner, Sam grabbed the arms of the sofa. Bracing himself, no doubt.

Libby grabbed the clipboard and looked over the notes she'd jotted during her time of exile, mentally modifying them beyond the scribbled list of impossible wishes that had filled her mind while she waited.

"I would strongly suggest that you add two conditions to the sale. First, as you have said yourself, it's vital for the owner to be a part of the camp. Since Sam already plans to be here full-time, it should be easy for him to participate fully in the program. I recommend that, as a condition of the sale, he must take on the job of a regular staff member for this summer, acting as a counselor while I teach him everything I can."

Myra tapped her pencil on the blotter. Sam glowered. "What are you pulling, Libby?"

"Pulling? Not a thing. I simply think that you've been gone for a long time, and there have been many changes since you were last here. Rather than jump in and try to learn all of them right away, it will be easier for you to understand the new systems if you are a counselor, working within the program." She pretended to check her notes, then looked up with a broad smile. "Of course you would be held to the same standards of conduct as any other staff. Live in the cabins, time off according to the schedule, drug testing, latrine duty and so on."

A muscle twitched in his cheek. "And if I don't obey all the staff rules, who will punish me? You?"

Well, if he was looking for a volunteer...

Rather than answer him directly, she appealed to Myra. "You have always followed the same rules as the counselors during the summer sessions, haven't you?"

A slight grimace played around the older woman's mouth. "Well, I must confess it's been a long time since I've slept in the cabins. But yes, I've done my share of latrine duty and dishes and craft house cleanup over the summers. I wouldn't have thought of suggesting it, but I believe it's a good idea. Working side by side with your staff lends a closeness and understanding that can't be duplicated."

"Fine." The scowl on Sam's face told Libby that *fine* wasn't his true sentiment. "I wasn't planning to spend the summer holed up in the office anyway, but if you think I need to lead a group, fine. I'll do it."

Libby looked down at her clipboard, focusing on the sunlight glinting off the silver clasp to keep Sam from seeing her grin. Mr. NHL was in for the workout of his life. By the time she finished with him, he'd be crawling back to the ice.

"But I'm living in the house," he continued, folding his arms across his chest. "Personal reasons."

And what was that supposed to mean? She'd never heard anything about him getting married, and a fast peek at his ring finger showed it to be empty. Did he have a honey he planned to bring along with him? She sucked in a hard breath. He wouldn't. He couldn't. That would never do.

"Does this personal reason have a name?"

He stared at her as if she were a puzzle he needed to put together, but wasn't sure where to start. Then his eyes lit up in a way that made her squirm with unease. A smile tugged at one corner of his mouth.

"Yes, actually." He all but purred the words. "A very nice name."

Oh, *crap.* He was planning to install a woman in his house.

Not that she cared. Sam Catalano had ceased to be anything but a heartbreaking memory the day she called him in tears to tell him her world had just fallen apart, and he hung up on her. To this day, the sound of a dial tone could still make her stomach twist. If some other woman was idiot enough to want Sam, she was more than welcome to him.

No, Libby's concern was solely for the camp.

"Are you married?"

His lips thinned. "No."

She clutched her clipboard. "Well, if this *personal reason* with the very nice name happens to be female, and you're not married, I strongly suggest you rethink your plan. Parents can be very particular if they think their kids are being exposed to something they consider unwholesome."

Over in the corner, Myra coughed. Sam's smile widened.

"Oh, don't worry," he said with far too much glee to trust. "I know all about what parents want for their kids."

Right. And she would be the one who ended up fielding

the phone calls from irate parents when Sam's so-called knowledge backfired.

"You said you had two suggestions." Sam's too-casual words cut into her indignation before it could reach full strength. "What's the other?"

She took her time in answering. "Well. It's just a formality, really. Shouldn't be a problem for you, since you've already eased Myra's mind about your history of walking away from things."

The sofa protested as he pushed upright. "Hey—"

She swiveled to face Myra, who watched their interplay with an expression somewhere between bafflement and amusement. "In all honesty, I still have concerns about Sam's plans for the camp."

"Ha. Thanks for stating the obvious, Lib."

She ignored him and carried on. "I would hate to see Overlook become just another plaything for him to use and discard—"

"Hey!"

"—or for him to ruin its reputation so it can become a money-losing tax shelter."

"Dammit, Libby, that's not—"

"I'm speaking now, thank you, Sam."

Guilt pricked at her heart when she saw the way Myra had twisted her fingers together. She gentled her voice and leaned forward. "Make him promise that he will continue to own it for at least three—no, five years. If he decides to give it up for any reason, it goes back to you. Automatically. No questions asked. And," she added, thoughts of poor Esther in her mind, "you don't have to repay any of the money."

Pink spots bloomed in Myra's cheeks. "That hardly seems fair," she said. "Once it's sold, it should be out of my hands. It doesn't seem right that I should—"

"No. Wait." Sam rose from the depths of the sofa with

a smoothness that reminded Libby with a start that even though he had retired, he was indeed still an athlete.

He crossed the room in two long strides and leaned over her, hands braced on the arms of her chair, leaning forward so she couldn't escape. He surrounded her, hijacking her senses. Eyes as deeply brown as the richest chocolate cake pinned her to the seat. The fresh scent of his aftershave tickled her nose and spun her back through time, to clandestine embraces behind the dining hall, stolen kisses beneath the dive raft, that last night when they had spread a blanket beneath the moon and—

"I want to add a condition of my own."

This close, his voice seemed to vibrate through her. She tightened her fingers on the clipboard but refused to look away. Though, when his gaze dropped to her lips and his own mouth quirked, she had one wild moment of wondering what kind of condition he was going to impose.

"Here's the deal." His words might have been directed at Myra, but his eyes never flickered away from her. "I *will* be here for at least five years. And I *will* take on the duties of a counselor for the summer. But I'm not the only one who needs to put her money where her mouth is, so to speak."

He leaned closer. He seemed to be searching her face, cataloging her every feature. Comparing her to the girl she used to be? Hunting for some weakness? If so, he was out of luck. She knew him too well. There was no way he could pull the wool over her eyes.

"Oh, for heaven's sake, Samuel, you're not playing hockey any longer. Must you loom over my assistant like some hulking thing?"

Myra's wry words brought an abrupt end to whatever game Sam was playing. He straightened, slowly and deliberately, as if he was calculating his actions to maximize the play of his muscles beneath his polo shirt.

Really. Yes, the man had great shoulders, and of course he moved with a quick grace that proved why he'd been dubbed The Cat. But did he have to put it on display?

"Libby says she'll stay through the summer as a favor to you, Myra. I believe she intends to do that. After all, she's taken the first step," he said, echoing the words she'd tossed at him just a few minutes earlier. "Libby, call me psychic, but I have this feeling you and I aren't always going to see eye to eye over the next few months."

From the corner of her eye, Libby saw Myra cover her grin with her hand.

"There might come a point when you decide you've had enough. When, for reasons I can't begin to imagine, you might decide you want to make me suffer. There are plenty of ways you could do that." He gave his pocket a quick pat before resuming his pacing. "The easiest, of course, would be for you to leave without notice."

Libby jumped from her chair, anger pulling her muscles tight. "You might find it easy to break a promise, Catalano, but I don't. I told Myra I would stay and that's exactly what I will do."

"Good." He didn't even bat an eye, which only amplified her temper. "Because if you, Libby, cooperate and work for me for the entire summer, then—well—you know that pavilion you always talked about? The one that's still not here?"

It took her a moment and another fast trip down memory lane to understand his meaning. When she got it, she could only stare at him through suspicious eyes.

"What about it?"

His smile made her think of an alligator right before it lunged.

"You see, Myra," he said as he swung back in her direction, "back when we were kids, Libby always said that the one thing this camp really needed was a waterfront pavilion.

Just down a bit from the swimming area, in that little inlet. Do you still like to hang out at the inlet, Libby?"

Her cheeks were probably flaming redder than a sugar maple in fall, but she would not let him get to her with his reference to the sheltered spot where they used to hide away and grab some privacy. And, not incidentally, each other.

Luckily, Myra jumped in before Libby could say anything she would regret as much as she now regretted the things that had happened at the inlet.

"You want to put a pavilion down there? Libby, all these years and you've never mentioned that. What a splendid idea."

"Isn't it, though?" Sam practically overflowed with enthusiasm. "It's something that's stuck with me. Can't you just picture it? A log structure, open to the water on one side and the forest on the other…maybe a fireplace made from local stone…space for picnic tables or chairs so we could have meetings or whatever down there… It would be perfect. Right down to the brass plaque on the front that says In Honor of Myra MacLean."

"Oh." Myra pressed her fingers to her lips and blinked. "Oh, my. Libby…Sam. This is too much."

Libby had to hand it to him. He was smooth. He'd just set himself up to be Mr. All-Star in Myra's books forever.

Did she buy the act? Not for a minute.

"Well. Sam. That's a lovely gesture. But let's say something happens. You push me too far and I decide I'm going, promise or no promise. What happens to the pavilion?"

"The minute you walk away, construction stops. Like that. No matter how close it is to being done." His voice dropped. "A permanent reminder of what might have been."

Oh, he was up to something. Of that she had no doubt. But she had given her word. And the longer she was here at camp, the easier it would be to make sure Sam didn't destroy the place before he threw in the towel the way she knew he would.

"Fine." She gave him a tight nod. "I'm in."

Even as she said it, she made a promise to herself: at the end of the summer, she would still be here. But Sam Catalano would be long gone.

CHAPTER THREE

THE REST OF SAM'S DAY passed in enough of a blur that he was able to put Libby out of his mind.

But not without serious effort.

After leaving the camp, he raced into town to conduct interviews with the three final candidates for the position of Casey's child-care provider. He mulled the choices while piloting his rental car back to the airport in Ottawa, called his favorite to make his offer during his layover in Toronto and got her affirmative answer when he landed in Windsor.

Two hours later he was sitting on his bed in the home he had recently sold, laptop propped on the mattress, smiling as he watched Casey laugh and wave at his cousins via video cam.

"Hey, Casey!" Ten-year-old Jody stuck her fingers in the corners of her mouth, stretched it wide and stuck her tongue out while crossing her eyes. Not to be outdone, her little brother, Andy, held his hands to his ears and flapped them, prompting Casey to dissolve into deep belly laughs.

Sam had been taking advantage of Casey's biweekly video call with his cousins to go over some of the never-ending paperwork that accompanied a change of home and jobs, but he found he couldn't tear his eyes away from his son. God, he loved it when Casey laughed. The way his eyes wrinkled, the way his double chin quivered, the slight hitch in the laugh as he chortled to an end.

He'd missed so much in Casey's first year of life. Sure,

he'd visited whenever he could, but it hadn't been enough. Never enough. He hadn't expected to leave hockey for a few years yet, had never thought he'd end up doing the single-parent thing, and God knew he would never have asked for things to end the way they had with Casey's mother. But he wasn't going to pretend that a part of him didn't light up every time he remembered that his kid would be waiting for him at the end of every day.

There was no way in hell he was going to let anyone steal that light away from him.

His phone chirped, pulling his focus back to business. It was a text from Casey's aunt Sharon, mother of the cousins currently on the screen and the Woman Most Likely to Threaten Sam's Existence. How could someone so frickin' misguided and pigheaded and just plain wrong have produced such great kids?

I'll be sending the kids to bed in a minute and then I will talk to Casey. I'd appreciate it if you weren't hovering in the background the whole time.

Oh, for the love of...

He's 18 months. Not leaving him alone.

Is your sister there?

Sam didn't dare curse out loud, not with Casey in the room and the cousins able to hear everything, but his thoughts were certainly tinted blue as he moved his papers, rolled off the bed, quickstepped over the dog and called for Brynn.

"You bellowed, big brother?" Brynn was already in her pink elephant pajamas—a day on Casey duty would do that to a person—but her smile was serene as she entered the room. Though as he showed her the texts from Sharon, the smile took a fast dive south.

"What is her problem?" Brynn's whisper was fierce as she handed back the phone. "I can't tell you how glad I'll be when this custody suit is behind us and we don't have to deal with her again. September can't get here fast enough."

"She'll always be his aunt. She's always going to want to see him."

"But will we always have to be so damned accommodating?" She raised a hand before he could answer. "I know, I know. It's what's best for Casey, not what's best for everyone else. I get it."

And she did. Brynn had put her life on hold for the past few months to help him with Casey while he was flying around the country rearranging his own existence. He hated to ask more of her, especially when it meant pulling her from her dearly earned downtime, but he did anyway.

"You'll hang with him for a few minutes while Sharon talks to him?"

Brynn rolled her eyes. "I'll do it."

"Thanks." He gave her a quick squeeze around the shoulders. "You're the best."

"And don't you forget it," she mumbled as she went to sit beside Casey.

"Watch the dog," he warned. "He'll go for the bed the minute I'm out of sight."

"Stay down, Finnegan," she said, but there was no strength behind the words. Sam groaned inside. Dog dander on the pillow was only slightly less disruptive to his sleep than a conversation with Sharon. And lucky him— he'd probably get to experience both in one night.

Sam leaned against the wall and sent another text to Sharon.

Brynn is in place. But I need to update you on some things so please stay on the line after you say goodbye to Casey.

Send me an email.

   He rolled his eyes.

This will be faster for both of us.

Email.

Sharon, you'll have questions. If you want answers, you'll stay on. This is a limited-time offer.

   Waiting…waiting…

Fine.

   He shoved the phone in his pocket and leaned back against the wall. Two women giving him grief in one day was about five too many. Though at least Libby had cause.
   Libby. Oh, God.
   Alone in the hall, surrounded by packing boxes, he remembered the moment in the office when she let down her guard and laughed with Myra over a private joke. Her hurt and anger had slipped away and for a second she had looked happy. Relaxed. Confident.
   And so much like Casey's mother that he'd had a hard time breathing.
   It had passed quickly. So fast, in fact, that he could almost convince himself it had been nothing more than a trick of the light. When he'd cornered her in the chair and really looked at her, he'd taken note of all the ways they were different—Libby's eyes were darker, Robin's nose had been

wider, Libby's mouth was fuller—and assured himself that the resemblance wasn't nearly as strong as he'd thought.

But damn, he hoped it didn't happen again. It left him unsettled in too many ways, raised too many questions that he was pretty sure would have no good answer.

"Hey, you. Lunkhead." Brynn elbowed him in the ribs, her arms full of a squirming, giggling toddler with a smooth gray rock in his hand. "I'll wrestle this guy into his pajamas. Her Majesty awaits."

Live the goal, he reminded himself, then returned to the bedroom feeling as though he should be strapping on a helmet and pads for protection against the blows he was about to take.

"Hello, Sharon." He lifted the laptop to his desk and settled himself in his softly squeaking leather chair, adjusting the screen to allow him to see the carefully coiffed blonde. "It sounds like Andy and Jody are excited about the start of summer vacation."

"Their time talking to Casey is supposed to be private."

For the love of… He bit back the curses pushing to be blurted out. Getting into a war of words with Sharon sure would feel good, but even he knew it wasn't justified in the long run. "Fine. Sorry. I'll cut right to it, then. Casey and I will be moving in a couple of weeks. Well, I'll go first to get things ready, then Brynn will bring him a few days later. I'll email you our new contact info, but I thought you might have questions."

"Moving?" For a moment Sharon seemed too flustered to speak, for which Sam gave thanks. "But he just— You just— Where?"

"I bought a camp." He stretched his legs, trying to ease the stiffness that lingered after too many hours in meetings and not enough time moving. "The one I used to go to when I was a kid. It's in the Thousand Islands, outside a place

called Comeback Cove. A bit closer to you than we are now."
Not that he thought she might be appeased by that fact.

Sure enough, Sharon's reaction was about as warm as
he'd expected.

"Are you insane? After all the changes that child has been
through in the past six months, all the upsets and reloca-
tions on top of losing his mother, and now you're going to
drag him someplace new again?"

He could remind her that it wasn't his fault Robin had
died. He could easily remind her that he had been grateful
to leave Casey with her in those first weeks after Robin's
death, and that Casey could have stayed longer if she hadn't
decided to sue him for custody. But Sharon had this habit
of developing a hearing problem when he tried to explain
himself, so he simply said, as mildly as he could fake, "This
is the last change. This will be home."

Sharon's bitter laugh told him she didn't believe him any
more than Libby had. And he used to be so convincing.

"It's a great place." Maybe he could skate around her
scorn by talking up the camp. "It's right on the St. Lawrence. There's forests and fields, and all the usual camp
activities. Most of the year it's used as a retreat center, but
six weeks every summer it's just for kids. He'll grow up
exploring the woods and playing in the river and learning
how to do archery and—"

"Archery? You're going to hand a bow and arrow over
to a toddler?"

"Of course not. I—"

"And what's going to happen when he's off exploring
and he wanders onto the archery field? You seriously think
a bunch of ten- or twelve-year-olds will stop to look for a
tiny little boy before they—"

Her voice broke. He watched her press a hand to her
mouth and breathe deeply, the way he was sure she'd read

about in some women's magazine, and then she continued.
"As for the river, and the forest and—dear God, are there
bears up there? If anything should happen to him…"

She finally lost her battle with her tears. Sam tried to be
sympathetic. Casey was Sharon's last link to Robin, the sister she'd lost so unexpectedly. He knew why she was desperate to hang on tight to the child. He really did.

But Casey was his.

While Robin found out she was pregnant, he had understood why she turned down his offer of marriage and
chose to move back to Nova Scotia, near her sister, even if
he didn't like it. He was on the road so much it had made
sense. And after Casey's birth, Robin had given their child
so much love and stability and security that Sam knew there
was no way he could upset things. If she hadn't died they
would have continued on that way until he retired.

But she *had* died. And Casey *was* his. And even though
Sharon had been Casey's child-care provider for most of
his life, even though she had begged Sam to let Casey stay
with her while he finished the season and made arrangements for his abrupt retirement, he had never intended for
his son to be with her permanently.

Sharon had had other ideas.

"I will take care of him," he said as soon as he thought
Sharon had regained enough control to listen to him. "You
know I don't want anything to happen to him any more
than you do."

"What are you planning to do there, Sam? Are you going
to spend your days walking the woods with him?"

"Of course not. I did some interviews today and hired a
woman with great references and experience to look after
him while I'm working."

"And what qualifies her to look after him? What can she
give him that I can't?"

Well, for one thing, she understood that a kid should be with his parent.

He knew that if he answered her question, he would be treated to a long list of reasons why Casey should live with her, including a two-parent home, cousins who were like siblings and no need for hired child-care providers. For one thing, he'd heard it all so many times that he could recite it from memory, like the chorus of a song he hated but heard too often to avoid.

More than that, though, was the fact that deep down, part of him couldn't help but wonder if she had a point. That maybe leaving Casey with her would have been the right thing to do. That maybe, no matter how much he loved and wanted his child, he really had made things harder for Casey by taking him away from the aunt and cousins who had been a more constant part of his little life than Sam himself had been until recently.

No. He couldn't start down that road. He had enough legitimate fears and doubts without adding to them.

"I already contacted the folks doing the home study and explained the situation. They'll come to the camp in August. Casey and I will be settled in by then, but there will still be plenty of time for you and your lawyer to see the report before the hearing."

Sharon sniffed. "I don't like this. It's too fast."

"Sorry, Sharon. I can't do anything to change the calendar. The summer sessions start at the end of the month, and I need to be moved in and ready to work before then."

"I don't see how this can be good for him. It's too much, too soon. Robin always said that once you got an idea in your head there was no stopping you, and now I see what she meant. It's all about what you need, isn't it, Sam?"

His toes curled into his sneakers. "It's about what Casey needs," he snapped, and hoped to hell he was telling the

truth. That being with him really was what was best for
his son. That he wasn't being a selfish bastard like his own
father, doing what he wanted and letting others pay the
consequences.

Stop the doubts and move on, Catalano.

"Watch for my email with the address," he said tightly.
And then, because he really did like her kids, he added,
"Give Andy and Jody a hug from me."

He ended the call before she could answer and leaned
against the back of his chair, blowing out his frustration.
His lawyer said there was no way Sharon could win custody, that her suit was pure desperation and no judge would
take a child away from a loving, competent biological parent. But he worried anyway.

And no amount of positive self-talk could make him stop
wondering how he was supposed to go on if he lost his son.

AFTER STUMBLING THROUGH the remainder of the day, preparing for camp, preparing for Myra to leave and preparing to
blot Sam from her mind until absolutely necessary, Libby
left work on time for the first time in forever. At last she
sat alone on the tiny back deck of the town house she had
shared with Gran. The slowly setting sun kissed her with
warmth. Soothing instrumental music sang through the
open windows. She had an extralarge glass of white wine by
her hand, and her laptop propped open on the wrought iron
table. With a hearty sip of liquid fortification, she opened
Google and typed in her search: *how to write a résumé.*

She had said she would stay for the summer and she
would. She owed it to Myra. She owed it to the camp. But
as the day went on, a lifetime of self-preservation instincts
had kicked in. She had no doubt whatsoever that Sam would
walk away. What she couldn't predict was the timing. It was

not out of the realm of possibility that she could find herself out of a job at the end of summer.

Rule number one in Libby's book of survival: take care of yourself. No one else is ever going to put you first.

If she'd ever doubted that truth, today's events had proven it with gift-wrapped vengeance. Not that she could blame Myra. Not really. But still…

It hurt.

A long sip of Riesling washed down the lump in her throat and sweetened the moistness from her eyes. This was her fault. Not Myra's, though she felt kind of…fragile… whenever she considered the way Myra had gone back on her promise. Not that she'd had any choice. Myra was in a lousy position, and Libby couldn't blame her, not in good conscience.

No, the fault was hers and hers alone. She'd knowingly violated rule number two. She had let herself be happy.

And just like that, her happiness had been snatched away.

She stared blankly at the screen as weariness washed through her. She should be used to this by now. God knew she'd survived worse. From the time her mother died when she was three, through the years when Gran did her best but still couldn't stay ahead of the wolves, right through to the double whammy of Gran losing the tuition money and Sam's slam-bam-thank-you-ma'am abandonment. She'd lived through all of those and come out stronger, tougher, fiercely determined to create the life she knew she wanted.

And she had done it. The diploma hanging on the wall, the town house that had been her same address for years now, both financed by the job she had found and made her own—all of these were proof positive that she knew how to work her way through whatever that bitch Fate decided to throw at her next. That she was indeed more than life had dealt her.

But how many times could one woman pull herself back up by her bootstraps before those straps finally broke?

Then she remembered the way Sam had loomed over her while she sat in her chair, so powerful, so damned sure of himself, and fresh anger gave her the boost she needed to push the weariness aside. She might have been knocked down again but she would be damned if she'd let her bootstraps break while Sam was watching. She could do this. She would write a kick-ass résumé and find a new job and bide her time. Save her money. And when he finally tired of his new toy—as she knew he would—she would be ready. The minute the camp reverted to Myra, Libby would be there, ready to turn over her life savings and mortgage her soul to make sure it became hers. No one was going to come between her and—

A child's excited shout cut through her thoughts. It seemed her neighbors were also taking advantage of the cool of the coming night. A moment later, a toy airplane sailed over the row of spirea shrubs that divided her backyard from the one next door, landing in the middle of her lawn.

"Mommy! My plane go Libby's!"

Grateful for the excuse to leave her private pity party, Libby left the shade of the deck for the fading sun of the lawn. She grabbed the plane off the grass—oops, time to cut it again—just as three-year-old Aidan Cooper squeezed through one of the many gaps in the row of bushes. Right behind him came his mother, Dani, who barely had to turn sideways to follow her son's path.

"Hey, buddy." Libby waved the plane in the air. "Are you looking for this?"

"Mine!" Aidan crossed the lawn in a mix of hops, runs and almost cartwheels. Libby held the plane just out of his reach and laughed as he danced around her.

"I don't know, Aidan. It's a really nice plane. I might want to jump on board and fly away somewhere."

"Mine! Libby! Mine!"

"Hmm. Well, maybe I could give it back. But what are you going to give me? I need something for fetching it for you, you know."

Right on cue, Aidan stood on tiptoe and pursed his lips. Libby leaned down for a sloppy wet kiss, then grabbed him around his soft waist and held him close until he squirmed out of her embrace.

"Tank you!" he yelled over his shoulder as he zoomed across the grass, toy in hand once more.

With a smile, Dani plucked a bit of branch from where it stuck to the sequins of her halter top, then brushed leaves from the denim cutoffs that barely covered her nonexistent behind.

"Sorry for barging in." She flipped her long blond hair over her shoulders. "We don't usually see you this early on a weeknight this time of year. Did you run away from camp?"

"More like the owner. Want to sit for a minute?"

"Sure." With the supreme self-confidence of the eternally gorgeous, Dani sauntered across the yard, cautioned her son against climbing the trees and took the extra chair on the deck. Libby slipped into the house, grabbed another glass and returned to the deck to pour a glass of wine for Dani, who accepted it with a smile and a nod of thanks.

"Lord, what a day." She sipped, then sighed with pleasure. "End-of-the-year concerts at two schools, and a doctor's appointment for this one." She nodded toward Aidan. "I just started a new job and the boss wasn't very happy about giving me the time, but what can you do?"

"Maybe you should try to get work as a juggler. It sounds like you're getting more than enough practice." Libby raised her own glass in a silent toast. "Aidan's not sick, is he?"

"Not now. He had another bout of tonsillitis and the doctor said one more this year and the tonsils have to be yanked." Her fingers clenched the stem of the glass. "Cross your fingers that it doesn't happen. I can't afford any more time off so soon."

"Fingers, toes and all nonessential appendages."

Dani sighed and shrugged. "All we can do is hope. So what do you mean, you ran away from the owner? I thought Myra worshipped the ground you walked on."

Libby reached for her glass. "Wait until you hear this." She launched into an abbreviated version of the events since Sam walked back into the office, carefully leaving out the precise extent of her former relationship with him.

"Then he said that if I play nice all summer, he'll build a waterfront pavilion for the camp. There's no way I can walk after that. What a…"

"Typical male. It's a lot easier to look like a hero than to act like one, that's for damned sure." Dani's nod carried the weight of bitter experience gained by bearing three children by three different baby daddies—though as Gran had often said, given the guys Dani chose, it was probably best that they didn't stick around after the pregnancy tests came back positive.

"So are you— Aidan Christopher Cooper, I see you. Don't even think of climbing that tree, young man. The last thing we need is for you to fall and break your arm." Dani shook her head. "So what are you going to do?"

"Buy a muzzle. Stay for the summer." She pointed to the laptop, still smack in the middle of the table. "Learn how to write a résumé."

"You've never written one?"

Libby shook her head. "I started at the camp right after high school, and Myra knew me so well that she didn't ask for one."

"You mean you've been working at that same place for, what, twenty years?"

"Twelve." Libby ran her fingers over her neck in search of wrinkles. Maybe it was time to buy a stronger moisturizer.

Dani whistled and pulled the laptop closer. "Okay. So the experience portion of your résumé will be a bit empty, but we can make up for that by highlighting the different duties that were part of the job."

"Um…Dani, what are you doing?"

The soft clack of the keys paused as Dani looked up from the keyboard. "Helping you."

Libby suddenly felt as exposed as though she'd been forced to remove her bra in public. "No, no, you don't need to do that. I'll figure this out. Really."

"Libby. Come on. What's the one thing I know how to do, other than pop out adorable kids?" Dani sat back triumphantly. "I can get a job from a place that's laying off and closing down. It's just like men. I can't keep them, but by God, I can get them."

This was true. But Libby couldn't stop from squirming a bit at the thought of Dani or anyone else taking over a task that should be hers.

"It's okay, Dani. Really. Thanks, but I'd rather do it myself."

"Libby, I know that accepting help is against your religion, but I love this stuff. Especially when it's not for me."

"I know, but…" Libby cast through her mind searching for a way to make Dani stop without hurting her feelings. In her experience, letting other people lend a hand, even with good intentions, only multiplied the odds of something going wrong. "It's just that…you know, I feel kind of silly being this age and not knowing how to do this. It's something I really should learn. I need to teach myself."

Aidan zoomed past making *bbbbrrrrooom* noises while

jerking his plane so violently that any passengers on board would certainly be pulverized. Dani watched him with a smile, then turned the laptop back toward Libby and grabbed her wine.

"Okay. But at least let me review it for you when you're done."

"Sure." Libby could do that.

Maybe.

Dani toyed with the stem of her glass. "So you're leaving camp."

"The minute summer's over. The sooner I can get away from Sam Catalano, the better."

"Sam— Wait a minute." Dani sat up higher in her chair. "The new owner is Sam Catalano? The Cold Ice guy?"

Libby closed her eyes and tried to purge her mind of the image Dani's words had dredged up, the picture that had caused months of frustrated channel flipping—Sam, clad in nothing but a towel, holding a bottle of body wash next to his face while he winked at the camera. The commercials had been a hit, spurring parodies on YouTube and lifting Sam from well-known hockey player to media darling. And, not coincidentally, causing Libby to clench her teeth so often that her dentist had had to discuss stress reduction techniques at her last checkup.

"Didn't I tell you it was him?"

"You were too busy calling him every other name in the book to use his real one."

"Oops." Libby shrugged. "Anyway, yeah. It's him."

Dani leaned forward, straining the fabric of her glittery halter in ways the designer had probably never intended. "I heard something about him. What was it?"

"Probably about him leaving his team. He was supposed to stay on for another couple of years, but at the end of this season he said, 'So long, I'm out of here,' and never really explained why."

"Those athletes are such divas. I bet he didn't get everything he wanted in his dressing room one night, so he took his puck and went home."

Libby started to agree, then stopped. Was Sam the type to storm off because someone hurt his feelings? She wanted to believe it, but couldn't. He might not have been able to man up and help her when she needed him, but that had nothing to do with his ego. Hypersensitivity wasn't among his laundry list of faults.

"I think, maybe, there had to be something else," she said slowly.

Dani pulled the laptop closer and typed in *Sam Catalano*. "I think… There was something, I swear… Yeah!" She pointed at the screen. Libby leaned closer, read the headline and reared back.

"Rehab?"

"Medical reasons." Dani framed the words with air quotes. "The question is, was it drugs or alcohol? Maybe both. Those hockey players take a beating out there. Painkillers would be a natural."

Oh, no. What had she started? With all the jobs Dani had collected over the years, she was tied into the town's gossip line tighter than the hairdressers down at the Comeback Curl.

"Dani, that article came from one of those tabloids that lurk at the checkout register. You can't believe what they say."

"You mean like the ones I've been freelancing for?"

Oops. How had she forgotten? After Dani had lost her job at the town newspaper, she had started supplementing her all-too-erratic income by watching for celebrities behaving badly while vacationing in the Thousand Islands, then sending pictures and articles to the tabloids.

Libby had no problem encouraging Sam to leave, but she wanted it to be a clean victory, not one brought about by slander.

"You can't write about him."

"Why not?"

"Because…because…" Much as she hated to defend the man, she couldn't condone splashing his life all over the tabloids. She fought hard, but she fought clean and fair. "Well, for one thing, he's not just here for a visit. He's a local business owner who is providing jobs for a good number of folks. Including me."

"You're planning to leave anyway." Dani tapped the screen on the laptop.

Not forever. "Come on, Dani. You have kids. How would you feel if you sent your kids to camp, then picked up something at the store that made it sound like the owner couldn't be trusted?"

"You know, Libby, I can't keep up with you. Ten minutes ago you were ready to toss him to the wolves. Now you're standing up for him."

"Not for him. For the camp, and the kids and the parents and the staff. The guy drives me crazy but whether I like it or not, he is the public face of Overlook, at least for the moment. You can't do anything that's going to bring the camp down. There's too many people relying on him." She placed a hand over Dani's. "You know better than anyone what the job market is like around here. Do you really want to do something that will leave even more people competing with you the next time you're hunting?"

"Fine. Okay. You've made your point." Dani sat back and crossed her arms. "But you have to promise that if he does anything slam-worthy, you'll call me before you call the cops."

Libby thought about Miss Personal Reasons with the Very Nice Name and had to bite her tongue before she blurted out anything that could be used the wrong way. Instead, she murmured something that Dani could interpret however she wished, then asked about Aidan's brothers and hoped Dani wouldn't return to the topic of Mr. Cold Ice.

She would bet her next paycheck that Myra hadn't considered the celebrity factor when she agreed to sell to Sam. Sure, it could mean great publicity for them, but they operated at full capacity most of the time anyway. All that could result from Sam's visibility would be a nuisance at best and trouble at the most.

Much like the man himself.

CHAPTER FOUR

Subject: Welcome, and a little light reading
Wednesday, June 6, 10:03 a.m.
From: LibbyK@Overlook.ca
To: SamC@Overlook.ca

Sam: Welcome to Overlook. Thanks for your patience while
we worked out the techno bugs. I'm attaching files containing the staff handbook, the disaster plan, the policies and
procedures, and the parent handbook so you'll have time
to familiarize yourself with everything before your arrival.

The timeline is much as it was when you last worked
here. Counselors and other staff will arrive Monday, June
25, for orientation and setup. Counselors-in-training will
join us Saturday 30th, and of course, the kids arrive July
1. I'm still working out your daily plan and will send ASAP.

Question: as you may remember, Myra always hosted
a barbecue the night before the campers arrived. Will you
want to do something similar? Cosmo needs to prepare
the menus.

Subject: Re: Welcome, and a little light reading
Friday, June 8, 1:42 a.m.
From: SamC@Overlook.ca
To: LibbyK@Overlook.ca

Yes to the barbecue.

I have the timeline tattooed on my forehead.

The handbooks look great. Can't wait to read them in

detail. Feel free to come pack up my house so I can dive right in.

Subject: Schedule
Friday, June 8, 8:56 a.m.
From: LibbyK@Overlook.ca
To: SamC@Overlook.ca

Sam, I realize you're quite busy these days, but I hope you will make to time to at least skim the handbooks. The transition will be easier for everyone if you are prepared for your duties.

I'll tell Cosmo about the barbecue. Will you need any help from me?

Here's your weekly schedule, broken down by day. You'll see I've given you time with a group and time in the office to ensure you have a well-rounded view of the entire operation.

Subject: Re: Schedule
Monday, June 11, 11:57 p.m.
From: SamC@Overlook.ca
To: LibbyK@Overlook.ca

The barbecue is covered.

Handbooks: be honest, Lib. You're going to tell me what to do anyway, so I'm not wasting my time reading it.

You have me scheduled from 6:00 a.m. until after ten each night. Not gonna happen. I can't start before eight, and I need to be in my house by eight-thirty or nine.

SAM FELT A TWINGE OF GUILT as he sent the email, but the sound of Casey's deep breathing over the monitor helped him push it aside. He'd missed enough of Casey's life already. No way in hell was he going to spend the entire sum-

mer so busy working off Libby's anger that he had no time
to spend with his own kid.

Carving out time for Casey wasn't being selfish. It was
being a good parent.

Subject: Schedule
Tuesday, June 12, 9:02 a.m.
From: LibbyK@Overlook.ca
To: SamC@Overlook.ca

Sam, do you have any memory of your time here at all? It's
a twenty-four-seven job and everyone has to give three
hundred percent. You can't set yourself certain hours and
expect everyone else to pick up your slack. Not without
hiring a boatload more staff to help cover what you should
be doing.

Subject: Re: Schedule
Wednesday, June 13, 11:36 p.m.
From: SamC@Overlook.ca
To: LibbyK@Overlook.ca

Then hire who we need.

Subject: Schedule
Thursday, June 14, 8:37 a.m.
From: LibbyK@Overlook.ca
To: SamC@Overlook.ca

Hire more staff now? Orientation starts in 11 days.

Subject: Re: Schedule
Monday, June 18, 1:56 a.m.
From: SamC@Overlook.ca
To: LibbyK@Overlook.ca

Then you'd better not waste any time.

AT THE END OF THE FIRST DAY of orientation, Libby walked into the office, took one look around her and let the screen door slam behind her.

"I'm going to kill him."

There was no answer, which was a good thing, since there was no one else in the room. If there had been an answer she would have known without a doubt that Sam had made her lose her grip on sanity. And he'd been back less than twenty-four hours. His furniture hadn't even arrived yet, for heaven's sake. She still had six and a half weeks to survive until the end of summer programming.

She'd promised Myra she would play nice, but right now, all she wanted to play was hide-and-seek—with Sam hiding in the Galapagos Islands and her not seeking.

Bad enough that he had waltzed back to camp after all these years, worse that he had bought the place, but now... now he was doing his damnedest to charm her staff. Okay, technically *his* staff, but still. She had done the interviews and hired them. She had shepherded most of them through at least two or three summers working at the camp. Many were back for their fourth or fifth year. They were reliable and trustworthy and dedicated.

And with one announcement of a pizza and karaoke night, Sam had them all eating out of his hand.

"Maybe I will kill him," Libby muttered as she sat down at her desk. "The heck with agreements. I'll kill him, the place will go back to Myra and as long as I get a jury made up of women, I won't get convicted. They would probably give me a medal for taking him out before he could get to anyone else."

Work, Libby. Focus on the work.

A fresh pile of camper forms had arrived that afternoon. She needed to get those logged in. After that, there were phone calls and emails to answer, most from parents with last-minute jitters. The canoe paddles she'd ordered hadn't arrived yet. She would have to track those down. And she'd had a thought for her résumé—

The pounding of footsteps on the steps made her clench her jaw. She knew those steps.

The door creaked open. She glanced up with a sigh.

"Hello, Sam."

He jerked at the sound of her voice, and she realized he hadn't known she was there—probably because he was so absorbed by the cell phone pressed to his ear. He glanced her way, waved and turned back to the door he hadn't closed.

"Right," he said into the phone. "Look, I have to go now....Uh-huh, no rest for the wicked....Yeah. You, too. Later."

Ah. Miss Personal Reasons must have called. Not for the first time, she wondered if this mystery woman with the very nice name was responsible for Sam's inability to work regular hours. Or if she was behind the long lag times between Libby's emails and Sam's replies. Or what she and Sam might be talking about that had caused him to cut his many calls short every time Libby approached.

It was more than him trying to have a private conversation. Between his evasiveness the day of the meeting, his elusive emails and now the parade of interrupted calls, she had the distinct impression he was hiding something from her.

Gran used to try to hide things from her, probably because she didn't want to worry Libby. But Libby would rather deal with the worst imaginable fact than walk around in dread, only to be blindsided.

Sam pocketed the phone and swiveled to focus on her, offering a grin that only a fool would believe.

"The door?" she said before he could start.

He glanced over his shoulder. "What? Does it do tricks?"

"You didn't close it. You haven't closed it the last five times you've entered this office."

"Oh. Sorry. Didn't notice."

Well, *duh,* she thought as he kicked the bottom of the door so it almost shut.

"So," he said as though there had been no disruption in his train of thought, "I thought you were down in your cabin. I was just gonna call you. The pizza's here."

"I know. I saw the delivery guy. If you ever do this again, make sure they know we want it delivered by someone who isn't trying out for NASCAR."

"Fine." He waited a moment, watching her, making her skin prickle. She didn't want him looking at her. Not while she worked, not while she ate, not while she breathed. It was too unsettling. Too intense. Too inclined to make her remember things best forgotten.

"Problem, Sam?"

"Aren't you coming down to eat?"

"No."

"You know this is it for food tonight."

"Yes, I know." She'd already had to deal with Cosmo's grumbling about last-minute changes and menus that would have to be rearranged and worries that this was setting a new and unpleasant precedent.

"So—" he began, but she stopped him with a sigh.

"I understand. This is dinner. But I'm a big girl, Sam, and I know how to take care of myself. Right now I am going to catch up on the work that would have been done this afternoon if *someone* hadn't made the morning sessions go overtime."

He offered her what he undoubtedly thought was a boyish grin. "Sorry about that. If I'd known we were on such a tight schedule, I wouldn't have suggested the game, okay? It seemed like a good way to get people to know each other."

"Most of the staff has already worked together. The ones who are truly new didn't need to get roped into playing Never Have I Ever with folks they'd just met. It was—" She stopped and rubbed the tightness out of her jaw. "In any case, I have things to finish. I'd appreciate it if you could let me get to it."

She turned back to the computer, hoping he'd take the hint. But after a full thirty seconds of tapping on the keyboard and ruffling the papers in front of her, he hadn't moved. She looked up and caught him watching her yet again.

"Something wrong?"

His shrug was too casual. "There's salad and wings, too. In case you don't want pizza because you're doing some low-carb thing."

Some low-carb—was he insinuating she needed to lose weight? After she'd starved herself from the minute he walked out of that first meeting until the start of orientation, just so she could wear her cutest shorts and make herself forget the horror of meeting him in her Emergency Bloat skirt?

"Work." She tapped the stack of forms and tried for a smile, but it probably looked more like a nervous tic. "Not carbs. Work."

His eyes clouded over, so fast she wouldn't have noticed if she hadn't spent years watching the emotions play across his face, committing each and every one of them to heart.

"You know," he said slowly, "there was a time when you would have been the first one down there, fighting to get your shot at the karaoke machine."

"There was also a time when I believed in Santa Claus and fairy tales. Then I grew up." Just in time, she stopped herself from suggesting that he might want to try growing up, too.

Faster than she could blink, he crossed the room and trapped her in her chair, one hand on either side just like before, as he squatted before her, eye to eye.

"Here's a radical thought, Lib. How about instead of hiding here in the office, you come down to the dining hall, have some fun with the staff and then we come back up here and I help you do the work."

Well, *that* was unexpected. The Sam she knew would never have been caught dead doing paperwork. She vividly recalled him bribing her to fill out an incident report after one of his campers tripped over a rock and needed stitches. If she recalled correctly, payment had taken the form of kisses on the deck. Kisses and groping and—

Oh, no. No no no no no. She could not start wandering down memory lane with Sam. Been there, done that, had the hair shirt to prove it.

She swiveled back to the computer, and Sam released his grip on the chair. "Thank you for the offer, but I'd rather get the work behind me first."

"All work and no play makes Libby a dull girl."

"I'll take my chances."

Eyes studiously fixed on the monitor, she didn't realize he had moved until he appeared at her side. She gave a little start and covered her mouth with her hand to hold back her squeak. Now she really knew why they called him The Cat.

"Libby." His voice was deep and warm and even more intimate than his nearness would have made her expect. "I know this isn't easy for you. But you can't avoid me all summer. I need to learn how to run this place, and you're the only one who can teach me. So how about we start over?"

A clean slate? Unlikely. Not without some serious explaining and apologizing. He had walked away from her when she needed him most. There wasn't enough grovel in the world to atone for that.

But…she had promised Myra she would help ease the transition.

And he was building the pavilion.

And she was going to have to work with him, be it good or bad.

She couldn't do anything about the sale, at least not yet. She couldn't undo what had happened between her and Sam. But for Myra's sake, and for the sake of everyone at the camp, she could show him how things worked.

"Fine. The most important thing to remember is that either you or I must be on the premises at all times when kids are here. No taking off into town on a whim, no scheduling off-site meetings for you on my day off, nothing. One of us must always be available. It's one of our biggest promises to parents."

"Got it. What next?"

If she wasn't going to get rid of him, she might as well start the training. "Pull up a chair for lesson one, camper information forms."

He sighed. "Paperwork. Why did it have to be paperwork?"

She bit back a smile and waited for him to grab a seat. Instead, he bent forward to read what was on the screen, looming over her. She scrunched sideways but he was all around her. His hair fell forward and his shirt gaped and she remembered the time she'd grabbed him by a similarly loose tee and hauled him close to her and silenced some smart-ass comment with a kiss that could have gone on forever if only the world hadn't continued to turn.

Oh, hell. She'd forgotten everything she'd ever learned in chemistry, physics and calculus. So why did her memory insist on serving up these tidbits whenever he got close?

She launched into a fast and furious explanation of the many camper forms, their purposes and how to record them on the master spreadsheet. She doubted it made any sense. It came out so fast and garbled that she didn't think she could have followed it, and she had been using the system for years.

"There," she said with relief. "Lesson one, complete."

"Yeah. Sure."

He sounded dazed and confused, and in fairness, she couldn't blame him.

But it was better to race through and send him on his way than continue to feel him hovering over her and tell herself he didn't make her feel…restless.

"That's enough for one night. Digest this, and tomorrow we'll tackle lesson two, filing."

"Fine." He straightened and stepped back. She breathed in again, and the hit of oxygen cleared her brain enough to make her remember something that had been tickling her brain since she sat down to attack the forms.

"By the way, I need your emergency information, too."

"Mine?"

"Yes, indeed. I need it from everyone—kids, staff, anyone."

"I'm the owner, not staff," he said after a moment.

"But you're living by counselor rules, remember? And face it, if anything happened to you here, our nurse would be your first responder. So hand it in."

His mouth set in a mulish line. Great.

She sighed and crossed her arms. "Are you still allergic to penicillin?"

His eyes widened. "You remember that?"

"Don't flatter yourself, Catalano," she said, though even she was amazed at how much of her previous knowledge was flooding back to her conscious awareness. "What would happen if, say, you finally pushed me too far and I whacked you over the head, then ran away? No one here would know."

"Fine. I'll fill out the damned form." A smile tugged at the corner of his mouth. "Are you planning to off me soon, Lib? Should I update my will?"

"That's entirely up to you, isn't it? Now get out of here and go back to your party. I'll be done faster that way."

"Fine." He took a step, then stopped and turned back to her. "But before I go, I— Look, what happened back then, when we were kids and I—"

"Hung up on me." Libby finished his sentence with clipped tones, pushing herself upright in her chair.

Hung up on me. The words were totally inappropriate for what she had felt. She had left camp that summer totally in love, amazed at what she and Sam had done, counting the minutes until they would start school together and could pick up where they'd left off. Then had come that horrible moment when Gran sat her down and said, "Oh, Libby, I don't know how to tell you, but there's a problem with your college money…."

Her first instinct had been to reach for Sam. She had walked away from her grandmother and closed herself in her room and called him.

She'd poured it all out to him. Cried so hard the words could barely slip through the tears. And when she was done, he had simply sighed, said, "I'm so sorry, Lib," and hung up.

She never heard from him again until the day he walked into the office and laid claim to the camp that should have been hers.

He crouched in front of her so his eyes were level with hers. He reached for her hands, but she jerked back against the cracked vinyl of the chair. Too much. Too soon. He flinched but didn't move away.

"I want you to know—I'm sorry. I never should have

done it, and I've lost count of how many times I've beat myself up for it over the years."

"Well," she said slowly. "Thank you."

He nodded.

She held her breath. This was the point when he was supposed to say why he did it, when he justified his actions. Not that there was any way to excuse it, but—

"Okay. Well." He stood and offered her a tentative grin. "Listen, there's something else I need to—"

A knock sounded at the door. "Libby? Are you in there?"

Libby scowled as her waterfront director walked into the office. What else had he planned to say? And how had she not heard Phoebe coming up the creaky steps? It was terrifyingly like the old days, when the rest of the world had seemed to operate on another plane whenever she was with Sam.

At least this time she knew that her sense-blocking passion was of the pissed-off variety.

Phoebe came to a sudden stop in the middle of the room, forehead furrowed, the multicolored beads in her hair clacking against each other as she looked from Libby to Sam and back again. "Hey, sorry. Didn't mean to interrupt anything."

Libby's cheeks burned as she thought of what Phoebe would have seen if she had walked in a few seconds earlier, when Sam had curved around her to inspect the screen.

"No interruption at all," Sam said with a wink. "I was just, uh, getting ready to head down to dinner."

Libby had never been punched in the stomach, but she had a pretty good idea that the sudden breathlessness she felt was a damned close approximation. Seriously? He barged in on her while she was working, messed up her staff, tossed her some half-assed excuse for an apology and then expected to just waltz out of the room like—

The door flew open again, this time admitting the craft

director. "Libby, we have— Oh." Her big blue eyes widened and her slight frown left her face, replaced by a goofy kind of smile. "Oh. Hi, Sam."

"Hi, Tanya."

Good Lord, was the girl blushing? Libby rubbed her forehead. Great. Tanya had picked Sam for her annual crush. It was going to be an even longer summer than she'd anticipated.

"What's up, ladies?" she asked, hoping they wouldn't hear the fatigue in her voice.

"I have some ideas. About our cabin." Phoebe looked at Tanya, who was alternating between staring at the floor and peeking through her lashes at Sam.

Sam himself shot a semiapologetic glance her way before edging toward the exit. "Okay. Well. I'll leave you ladies to your discussion. Catch you later, Libby."

Coward.

The minute the door slammed behind him she massaged her forehead, caught somewhere between old hurts and frustration and a vague disappointment, as if she'd been on the brink of something and had it snatched away from her. Which, in a way, she had.

"Libby?" Phoebe's voice was small. "Are you okay?"

Libby shook her head and pulled herself upright. She would not, could not fall apart now. There were questions to be answered, people to be reassured, papers to be pushed. She still had a pile of work before she could call it a night. Her job was waiting.

Somehow, the prospect wasn't quite as compelling as it had been before Sam waltzed in.

A COUPLE OF HOURS LATER, Sam grabbed a slice of pizza from the box left on the serving table in the deserted dining hall and spied exactly what he needed in the far corner of the dim, echoing space: a place to hide.

He didn't need long. A couple of minutes, just enough to catch his breath and have a bite in peace. And if he remembered correctly, the floor-to-ceiling stone fireplace halfway down the wall provided a small but private corner on the other side. He kept his steps as quiet as possible until he reached the spot. Yep. He could prop himself at the nearest picnic table, watch the stars from the window, but no one could see him unless they knew where to look. Which was a damned good thing because he needed a minute to himself.

Sharon had called during dinner to try to talk him out of moving Casey. Brynn, stuck with the task of closing up the house and supervising the move, had done an amazing job but still had needed to run an endless stream of questions past him. Casey had been fretful and fussy the last time they talked.

And on top of all that, he was supposed to learn about his new staff and his new job and line up a pediatrician and stock the house with groceries and still have the energy to convince himself that he was doing the right thing.

Oh, and mollify Libby enough that he could tell her about Casey without feeling like he was pouring salt into wounds that he had caused.

He had hoped that the pavilion plans would do the trick, but when he showed them to her that morning, she had brushed them aside with barely a glance. The pizza night had turned out to be another mistake. Shit, he'd even pretended to be interested in paperwork. He was running out of ideas, and worse, running out of time. Brynn would be there with Casey in just three days.

He was going to have to tell her. Soon, before it became an issue.

As soon as he finished catching his breath.

He took a slug of coffee, gasped at the unexpected heat and backhanded the drops away from his mouth as the door creaked open.

Libby stepped inside. From where he sat he could see her give the hall a quick once-over. Seated in the shadow of the fireplace as he was, with her eyes still adjusting from the bright glare of sunset to the relative shadows inside, she probably hadn't seen him. Fine by him. He'd give her a moment to do what she'd come for, then he'd scrape together his brain cells, chase her down and come clean with her.

"Cosmo?" she called in the direction of the kitchen. "Hey, Cosmo, are you there?"

"Just a minute."

As far as Sam could tell, Cosmo hadn't changed a bit since he first barked an order at preteen Sam and almost made him wet his pants. He was still big, still burly and still inclined to wearing brightly flowered Hawaiian shirts beneath his apron. Sam had yet to have a conversation with the man in his new position as owner that hadn't ended with Cosmo grunting and telling him he had a hell of a lot to learn.

Right. Just in case Sam wasn't painfully aware of that already.

"What's up?" Cosmo emerged from his lair, wiping his hands on a towel.

"I'm doing a staff campfire tomorrow night. Do we have enough marshmallows for s'mores?"

"We should have plenty. Thanks for checking."

"Just doing my job." She grabbed the clipboard from the table and flipped through the papers. "Hey, have you seen Sam around?"

"Can't say I have." He tossed the towel over his shoulder. "Course, can't say I've been looking, either."

Sam gritted his teeth and eased deeper into the corner,

pressing himself against the cold stone of the fireplace. Libby laughed, soft and low, and he held his breath so as not to miss whatever might come next.

"Now, Cosmo, is that any way to talk about your new boss?"

"Humph. Just because his name's on the deed, it don't mean he's the boss."

Sam was seized by a sudden urge to start handing out pink slips.

"Give the devil his due," Libby said. "He's doing everything I tell him to do."

Libby was defending him?

"There ya go," Cosmo replied. "Y'ever hear tell of a boss who lets someone else tell him what to do?"

Well, hell. Sam was more than ready to turn that trend around. Step one: tell Cosmo where to go.

Libby laughed again, a bit more freely this time, which made Sam's jaw tighten with words that could never be said. "Be that as it may, if you see him, would you please be a doll and tell him I'm heading into town tonight? I'll be back before the morning session."

"Sure thing. Got anything else for me to tell him?"

"What do you mean?"

"Like if he doesn't have the brains to stay away from you this time around, he's gonna wish he had?"

Sam was too far away and the shadows were too deep to see if Libby blushed or not, but he'd bet his Stanley Cup ring that her cheeks were firing almost as red as her hair. "I don't know what you mean."

"I've been here a lot longer than you have, missy. There's not much that gets past me. I saw the way you two were that summer. Velcro. Myra thought she was going to have to turn a hose on you sometimes."

Sam grinned to himself. And they thought they had been so surreptitious.

"I shared Sam's cabin that year, you know. Saw him sneaking back in that last night. Stupid fool was practically glowing."

"I really should go," Libby said, and stepped toward the door.

Cosmo's hand shot out and grabbed her arm. "Funny thing," he said. "You two were all over each other when it came time to say goodbye, but not two weeks later, there you were in Myra's office, hunting for a job instead of going off to school, and turning all white and pinched whenever Sam's name came up."

Ah, damn. He'd known it had to have been hard on her. But it was one thing to know that he'd hurt her, and a totally different thing to hear Cosmo, of all people, lay it out so plainly.

"Not much of one for sticking around after the fun, is he?"

Cosmo's question was quiet but still packed a punch—one that went straight to Sam's gut. Especially when Libby sighed softly and said, "It doesn't seem that way, does it?"

It's not what you think, Libby. There's so much you don't know.

He was halfway to his feet, ready to reveal himself and pull her out of the room and tell her everything about then and now, but she picked up her clipboard and pasted on a smile that he could see was fake, even from the other side of the hall.

"Listen," she said, "this is way too depressing for such a gorgeous night, okay? Let's save it for another time."

"Like when?" Cosmo asked. "After Sam fires you?"

"He can't fire me. He needs me—well, someone with

my qualifications, and I happen to be the most convenient. I'm the one who's calling a halt."

"Huh. First Myra, then you. Place is going to the dogs."

Her smile was sad. "Thanks. Oh, I talked to Myra last night. She said to say hi to you, and that she can't eat meat loaf anymore because it makes her miss you."

"Yeah? Well, if you talk to her again, tell her…"

"What?"

He waved her away. "Nothing. Forget I said anything. I have to finish cleaning up."

He picked up the pizza box and lumbered back into the kitchen. Sam crushed his napkin in his hand, then readied himself to stand. It was time to make his move.

Libby watched Cosmo go, nibbling on her lip in a way that went straight to his groin, then shook her head. She set her clipboard on the closest table, reached both arms overhead and stretched toward the beamed ceiling. Face tilted up, she swayed in place as if to undo the kinks in her back. Her braid danced behind her and her hips rocked from side to side and her dark blue Overlook T-shirt molded itself to her breasts and his mouth went dry.

Because when she made herself taller this way and let herself relax, when the shadows blurred her features and let him see nothing but hair and curves—he couldn't deny the truth anymore.

Libby and Robin could have been sisters.

With a sigh, she gathered up the clipboard and slipped out the door with barely a sound. He knew he should follow her, knew he should chase her down and bring her up to speed, but he couldn't. Not when his brain was jumping between memories of Robin and thoughts of Libby. And who he had been with each of them. And the moment earlier in the evening when he leaned over Libby's shoulder, pretending to pay attention to the numbers on the screen, when he had placed a hand on her shoulder and inhaled the last traces of her coconut shampoo and his muscles had started to purr in recognition.

But which woman had he recognized?

CHAPTER FIVE

LIBBY HAD BEEN SLEEPING in the cabins with her staff, just to save time, but after her run-in with Sam she thought it best to head back to the town house for the night. She had never sleepwalked to her knowledge, but she didn't trust herself if the inclination should kick in that night. She might find herself jerking awake just after tossing Sam into the cold waters of the river.

Or, worse—she might find herself sleep-wandering up to his cabin to see how it would feel to have him hovering over her, breathing softly on her neck once more. Because while her brain knew that Sam was a temptation best left in her very distant past, her hormones had chosen those moments when they were alone in the office to come out of hibernation. Lousy timing. Truly lousy choice of person to rouse them.

She tossed her keys on the table, stripped off her camp clothes and treated herself to a very long, very relaxing shower. Sam had been her first lover. It made total biological sense that he would be imprinted on her in some primordial manner, that her body would recognize him in ways that her brain knew should not be indulged. But this time she had knowledge on her side. Knowledge and the fact that, given his history, Sam would likely slip up and make an ass of himself sooner or later. If she was lucky, it would be a thorough enough fall that even her stupid hormones would get the message.

She let herself sleep a bit later the next morning, indulging in the comfort of a real bed and a few moments of total peace. When she did pull herself from the covers she lingered over her coffee while tweaking her résumé and composing a cheerful email to Myra. She took a few moments to go through the refrigerator and toss some perishables, then gathered up her library books before finally heading out the door.

The library was one of her favorite places in town. Comeback Cove, like so many settlements in the Thousand Islands, had a rich history that revolved around both the river and their proximity to the States. Shipwrecks and pirates and rumrunners lived on in both local lore and the many themed gift shops that lined the main streets. But the library had opted to feature the story she loved most, that of a rumrunner who dared to fall in love with a rich summer girl and then died in a shoot-out on the water before revealing the location of a rumored hidden treasure. Thus, each summer the library put together treasure hunts and highlighted books of other supposed lost riches—and, for the older patrons, other tales of star-crossed lovers.

She dropped off her books at Returns, stopped to talk to the volunteer behind the circulation desk and had just headed for the children's room to pick up a few books for the camp when she spied one of Gran's friends, Verna Collins, loading up on board books. Years of regular tennis games had left the woman fit and fast enough to ride herd on the Sunday school classes she still led, just as she had once taught Libby.

"Mrs. Collins, how are you?"

They chatted for a few moments about mutual friends and the latest escapades of Verna's out-of-town grandchildren, until Libby checked her watch.

"Oops. It's later than I realized. I need to grab some books and get out to the camp."

Verna nodded and waved her away. "You go on. I'm sure we'll get plenty of chances to catch up over the summer."

"Not that many," Libby reminded her with a short laugh. "I don't make it into town much once the campers arrive."

"Oh, I know that. I mean, what with me working out there now."

Working at the camp? What? Verna wasn't on any of the staff lists Libby had seen. Unless Sam had hired her himself, to do—what? Keep his house clean for him and the unnamed person he was working so hard to hide from her?

The anger she'd managed to tamp down reared its head once more. Did Miss Hidden From Libby know that Sam was in the habit of leaning too close when looking at computer screens, talking in a voice low and soft enough to guarantee flashbacks and wholly inappropriate tingles?

Not that she cared. Whatever happened between Sam and his—whatever—was of absolutely no concern to her. Except, of course, for the phone calls she would end up fielding from outraged parents.

Verna looked at Libby as if wondering who had stolen all her marbles. "Well, yes. I thought for sure you knew. I'll be starting in a couple of days. You know." She hefted the pile of board books. "I'll be looking after Casey. Mr. Catalano's little boy."

SAM WAS DOWN AT THE INLET, talking to the contractor about the schedule for the pavilion construction, when the walkie-talkie at his hip crackled.

"Catalano?"

He winced inside. Libby. And judging from the way she had barked out his name, she wasn't happy.

He tossed an apology to the contractor, walked a few

steps toward the woods in an illusion of privacy and pulled
the walkie-talkie free.

"Hey, Lib. What's up?"

"We need to talk. Now. You have five minutes to get your
sorry self up to your house or I swear I am going to—to—
to hunt you down and do this in front of anyone who might
be within hearing distance. And trust me, this is not a conversation that you will want other people to hear."

Oh, shit. There was only one thing he could think of that
would leave her spitting fury this way. Why the hell hadn't
he made himself tell her already?

"I'll be there in ten."

Before she could say anything else, he hit the power button. She'd said she would hunt him down, but he knew, as
did she, that it would take longer than ten minutes for her
to find him. She would wait.

In the meantime, he'd bought himself a few moments in
which to figure out how to handle the inexcusable without
coming out with the total truth. Because somehow, he didn't
think that saying, *Sorry, I tried to tell you about my kid but
I got freaked out because his mother looked like you and
I'm worried I might have got you two mixed up in my mind*
was going to improve the situation.

He made his apologies to the contractor and trudged up
the hill. For what seemed like the first time ever, he didn't
run into anyone else on his way. Maybe they'd all heard
Libby's blast over the walkie-talkie and ducked into the
woods for shelter.

He couldn't really blame them.

Things were so quiet that when he heard his name being
called as he passed the dining hall, he first thought it was
his imagination. But when he paused and looked around,
he saw Cosmo snapping a towel in the wind—whether to

get Sam's attention or to give him the mother of all rat-tails, he couldn't decide.

"What is it, Cosmo?"

"Got a problem. One of the fridges is on its way out. You have to call the repair guy."

Sam was still learning the ins and outs of who did what, but one thing that had been clear to him even when he was a camper was that when it came to the kitchens, Cosmo was God. He didn't ask permission and no one interfered with his sovereign domain.

"What do you mean I need to call? Is this a test to see if I get the right person out here? You've been doing this for-ever, Cos. You make the call."

Beefy arms crossed over a burly chest. "Afraid to get your hands dirty with some real work?"

Sam clenched his jaw as he thought of the eighteen hours he'd put in the day before, and the even longer one ahead of him. "Dammit, I don't have time for this. You've been rid-ing my ass since I got here. If you have something to say to me, say it. Stop this damned nit-picking, expecting me to do things that I know there's no way in hell you expected Myra to do for you."

Cosmo pulled himself up straighter. Something flashed in his eyes at the mention of Myra, but Sam was too pissed off to try to analyze it then.

"Okay, then. You want it straight? You got it. I don't know what kind of games you're playing, but it takes a hell of a lot to make Libby as angry as she is right now. And let me tell you this. She doesn't get bent out of shape with-out good reason. Whatever you pulled, you got her where it hurts." He jabbed a finger in Sam's chest. "You hurt her, you answer to me."

Reassuring as it was to know that Cosmo was capable of

actual affection, this wasn't the way Sam wanted to make
the discovery.

"You know," he said as he plucked the older man's finger from his chest, "I get that Libby's been here forever. I
get that you want to protect her from the big bad wolf. But
that's not going to change things." He stepped back, arms
flung wide. "You don't want me here? Tough. I'm here,
and I'm here to stay. You don't like it? Walk. But you're
gonna have to be the one to do it, because it's sure as hell
not gonna be me."

Without waiting to hear whatever Cosmo might have to
say, he turned back to the road. Adrenaline pumped through
him, pushing him up the hill, readying him for whatever
was going to happen next.

Just like being back on the ice all over again.

Just as she had said, Libby was waiting at his house,
pacing in front of the door with that ever-loving clipboard
clutched to her chest and smoke all but pouring out of her
ears. The minute he rounded the corner she double-timed
it across the grass to meet him.

"Why the hell didn't you tell me you were bringing a
kid to camp?"

"Because you spent my first meeting snarling at me and
the next two weeks planning to overwork me and my first
day back trying to pretend I wasn't here. Also, unlike you,
I have a personal life outside this place. *Personal.* As in, it
was none of your business."

Wrong answer. He knew it even before he finished saying it, but there was no backtracking now.

"Of all the— Look. I don't care how many women you've
deluded over the years, and I don't care how many kids you
have scattered across the continent. But if you're bringing
one here, I need to know."

"Well, hell. Forgive me for having a life that doesn't revolve around you. You want me to say the words? Here you go. Libby, my son is moving in. Tomorrow. Oh, and since you have to know every single thing that's going on around here, let me tell you this. There's a dog, too."

"A—"

For the first time in his memory, Libby appeared speechless. Her mouth sagged open and red spots flared in her cheeks, and if he wasn't so sick and tired of dancing to her tune, he would have laughed at the way the words seemed to have been stolen from her brain.

"That's right, Libby. A dog. A big Lab."

Whatever had been interfering with her ability to speak wore off too damned fast. "Do you have any idea how complicated things just became?"

"Nope." He bounced in his shoes, back in his element. She wanted a fight? He was more than ready to give her one. "But I bet you're just dying to tell me, aren't you?"

"Yeah, Sam. I am. You deliberately misled me. You thought it was so cute to string me along, make me think you had a woman coming here, when all along…" She closed her eyes in what he was sure was a silent scream, given the way her fingers tightened on the clipboard. "What are you going to do with a dog? Huh, Sam? What are you going to do about kids with allergies? Or when the dog gets loose and sees all the campers as trespassers on his territory?"

"I'll deal with it."

"Sure you will. The same way you keep disappearing from meetings to talk with the contractor, or left me to interview and hire all the new staff needed to accommodate your schedule restrictions, or expect me to smooth things over with Cosmo after you messed up his meals, or—"

"Maybe that's because you've been pouncing on everything before I have a chance to deal with it. Maybe because you just love jumping in and being the one who fixes every-

thing so you can look like a goddamned martyr saint while
I look like some idiot who just fell off the truck."

Her eyes narrowed. "I am doing what's best for the
camp."

"Bullshit. You're doing what's best for Libby Kovak."
He grabbed the clipboard and yanked it from her unsus-
pecting fingers. "You know what your problem is, Libby?
You need to get—"

"So help me, if you say what I think you're going to say,
I will sue you for sexual harassment faster than you can say
it was just a mistake."

He blinked. She thought he was insinuating she needed
to get laid? Holy... Never mind that it was true. He would
never be idiot enough to say it.

"You. Need. To. Get. A. Life." He waved the clipboard
in her face. "You live, breathe and probably dream about
this place, and I wouldn't give a rat's ass except it means
you can't let go. This is your little empire and you are
queen and you won't ease up because without it, you'll
have nothing."

"Well, thank you for the life advice, Dr. Phil."

"Go ahead, Lib. Laugh. I have news for you." He leaned
in close enough to smell the hint of coconut underlying the
pine scent that he would forever associate with her. "Maybe
I should have told you sooner, but you know what? This is
my kid we're talking about. Not a complication. My *son*.
The reason for my every frickin' breath. Believe it or not,
he comes before the camp. He is more important than the
camp. And you—" he shoved the clipboard back at her
"—would be smart to keep that in mind."

She gave him a look that he was pretty sure was the kind
of expression usually seen on marauding hordes, yanked
the clipboard from his fingers and snapped her mouth shut.

Without another word she marched away from the house and down toward the office.

So much for making nice before he told her the truth.

YOU NEED TO GET A LIFE.

Sam's words pounded through Libby as she stalked down the path to the dining hall. She let the door slam behind her, startling Phoebe and Alex, the counselor assigned to double-team with Sam, who were lurking in the corner but who jerked apart at Libby's arrival. Phoebe gave her shirt a semisurreptitious tug.

"Libby. Hey. How are you— Whoa." Phoebe stepped back and reached for Alex's hand. "Are you okay?"

"Just ducky." Libby strong-armed the swinging doors to the kitchen and scanned the alien world of butcher block and stainless steel. "Cosmo?"

No answer.

"Cosmo?" she repeated, louder this time, but the only answer was a small voice from behind her.

"He went down to his cabin," Phoebe said.

Well, duh. If Libby hadn't been so furious she couldn't think straight, she would have realized that Phoebe and Alex wouldn't have been playing tonsil hockey with the cook in residence.

"Is it an emergency? Do you need me to get him?" Alex sounded all too eager to escape, which told Libby everything she needed to know about what kind of an impression she was making on her—correction, on *Sam's*—staff. She forced herself to take a deep breath and dug up something that she hoped resembled a smile.

"No. I just need something, but I'll leave him a note. Thank you."

Alex nodded and disappeared back into the dining area.

She heard whispers, then the door closing as he and Phoebe undoubtedly got away while the getting was good.

"Cowards," she shot in their direction, but there was no heat in the word.

She opened cupboards and drawers until she found what she was looking for—a five-pound bag of chocolate chips. She slung it over her shoulder, scribbled a message for Cosmo and hoofed it back to the office.

You need to get a life. You can't let go. You're doing what's best for Libby Kovak.

Seriously? He had just pulled the bonehead move of the century, and he was accusing *her* of looking out for number one?

The door to the office stood wide-open to the critters and the elements, causing her to narrow her eyes and fling some more mental arrows in Sam's direction. She slammed it closed, took a step and smacked her ankle into a file cabinet drawer that he had undoubtedly left open.

"That miserable, puck-brained son of a—" She gave the drawer a vicious kick and let out a satisfied *hunh* when it latched. Then she hobbled to her desk, slid the bag of chocolate chips off her shoulder and tore it open.

There was a reason God had given chocolate to the world. She was pretty sure it had something to do with the continuation of the species.

She tossed a handful of the chips into her mouth, chomping with satisfaction before turning to the computer. Sam the idiot had also left a file open on the desktop—a file filled with staff information.

Come on. He left stuff like this lying open for anyone to see, and he had the nerve to hurl insults at her?

You can't let go.

With a few clicks she accessed her private email. She scanned her in-box quickly, noting with a pang that Myra had replied to her, but ignored the posts while she opened a blank email. A few quick sentences, a fast attachment and she hit Send before she could change her mind.

There. She shoved another handful of chocolate chips into her mouth and fist-pumped the air when the your-message-has-been-sent screen appeared.

"That's right, Catalano," she said to the empty room. "I'm just looking out for number one."

The words were scarcely out of her mouth when the impact of her actions began to sink in. She had just applied for a job. A teaching job. And she hadn't done it after careful consideration, but in a reactionary "I'll show you" fury.

Oh, great. She hoped to hell her cover email had made some kind of sense. Otherwise she might have killed her chances at one of the few local teaching positions before she even had a chance.

"It's all his fault," she muttered around a mouthful of chocolate. "Him and his secrets and his games and his—"

I have a kid.

Well, of course he did. Why wouldn't he? He'd had a big, loving family while she had only Gran. He'd had a free ride to a degree that he then turned his back on, while she squeezed classes and student teaching around work and a needy grandmother. He had the Stanley Cup and romances with starlets and a commercial that made him an object of desire for a good chunk of the female population of North America, while she had…while she had…

While she had the camp. Until he took it from her.

Which did *not* mean she needed to get a life.

It just meant that the life in question had just had another chunk ripped out of it.

HE'D MANAGED TO PISS OFF two members of his staff in twenty minutes. One more and Sam would have a frickin' hat trick.

If he'd had a brain he would have holed up in the house
for a beer's worth of unpacking, but instead Sam watched
Libby disappear around the corner, then hightailed it down
to the waterfront. There was nothing like hauling rocks to
work off the adrenaline rush that came with a good fight.

Because much as he hated to admit it, Sam felt more
pumped than he had in weeks.

He curled his fingers around a hunk of solid something,
grunted and heaved. He'd only been a camp owner for a
couple of weeks. He'd been a hockey player since he was
old enough to make the stick connect with a puck, close to
thirty years. Hockey players didn't do subtle. They didn't do
nit-picking. Hockey players went for the goal. Anything and
anyone that got between them and the goal was fair game.

He'd be a liar if he tried to pretend he didn't miss the
clear focus of hockey. He'd be a damned liar if he tried to
convince himself that he'd handled the Libby situation well.

But God, it had felt good to be on the edge again.

He had the old feeling back, the awareness of his skin and
his muscles that had been such a part of flying over the ice.
He'd felt back in his element up there with Libby, dodging,
shooting, drawing a line and letting her know which way
it lay. He was probably going to strain something by shoving around rocks that were too heavy to lift alone, but right
now he felt like he could haul enough boulders to dam the
whole St. Lawrence.

He owed Libby an apology. He knew that. He also owed
her an explanation, though he still had no idea what the hell
he was supposed to say to her.

But as he dropped a giant stone on top of the pile, he
couldn't keep from grinning.

He still had a thousand worries and he still had screwed
up, but somehow he couldn't help feeling like he was finally
back where he belonged. Back to himself.

CHAPTER SIX

LIBBY SPENT THE REST of the day attacking her to-do list. She flew through tasks with a focus and efficiency that frightened even her. She debated going back to the town house that night, but two times in a row was too much at this point in the preparations. She also didn't want anyone to think that Sam had the power to drive her away from camp. So she decided to stay. The fact that she wouldn't be able to sleep was inconsequential. She was there, ready to hear Sam's apology and/or explanation whenever he should decide to offer them.

Not that she was holding her breath.

She dealt with the filing and went to dinner and led a session on discipline, congratulating herself when she got through the whole thing without once making eye contact with Sam or referring to him as an example of someone in need of correction. She did notice that he abandoned his usual seat at the back of the dining hall to stand up near the front, off to her side, as if he were an emcee waiting to resume running the program as soon as she finished her portion. It left her rattled, but she refused to let him see it.

She did, however, allow herself a few moments of wondering about the teaching job she had applied to. As she stood at the front of the room, leading the counselors through theory and examples, she couldn't help but think how it might feel to lead a group of third-grade students in the same way. Would they be more or less attentive? Would they need more explanation? Would she be able to handle months of working inside without regular trips outdoors to walk her rounds and refuel herself with a shot of blue sky and green trees?

When the session was over and staff had been dispersed with instructions to get a good night's sleep because there was another full day ahead, she watched Sam trudge off to his cabin without a word to anyone. That was unusual.

Come to think of it, everyone had seemed somewhat subdued that night. Not just during her talk, but before that, at dinner. She would have liked to blame it on exhaustion but she had a guilty feeling that news of her shouting match with Sam had left everyone uneasy and uncertain.

Not exactly the greatest way to get people psyched for the arrival of the kids in a few days.

In the good old days, when Myra was in charge, things would never have reached this point. Libby was great at organization and motivation, but Myra had always been the one who saw the potential personality issues and headed them off before they could reach a crisis point.

On an impulse, Libby made her way to her car—the one place at camp where she could be assured of both a little privacy and a decent cell phone connection—and called Myra.

"Libby, dear!" Myra sounded tired but happy, the way Libby always thought of her. "How are you? And Sam, and everyone? And Cosmo. Does he... Has he adjusted?"

Libby gave Myra the high points first: the staff members were starting to work as a team, Cosmo was only mildly grumpier than usual, they were a bit behind schedule with the cabin and activity area prep but she was sure they would be ready to start checking kids in on Sunday afternoon. They talked about Myra's adjustment to life with her sister, and how she and Esther were planning a trip to Victoria in a couple of weeks.

"Esther is still well enough to do something like that?" Libby asked.

"She has more good times than bad," Myra said slowly. "We want to make the most of them while we can."

Suddenly, Libby's problems with Sam seemed small and petty. She couldn't dump her worries on Myra. That would be the worst kind of thoughtlessness.

But before she could redirect the conversation to happier topics, Myra jumped in. "I spoke to Verna Collins today. She told me she ran into you at the library."

Oh, Lordy. Trust the small-town gossip line to beat her to the punch even after Myra had moved.

"She said she gave you quite a surprise."

Libby slumped lower in her seat. "Well, yeah. Not her fault, though. Really. I hope she doesn't feel guilty or anything."

"Heavens, no. Verna is far too wise to waste energy on that. But she was worried about you. She said you seemed rather upset."

That was one way to describe it. "I was…not very happy. This is something I should have found out a long time ago. It's going to have a major impact on Sam's ability to do the job, which is absolutely okay. He has a kid…he needs to be with the kid. That's fine. But I do the scheduling. I should have known."

"Yes, you should have, and I'm very surprised that Sam didn't tell you already. He assured me he would, once he'd had a chance to smooth things over with you."

"Smooth things over? He said that?" She couldn't hold back a sigh. "Myra, if he was going to wait for that to happen, I wouldn't have found out about this until the kid was in high school."

Myra's familiar *hmm* carried across the miles, making her sound so close and reliable that tears pricked at the back of Libby's eyes. The camp had been one of the few constants in Libby's life. So had Myra. From her first summer at Overlook when she was eleven, Myra had been a steady oasis in an otherwise rocky life. Libby would never forget the day, a couple of years after she started working for Myra, when she was weeding the files and found a folder with her name on it. Inside she found a note from her fifth grade teacher recommending her for one of that year's free camperships. There followed a series of other correspondence, copies of letters between Myra and Gran and other teachers, all ensuring that Myra always knew how to find Libby and bring her back to camp for free each year.

When Myra found her crying over the file, she had pressed a tissue into Libby's hand, placed a gentle hand on her shoulder and said the words that had carried Libby through many a hard time since then: "I always knew you could be more than life had dealt you, dear."

"Libby," Myra asked now, "did Sam say why he hadn't mentioned this fact to you?"

"He said it was none of my business." Her fingers tightened on the phone at the memory.

"Oh, dear. And that was all?"

"No." Libby breathed out her anger, fogging up the windshield, so as not to make things any harder for Myra. "There were some other points. Mostly about me."

"I see."

Myra might have been waiting for more details, but Libby refused to go into specifics. For one thing, repeating Sam's accusations would only make her angry all over again. For another, Myra shouldn't have had to hear even this much.

"I'm sure we'll work it all out somehow," Libby said. "Meanwhile, have you read any—"

"Would you say that things between you and Sam are any better now than when he arrived?"

So much for hoping Myra would let it drop. "Excuse me?"

Myra sighed. "Libby, it's no secret that you and Sam had some sort of very painful falling-out in the past. I understand how that would make things awkward at first. But has there been any improvement?"

For some stupid reason, her mind immediately threw up the memory of Sam leaning over her the night before. Her toes curled.

"There have been a couple of times when I thought there might be some hope. But…"

"Ah. And what have you done to address that problem?"

"Me?"

Okay. Myra didn't know what had happened. She couldn't know that Sam was the one who had walked away, who had kept secrets, who had—

"Exactly. What have you done to improve things between you and Sam? Because, Libby, dear, please don't take this the wrong way, but I have known you since you were quite young. I know how determined you are. If you had decided to work on creating a more peaceful working relationship between you and Sam, I have no doubt whatsoever that it would have happened within three hours of his arrival."

The impact of Myra's words sank in, making Libby slide even lower in her car seat as the events of the past weeks rolled through her memory. She remembered Sam showing her the plans for the pavilion, and the way she had brushed him off; Sam coaxing her down to pizza and karaoke night, only to have her self-righteously proclaim that she needed to work; Sam asking her for guidance in learning the job, only to have her try to dissuade him with paperwork.

The awful truth hit her like a cold river wave flat in the face. Sam had screwed up, but in between, he had been trying to make things better between them. And she…

"Oh, crap. I have been such a bitch."

"I doubt that it went that far. And let's be honest, dear. You were probably focusing your anger on him because you didn't want to be mad at me."

Myra's suggestion sounded a little too on-target for the sake of Libby's conscience.

"But," Myra continued, "I do wonder if half the reason he found it difficult to open up to you was because you were too busy keeping yourself firmly closed off."

Myra was right. Sam had been trying to build a bridge between them. A clumsy, awkward one, to be sure, filled with gaping holes left by old hurts, but a bridge nonetheless.

And Libby had not only refused to meet him halfway, she'd been too determined to cling to the past to take even a baby step forward.

Worse, as she remembered the way her body had reacted to his nearness the previous night, she had a horrible feeling that a lot of her reluctance to move forward had very little to do with what Sam had done to her in the past and a whole lot to do with what she feared could happen between them in the future if she didn't throw a pile of nasty between them.

She was better than that. She would do better than that. Starting right that minute.

She thanked Myra and said her goodbyes while climbing out of the car and navigating the path to Sam's place. She slipped the phone into the pocket of her shorts, knocked at the door before she could talk herself out of it and twisted her shirttail between her fingers, smoothing it while waiting for Sam to answer.

The door opened.

He stood before her, framed by the opening and backlit by the light of his living room. Wet hair and blue flannel sleep pants told her she'd caught him on his way to bed. The absence of anything above his waist—and the accompanying spike in her heart rate—told her that her suspicions as to why she'd been behaving so very badly were dead-on.

"Lib." He spoke cautiously, as if waiting for a shoe to drop.

"Hi. I…" Crap. What was she supposed to say? She should have waited until tomorrow, should have given herself a chance to figure out the best way to—

No. No, she needed to do this now. And if her words weren't as polished as she would like, well, maybe that would make it easier for him to hear that they were coming straight from her heart.

"We still need to talk about how to handle things. About your son, I mean. But I—"

"Casey." Sam crossed his arms over his chest. She tried not to look.

"Sorry?"

"His name is Casey."

"Oh. Of course. Well…" She inhaled to steady herself and caught the subtle peppery scent of his body wash. The tiny corner of her brain still operating on a rational level noted that it wasn't the stuff from his commercials. "I just wanted to say…I'm still not happy about the way you kept this from me, and we will need to figure out how to make this all work. Tomorrow."

"He'll be here late tomorrow morning." Something flickered in his eyes. "He usually naps in the afternoon."

"Okay. I… If you can jot down his schedule for me first thing tomorrow morning, I can look at ways to work around it, and then we can go over things while he naps. Will that work for you?"

"It should." His head dipped to one side. He shifted a little, narrowing his stance so he didn't look quite so intimidating. For the first time she realized that he had probably been ready for another blast from her.

"I'm still not happy about the timing of this. But I wanted to say…I…"

His eyes narrowed. She pushed the words out before she could stop herself.

"I realized tonight that I wasn't exactly making it easier for you to tell me things. That I was deliberately making things more unpleasant between us than they needed to be. And I just want to say, I shouldn't have done that. I'm sorry."

He studied her as if waiting for her to change her mind. After a moment his shoulders relaxed and his hands slipped down to his sides.

"Thanks." He hesitated before adding, "And for the record, I know I should have been more up-front. You deserved that. I didn't mean to make things more complicated for you, and I blew it. I'm sorry."

The big *why* burned inside her, pushing to be asked, but she bit it back. She deserved some answers, absolutely. But she could wait. She—they—needed time to take the raw edge off everything that had been said and done.

So she murmured her thanks for his apology and stuck out her hand.

"Fresh start?"

His palm brushed hers. Awareness, heat, memories shot through her, and she had a terrifying moment of wondering if she had bitten off a far more potent mix than even she could chew.

Then his hand enveloped hers, surrounding it, and he grinned in that old cocksure way, and even though she knew things were still dicey, knew they had some rocky times ahead, she had this feeling that maybe—just maybe—they would get through this.

There had once been a time when she had believed she

could do anything with Sam on her side. She was no longer that naive.

But maybe, perhaps, they could make it through the summer together.

THE NEXT MORNING, Libby was halfway through the final session on camp policies and guidelines when Sam pulled his phone from his pocket, grinned like an idiot and practically ran out of the dining hall. Her gut contracted.

His son must have arrived.

She was ready for this. She had spent half the night talking herself into some form of preparedness. So he had a child. Big deal. He was thirty, just a few months older than her. Okay, so no one had ever mentioned him having a kid, and she hadn't ever heard of him getting married or being involved with anyone longer than maybe thirty seconds—and with everything else, she had never thought to ask about the kid's mom—but then, many people had a baby or two by the time they turned thirty. Just look at Dani. She was a good four, maybe five years younger than Libby, and she had three of them.

Hmmm. Maybe Dani wasn't the best comparison.

In any case, by the time the session ended and Libby headed toward the office to sneak in some paperwork before lunch, she was sure that she was ready. Really, the fact that Sam had a child was good. It was a vivid and undeniable reminder that the past was in the past, they had both moved on and from here on out theirs would be a strictly platonic business relationship.

Not that she had ever had any intention of forgetting that in the first place, but a well-placed reminder was always helpful.

"Hey, Libby." Phoebe scooted up beside Libby, halting her progress toward the office. Tanya, of course, was right behind Phoebe, but unlike her, Tanya wasn't looking anywhere near Libby. No, Tanya's big blue eyes were dancing a jig between the office and the path up the hill to Sam's place. Looking for her new true love, no doubt.

Libby sighed. God protect her from overactive imaginations and hormones.

"What's up?" she asked Phoebe.

"You're going to eat lunch with us, right? I know you have to go check on the office stuff, but I had some ideas for the opening campfire that I want to run past you. So when you come back, make sure you— Hello, who's this?"

Libby followed Phoebe's gaze to the crest of the hill, where a pretty brunette in a swirly blue-dotted sundress was double-timing it down the path.

The mother? she thought, and something hard and hot twisted inside her until the brunette waved and burst into a jog.

"Libby!" she called. "Oh, my gosh, Libby, is that really you?"

It took a moment. A moment and a squint and a fast readjustment of old memories with the reality of the woman running toward her with open arms. Then recognition kicked in and laughter bubbled out as Libby recognized Sam's little sister.

"Brynn! What are you doing here?" Libby met Brynn for a squealing hug, then released her for a long inspection. "Let me see you. Wow. You look fabulous!"

From the corner of her eye, Libby saw Phoebe nudge Tanya in the ribs and nod in her direction.

"You, too," Brynn said. "Which is, you know, totally amazing. Since you've had to put up with my beast of a brother, I mean."

Libby wouldn't even dream of challenging Brynn's assessment. "Where is the beast, anyway?"

"Right behind me. He had to tie up the dog. I told him, look, mister, if you think I'm wrestling that damned dog for one more minute after I drove all this way in your boring grown-up car with it slobbering all over me, then you can—"

Brynn stopped as Sam crested the hill. At least, Libby thought Brynn stopped talking. It was hard to be certain over the sudden rush of blood pounding in her ears. Her jaw sagged and she jerked forward at the sight of Sam walking toward her, for once moving slowly as he matched his steps to those of the child whose hand he held.

Wisps of strawberry-blond hair danced like dandelion fluff across the little one's head. Deep brown eyes peered at her above cheeks that were flushed from sleep. Chubby arms and toes that poked out from denim shorts and a miniature Overlook shirt simply begged to be tickled.

Beside her, Phoebe let out a soft *meep*. Tanya clapped her hands to her mouth and fled.

Libby took in the hair, the eyes, the full mouth, and let her clipboard sag to her side.

The child paused and looked down the hill, over the camp and toward the river. His eyes doubled in size. His bottom lip shook. Even from where she stood, she could see the way his grip on Sam's hand tightened, the way he edged closer to Sam's leg and looked up at Sam with an expression that said *I'm lost and scared but I know you'll make it okay.*

And she remembered when she had been the one who was lost and scared. After the accident that left her mother too silent in the crumpled front seat of their car, after the police officer had lifted Libby out of her car seat in the back, after the sirens and the flashing lights and the hours when no one would tell her when she could see her mommy. Gran had walked into the police station and taken Libby's hand, and Libby had held on tight. She knew that Gran was the only person standing between her and a world that had suddenly turned inside out. She had gripped Gran's hand and refused to let go, clinging to her the way this little one was clinging to Sam.

It's okay, sweetheart. Casey. I know how you feel. I promise you, you'll be okay.

But as heart wrenching as Casey was, he wasn't the reason for the way her heart seemed to have reached up into her throat and yanked everything tight and closed. No, that honor went to Sam.

No matter what Sam had put her through, she knew that he could be tender and caring. She'd seen him console homesick campers and talk a kid through a panic attack and keep a straight face while holding tight to a boy being readied for stitches. She'd seen him in the moonlight, his eyes filled with wonder and want as he pulled her close and kissed his way down her body.

But she had never seen anything that came close to the fierce love in his face as he swooped this little one into his arms and cradled him tight while walking closer.

"Casey," he said in a voice that was lower and gentler than she had ever heard, "this is Libby. She's going to be at the camp for the summer. That makes you a lucky little guy, because she's a very special lady."

Sam tore his gaze away from his child to look at her, and her breath froze in her chest. He shifted the boy higher on his shoulder, tightening his grip.

"Libby, this is Casey. My son."

ONE LOOK AT THE SHOCK that had claimed Libby's face when she saw Casey, and Sam knew things were still not right. Especially when, as soon as she had fussed over the boy and said all the right things, she slipped away from the crowd that had gathered and headed for the office.

He wanted to follow her. But sense told him that the best thing he could do would be to give her some time, then get everything straightened out during their meeting.

He took Casey into the kitchen and introduced him to Cosmo, who gave Sam an assessing look, grunted and immediately offered Casey a hunk of cheese that was almost as big as his head. Sam carried Casey and his giant wedge of cheddar into the main part of the dining hall and gave everyone on staff a few minutes to coo and fuss over the boy before announcing that it was family time. The counselors laughed and waved him off with promises that they could handle things for the afternoon. His job was to spend time with Casey.

And he did. He talked to Brynn and cooked Casey's favorite tiny pasta and helped his son see that, look, here's your high chair, and here's your *Sesame Street* plate and here's your daddy shooting peas into the net just like always. He changed Casey's diaper and sang "Three Little Monkeys" while rocking him in the regular chair, and when he settled Casey in his crib for a belated nap, he made sure that Casey noticed the picture of Robin on the dresser, just like always.

There. Not even Sharon could say he wasn't doing everything he could to make this transition as easy as possible for his child.

Too bad he hadn't given as much thought to other people's feelings.

No sooner had he come downstairs after dropping a final kiss on his son's velvet cheek than Brynn met him in the living room with a pitcher of iced coffee.

"Here." She pressed it into his hands. "Take this out to the porch. I already set out some glasses and cookies."

"Why?"

"Because Libby will be here in five minutes, and you're

going to have to work very hard to make up for whatever bomb you dropped on her."

"Crap." His shoulders sagged. "I wasn't imagining it, huh?"

"Nope. Please tell me that Casey wasn't a surprise to her."

"Not totally."

"So what do you think made her look like she'd been sucker punched?"

He had a suspicion. Or maybe that was just his own guilty conscience, still blaring the Libby-Robin tango at such a high volume that it drowned out all other possibilities.

He was ready to explain things to Brynn but the beep of an incoming text message made him stop. He checked his phone. His heart rate spiked.

"Libby's on her way," he said.

"Sucks to be you."

"Want to play mediator?"

Brynn shook her head, rolled her eyes and pointed to the porch.

"Go practice your groveling," she said. "You're gonna need it."

CHAPTER SEVEN

How the hell had she ever thought she was ready to see Sam as a father?

Libby stood at the door to the office, forcing herself to breathe slowly in an attempt to steady the racing of her heart. Thus far, it wasn't working.

She thought—hoped—she had covered her reaction well enough to keep from becoming the latest buzz on the Overlook gossip line. She had said hello to Casey and made what she hoped were the appropriate noises about how gorgeous and strong he was, and asked Brynn what she was doing these days, and laughed along with the others when Casey demanded to be put down then promptly fell on his well-padded little rump. She thought she had even congratulated Sam.

Then she had made an excuse about work and fled into the office, through the door Sam had left open *again,* where she closed herself off from the world and leaned against the wall and groaned.

Sam was a parent. Somehow, she had been so fixated on the presence of the child that she had managed to gloss over the fact that she would be looking at Sam through a different lens. He was a *daddy,* and probably a very good one, if the love in his eyes and the way little Casey had clung to him were any indication.

Maybe that was the difference. When she had thought of him as simply a father, well, that implied a level of involvement she could handle. Remote. Not too hands-on. Possibly even Victorian.

But Sam was a daddy.

Libby didn't have much experience with daddies. The "father" space on her own birth certificate was a taunting blank. According to Gran, her paternal DNA came from a tourist who "blew through town one weekend and left your mother with an extraspecial souvenir." The closest thing she had ever had to a father figure was probably Cosmo, and if that wasn't a thought to leave a gal gasping, she didn't know what was.

A daddy, though... That was a whole other story. Daddies took care of their children and put them first and turned themselves inside out to make sure their children always knew they were loved and wanted. At least, that was how it had looked to her as a little girl when she watched her friends with their families. Daddies stood between their kids and the world, keeping their lives safe and secure and stable.

She hadn't known that Sam had that in him.

Or—was it just that she didn't want to believe it?

The ringing of her phone cut through her confusion. She shook her head, pulled her phone from her pocket and checked the display. Dani.

Oh, goody.

"Hi, Dani. What's up?"

"I need a favor."

Libby frowned, not at the request, but at the unusual huskiness in Dani's voice. "You sound awful. Are you sick?"

"Nah, though I probably will be if I don't get some sleep soon. Liam came down with a bad cold, and now Aidan has it, and—Aidan, stop hitting your brother!—and I'm just waiting for it to turn into tonsillitis. Plus one of the women at work quit without notice, so that's been insane, and…anyway. My lawn mower died, and I can't deal with fixing it right now."

Translation: she probably couldn't afford to fix it right now. "Mine is in the shed behind the house. You have my house key, right?"

"Right."

"Okay. The key to the shed is hanging by my back door. It's the one with the key chain that looks like an outhouse. There should be plenty of gas in the mower."

"Thanks,° Libby. You're the—"

Whatever Dani was about to say was cut off by a loud crash.

"Liam! Damn, you know better than to—Libby, sorry, I have to run. There's marbles all over the floor. Thanks a million."

Libby ended the call, checked the clock and saw that it was time for her to meet with Sam, to hash out the details of meshing his job at camp with his job as Daddy. Quickly, before she could let herself hunt up an excuse, she sent him a fast text that she was on her way.

There. She'd committed herself. She had to talk to him now.

She just hoped she could get through it without making an even bigger idiot of herself than she probably already had.

SAM CARRIED THE PITCHER of iced coffee to the porch, setting it beside the plate of little sugary things Brynn had set out.

A soft knock sounded from the front of the house. Libby had arrived.

He inched the plate closer to the center of the table—then back to the first place—then over to the far edge before giving up in defeat and moving to stare out at the river while

Brynn exclaimed over Libby's hair, efficiency and ability to put up with him. Between the two of them, he was doomed.

Finally, he sensed more than saw Libby hovering at the entry to the porch.

"Hi," she said carefully. "Did Casey go down for his nap okay?"

Casey. That was who he needed to focus on right now. Not himself, not Libby, though she definitely deserved some attention. Casey.

"Out like a light." He pulled himself from the screen and returned to the table, where he poured two glasses of coffee.

Ice clinked.

Liquid sloshed.

No one spoke.

He handed a glass to Libby, taking great care to avoid brushing her fingers, then forced himself to face her.

A casual observer would never know she'd had the stuffing yanked out of her. But he knew that her eyes didn't usually hold that wariness, that her grip on her clipboard didn't usually leave her knuckles white.

It was the pinched look around her mouth that finally made him man up and speak.

"I owe you an explanation. Among other things."

She pulled the clipboard closer to her chest. A small movement, barely visible, but he had to force his feet to stay planted where they were instead of carrying him across the porch to wrap her in a hug and rock her back and forth until all the tension slipped out of her.

Yeah, that would go over really well.

Lucky for him, any inclination to move was halted by a sudden tickle in his nose. He ducked his face into his elbow and let loose with a sneeze that could have rattled the windows if they'd been closed.

"Bless you," she said automatically, then frowned and took a step back.

"Are you catching a cold?"

"No," he said with a sigh. "It's allergies. The dog."

As if on cue, Finnegan strolled into the room and dropped a rubber chicken at Sam's feet.

"Libby, meet Finnegan," he said before another sneeze set in. Finnegan sat and waited for the silly human trick to be done, then whined softly and pushed the chicken forward with his paw.

"Sorry, fella." Sam picked up the toy, tossed it out of the room, then quickly shut the porch doors. Too late; another sneeze nabbed him.

"Sorry about that," he said after blowing his nose. "It's usually not this bad. Every time I'm away from him for a few days, I have to get used to him all over again."

"Why do you have a dog if you're allergic?"

He waved her into a chair before seating himself beside the table. He plucked one of the sugary things off the plate before realizing that if he tried to eat anything, he would probably end up choking on his own nervousness.

"He's Casey's dog. When Casey came to me, Finnegan came, too."

A thousand questions flitted across her face, all in the space of her simple "Oh."

He sighed and dropped into a chair. "Let me give you the condensed version. A few years ago, I had a very nice neighbor named Robin. We were friends. Then for a while, we were more than friends, and we had Casey."

Libby perched on the edge of her chair, the clipboard balanced on her knees.

"We never—well. It's complicated." And could lead to an inadvertent revelation about Sharon, which was a step he was not prepared to take. This discussion was difficult enough without throwing in a mention of the lawsuit. "Robin and I had a system that worked for us. Casey lived with her not far from Halifax. I visited whenever I could. It was all very adult and reasonable, and we were managing just fine." He drew in a deep breath. "Then six—no, seven months ago now—Robin died."

"What?"

Libby looked as if she wasn't sure whether she should fall back in her chair or jump up and run away. Pretty much the way he had reacted when he got the news, come to think of it.

"It was one of those freak things. Aneurysm. One day she had a headache, then she was in the hospital, then she was gone."

She cupped her hands over her mouth. Her eyes, barely visible above her fingers, were soft and disbelieving.

At last she dragged her hands back down and shook her head. "I am so, so sorry."

"Thanks."

"So that was when Casey came to you. With Finnegan."

"Sort of." He backtracked quickly before the curiosity on her face could lead her to questions he didn't want her entertaining. "I was near the end of the regular season, and we were fighting for a play-off berth. I had a responsibility to my team. Brynn was able to take time off and come help me while I finished things up."

"And while you were getting everything set here."

"Yeah."

"You're lucky you have her."

"Don't I know it."

She nodded, but the action was hollow. More of a time-marker than an agreement, he could tell.

Then she looked over at him, and he felt like he'd just taken an elbow to the head. "Why the big secret?"

The seventy-five-million-dollar question, and he couldn't answer it.

"That was a mistake."

"Agreed. But that wasn't my question."

"I'm sorry. It's personal."

As if she had expected the answer, she pushed out of her chair and took the place he'd occupied by the screen, staring out over the campground without seeing, much the way he had.

"I should have been told."

"I'm sorry."

She shook her head, small pink spots forming on her cheeks. "No, Sam. No. You're not getting out of this one with a simple 'I'm sorry,' okay? I should have known."

"I had reasons, Lib. Good reasons."

"I'm sure you did. You're an old hand at doing what you want and then skipping away without a word of explanation, aren't you?"

Oh, no. He wasn't going there. The last thing he needed was to get her thinking of old wounds once again. "Don't drag the past into this, Libby."

"Don't…" She looked to the walls, exasperation practically pouring off her, her free hand reaching up to fist in her hair. She breathed in deep and held it for a second. Probably trying to calm herself, for when she spoke again, her words were clipped and tight. "Fine. Setting aside everything that happened once upon a time, Sam, you still should have told me."

She should have known about the dog and the scheduling. No question about that. But was she entitled to more? She wasn't part of his life. She was his employee. A very enticing employee with whom he had a tangled history, sure, but that was it. It wasn't as if he were trying to pick up where they had left off. Even if she'd made it abundantly clear that there was no chance of that, well, heck. In a show-down between the camp and Casey, her heart would fall to the camp. He was sure of it.

He studied her, trying to figure out what lay behind that shield of a clipboard. She flushed a bit but held his gaze as he tried to decipher what she was hiding. There was more than anger there, he could tell. It was more like she was... hurt.

He'd hurt her.

Ah, crap.

"You have a point," he said with a sigh.

She jerked back. Not much, just enough to make her cheeks flush and bring a small smile of surprise to the corner of his mouth.

"Here's the thing, Lib. I got shoved onto the full-time parent track without warning. I'm not complaining, believe me. I thank God every day that I was able to make the changes I had to make when Casey needed me." He picked up his glass and absently rubbed his finger around the edge. "But I'm still learning how to balance it all, you know? Everything I do now goes through the Casey lens. Is this what's best for him? What will he need?"

"I understand that. But—"

"Lib." He scooched forward, hoping and praying she could see that he really meant this. "I... Sometimes, when I'm juggling lots of different people, lots of different needs...sometimes I make the wrong decisions. Ones I regret, even years later."

She reached for her clipboard.

"I figured out how to make the camp work for Casey. I forgot about making him work for the camp. And for you." He looked her straight in the eye and added, softly, "For that, I'm sorry."

She seemed to be in some kind of inner debate. He held

his breath while she bit down on her lip and looked at the ceiling, the naked wall, anywhere but at him.

She sighed. "No more surprises. At least nothing like that, okay?"

The matter of the lawsuit flashed through his mind. Should he tell her?

No. There was no need. Court wasn't until September, when she would more than likely be gone. There was no reason for her to hear about it. No reason to put himself through the unpleasantness of telling her, of having it hovering between them each time they spoke, of having her wonder if he could do his job with that hanging over his head. He was doing enough of that on his own.

"That's all I've got."

She bit down on her lip and looked away.

He held his breath.

Then, at last, she met his gaze again, nodded and offered him the barest bones of a smile.

"Thank you."

It wasn't much. A whisper and a quirk of the mouth before she focused on the clipboard and started talking schedule. That was it.

But Sam could swear the earth shifted a little on its axis when Libby smiled at him, no matter how reluctantly.

LIBBY WALKED INTO THE OFFICE on the last day of orientation, checked her clipboard and frowned. The to-do list was going down, but it was still fuller than she would have liked. For every item she checked off it seemed she was adding two or three more, which wasn't unusual. She could handle that. But removing Myra from the mix and adding Sam had complicated things in ways she hadn't anticipated.

It didn't help that she herself seemed incapable of working when Casey was around. He spent most of his time in the house with Mrs. Collins, but Sam had developed a habit of bringing him along for meals, or having him pop into the office for kisses before naptime. And Libby could not make herself keep working when that strawberry-blond head poked around the door and whispered a loud, "Biiiibby?"

But she'd spent the morning running from one end of the camp to the other. Sam was down in the cabins, hauling mattresses. She needed a break. Five minutes to sit alone on the sofa with an iced coffee and do nothing but stare at the walls. Then she would be ready to dive back in.

But no sooner had she raided the minifridge in the corner for her caffeine stash than her gaze fell on the folder containing the plans for the pavilion and her fingers started to twitch.

She wanted to look at the plans.

Of course she had seen them. Sam had shown them to her within an hour of his return, but she had been too busy trying to push him away to pay attention to them.

Now, though... Now she could focus on them. Now that she wasn't busy tearing down bridges, she could give the plans the thorough inspection they deserved.

Besides—she really, really wanted to see what Sam had in mind.

She peeked out the window. The road down to the dining hall and the rest of the camp was deserted. She crept to the door, opened it cautiously, then peered all around, double-checking the paths to the staff parking lot and the house, in case he was wandering down either of those. Because, while she was desperate to have a look, she wasn't quite ready for Sam to know about that desperation.

The coast was clear.

Moving quickly, she returned to the table and pulled the papers from the envelope. She skipped past the pages with the specs and the lists of options, and went right to the one that mattered—the artist's rendering of the completed pavilion.

"Oh, wow," she breathed.

It was perfect. Sam must have given the architect photos of the inlet, because the background was exactly as she remembered it, right down to the rock peeking out of the water at the bend in the river. But the pavilion itself was what made her bring her fingers to her lips to hold back a squeak of happiness.

It was going to be long and gently curved, following the riverbank. The roof hung lower to the ground on the side closest to the water, not enough to totally block the view but enough to provide a bit more shelter if there was a light rain. A massive stone fireplace that opened front and back divided the structure into two spaces, one twice as long as the other. Restrooms and a small kitchen flanked the fireplace. Libby could immediately picture staff meetings happening in the smaller space and end-of-session award ceremonies in the larger one.

She slipped the plans back into the folder with a sigh. The structure Sam had planned was everything she had described to him when they talked about it all those years ago. The camp deserved the pavilion. Myra deserved the honor.

But much as she didn't want to, she couldn't help but wonder at the way Sam had carried her dream with him all this time.

THE OWNER'S BARBECUE on the night before check-in had always been one of Sam's favorite camp traditions when he had been a counselor, both in training and for real, and he had no intention of doing away with it now that he was in charge.

Orientation and setup were finished. The cabins were ready. With the arrival of the counselor trainees that morning, the staff was complete. All that was needed was about one hundred and forty kids and the camp would be humming.

Sam did choose to make one change. While Myra had always kept it a working party, with folks helping with the grilling and the food prep, Sam decided that at least this once he would go all out. The cries of appreciation from the staff as they arrived to the pig roast he'd arranged, followed by relaxed laughter and sighs of contentment, told him it was a wise choice.

"Catered, huh?" Libby stood beside him at the entrance to the dining hall, surveying the happy crowd. "Interesting choice."

He shifted Casey higher on his shoulder. "They've all worked hard this week to get everything ready. I figured everyone could use a night off."

She scanned the room once more, then gave a nod of approval. "I think you're right. This was a good idea."

Libby agreed with him? Damn. She really had meant it when she said she was ready to give them a fresh start.

Bolstered by the thought, he decided to push the envelope a bit. "When I say everyone has earned a night off, that includes you." With his free hand, he plucked the clipboard from her hands before she had a chance to react.

Her eyes widened. "But I—"

"Uh-uh. You're not getting this back for at least an hour." When she sputtered, he shook his head and lifted the offending object above her reach.

"Forget it, Lib. Like it or not, you're having some downtime. You're gonna eat a relaxed meal, and listen to some bad jokes and laugh. And I bet you'll end up so refreshed that you sail through tomorrow and end up saying it was your easiest first day ever."

"Not likely," she said, but there was no force behind her

words. She must have needed the break even more than he realized.

Casey chose that moment to twist himself around from his over-the-shoulder perch. His hair brushed Sam's cheek as his small head leaned up against Sam's jaw.

"Did you get bored with the scenery back there, squirt?" Sam patted Casey's bottom. Not soggy. Yay.

"Hi, sweetpea." Libby's face brightened as she leaned in and offered her hand to the child, palm up. "Are you having fun?"

Casey looked from her hand to her face, then slowly placed his palm over hers. "Bibby!"

"That's right. Do you remember what Leo the Lion says?"

Having been well trained by Libby, who Sam could swear knew more kid songs than all four Wiggles combined, Casey immediately let loose with a fierce roar.

"That's right!" She glowed as she leaned closer, laughing and light. "You learned that so fast!"

"Yeah, the Nobel people are already planning to give him a call," Sam said, but on the inside he was doing a serious little pride dance. Not only was his kid bright, he also had a head start on how to impress women.

"Do you know about the eensy-weensy spider?" Libby took Casey's hands in hers and moved them through the motions of the song, clapping them together with a gleeful "Yay for the spider!" when she was done.

She was so good with Casey. So easy. He knew too many people who gave his kid a passing hello and then returned their focus to him, intent on impressing Mr. Cold Ice. Or those who knew about Robin would continue to talk brightly to Sam while sneaking speculative glances at Casey, as if they were measuring his adjustment level or something.

Libby did neither of those. She just sang to Casey and

made him giggle, and Sam wasn't sure whose smile warmed his heart more.

Casey lasted through one more round of the song before lurching forward, arms outstretched.

"Bibby!"

Her arms closed around him effortlessly as she shifted him to her hip, falling immediately into a side-to-side sway when Casey tucked his head into her shoulder.

Sam was impressed. Libby might be the most efficient and determined woman he knew, but in a heartbeat she could transform into this nurturing, humming person who created a tiny oasis of calm and togetherness in the middle of the bustling hall.

A hand landed on his shoulder. He knew it was Brynn from the fuchsia nails digging into his skin, even before she let loose with a soft but most emphatic swearword. He thought she had simply lost her balance until he twisted sideways and saw the way she stared at Libby and Casey, eyes wide, a hand over her mouth.

And if he'd had any last hopes that the resemblance between Libby and Robin was his guilty conscience playing tricks on him, they had just been blown to hell.

CHAPTER EIGHT

THE NIGHT BEFORE the campers arrived always challenged Libby's ability to sleep. This year was worse than ever. Between worries about how Mr. Cold Ice might complicate the flow of traffic through the various stations, worries about parents who might not have read the letter telling them of Myra's departure, and worries about Cosmo's sudden and unexplained insistence on removing meat loaf from all the menus, she spent far too many precious minutes staring at the familiar knothole in the ceiling above her bunk. Not that she could really see it in the dark. She just knew it was there, round and swirly.

Just like she knew that the real reason she couldn't sleep had very little to do with camp worries and a whole lot to do with something Brynn had said in the middle of the barbecue. Libby hadn't been able to catch it all in the buzz around them, but there had been something about the last time Brynn had been at camp, and some crisis with the family. Something about their world going to hell and back. Those were the words that were drumming through her in a can't-sleep rhythm.

Because the last time Brynn came to camp was the last time Sam was there, too. Right before he did the inexplicable.

And Libby wanted to know more.

Finally admitting that she wasn't going to be drifting away to dreamland anytime soon, she threw off her blanket, shoved her feet into her fuzzy slippers and grabbed her flashlight. Five minutes later she was in the office, making a mug of hot chocolate and booting up the computer. Not the camp's, but her personal laptop.

Research time.

While her machine wheezed to life, she checked voice mail. Three parents checking on their kids, one supplier, an inquiry about a last-minute opening and then a message so garbled by a child's background wailing that she had to play it twice to catch the words.

"Libby, it's Dani. I'm all done with your lawn mower, but could I maybe use your weed trimmer, too? Mine has disappeared. I think one of the kids took it apart. Give me a call, but don't be surprised if it takes me a while to get back to you. Aidan has tonsillitis. You know what that means."

Oh, *crap*. Poor Aidan. Poor Dani.

She made a note to call Dani in the morning, then pushed her neighbor worries aside and paid a quick visit to Google, where she found over nine hundred thousand references to Sam. She needed to start digging.

She made quick work of the gossip pieces linking him with starlets and country singers. She found nothing referencing either Robin or Casey, which seemed odd at first. But then, it sounded as though Robin had been a regular Josephine. It might have been that the starlets and singers were the ones who had attracted attention more than Sam, at least until he became the Cold Ice man. If he and Robin had kept things quiet... And he had said she'd moved before Casey was born....

She sipped her drink, savoring the smooth heat, and concentrated on the task at hand. She knew a heck of a lot about Sam's first eighteen years and a decent smattering of his current life. But there was over a decade in there that was ripe for mining. She had always been a great researcher.

Surely if she looked hard enough, she could find some kind of clue as to what the man was hiding behind that smile.

An hour later, her cocoa was gone and her neck was cramped, but she barely noticed. For there, buried in the middle of a fluff piece from his college paper, Libby saw words that had her leaning forward to be sure she was reading correctly.

The article had been written just a couple of years ago, when Sam's team won the Stanley Cup. It was a "we're so proud of our alumni" piece that had first made her cringe, because how could someone be considered an alumnus if he left midway through his second year?

But the story turned out to be a treasure chest of memories from people who had known Sam—coaches, professors, even a few of his old college teammates. And there, halfway down the page, she found unexpected gold.

"Of course, he had a rough start to his first year," said Coach Lyon, then an assistant coach of the Ice Cats. "Not two weeks before classes started, his mother landed in the hospital, and his father, from what I remember, took a powder. Sam wasn't just any incoming freshman. He was the rock of his family. It was a heartbreaker, no doubt about it, but I'll never forget his focus on the ice. Before that, he was just another kid using an athletic scholarship to pay for school, but after that…it was like he had to get good and he had to do it fast. Because, you know, there was a whole family depending on him."

Libby leaned back against her chair and covered her mouth with her hands. The words seemed to leap from the screen to lodge in her brain.

Not two weeks before classes started.

That would have been right after he left camp—a perfect fit with what she'd heard from Brynn.

Right after he kissed her goodbye and promised her that it wasn't the end for them.

His mother landed in the hospital and his father, from what I remember, took a powder.

Sam was the oldest of four. If this coach's memory was correct—and dear God, could anyone forget something like that?—then in the space of a few days, Sam had been pushed from a carefree youth who was playing hockey to put himself through college, to someone who had to look after a whole boatload of scared and hurting people.

He had to get good and he had to do it fast. Because, you know, there was a whole family depending on him.

Maybe Sam hadn't left school in his second year in search of fame and glory. Maybe he'd been searching for nothing more than a paycheck to support the family that needed him.

And maybe, when she had called him with her own heartbreak…maybe he'd had a hell of a good reason to hang up.

LATE THAT NIGHT, when Casey was soundly asleep and Sam had finally surrendered after a couple of hours of unpacking boxes and moving furniture, he grabbed a beer from the fridge and retreated to the quiet shadows of the porch. He dropped into the Adirondack chair, then winced.

"I have got to get some softer chairs for out here," he said. A very unladylike snort came from the other seat.

"You're telling me," Brynn said. "I hereby volunteer to

do the honors on my way out of town tomorrow. Your credit card and I have had some lovely times together the past few months. I'm going to miss it."

"I bet you will." And then, because the light was off and it was easier to be sappy in the dark, he added, "There's no way I can thank you enough for everything you've done for me and Casey."

"Yeah, so, you'll now be in my debt for all eternity. I like that." Her voice dropped as she added, "I'm glad you asked. It's been kind of a wild ride, but I wouldn't have wanted to be anywhere else."

He nodded even though he knew she couldn't see it. She would know, though. She was good that way.

"It's pretty here," she said. "When we were kids, here for camp, I didn't really notice how gorgeous it was. No wonder you jumped at the chance to come back."

He stared into the night. He never realized there could be so many shades of darkness, from the deep black of the forests to the glinting onyx of the river and the shadowy dark of the areas on the fringe of the few lights left gleaming. Stillness had settled all around them. Other than a few distant animal calls and the gentle ringing of the wind chimes Brynn had hung outside the door—and, of course, the soft hum of Casey's monitor—the world was silent. Pride swelled within him as it hit him: this was his. His life, his future, his home.

"Yeah. Yeah, it's a damned fine place."

A soft rustling told him that Brynn was shifting in her chair. Uh-oh. A restless Brynn usually meant he was in for something.

"So." Her voice was far too bright. "Interesting how Libby could be a stunt double for Robin, isn't it?"

Ah, crap. So much for hoping Brynn would leave without mentioning it.

"Not that it's that obvious," she continued, as if he'd agreed. "Sure, the hair is about the same color, and they both have freckles. And I'd say Libby is about the same height as Robin was, maybe a little shorter. Robin was definitely prettier than Libby, and more—oh, I don't know—willowy, I guess you'd say. But it's more the way they carried themselves. Libby is just as brisk and no-nonsense as Robin was. She doesn't smile as much as Robin did, but then, she has a lot on her mind right now."

And Libby's voice was close enough to Robin's that he was pretty sure if he had to tell them apart on the phone, he couldn't have done it, at least not a month ago. Not that he was going to admit that to Brynn.

Sam had never tried to pretend that he and Robin were seriously in love, even when he proposed, and neither had she. Maybe if he hadn't been gone so much...maybe if life had progressed according to plan, and he had ended up living in the same town as her and Casey after he retired...

But she was gone, and he was here and, damn, he wished he knew what it all meant.

"Of course, it could make perfect sense," Brynn said. "Guys have a favorite type, just like women are either into Daniel Craig or Hugh Jackman. It's not unreasonable to think your type could be organized, efficient redheads."

He liked that theory. A lot.

"It also could be that you've been carrying a torch for Libby all these years."

And, bingo. One hot button, pushed.

"You don't have to sound so friggin' cheerful about the whole thing."

"I can sound any way I want about it, big brother." Ripples in the darkness told him she was on the move. She waltzed past, pausing only long enough to pat his head in a way that was definitely not reassuring. "But then, I'm not the one who has to live with those questions. Am I?"

She left, but the worries she'd unleashed lingered behind her like an old wound aching in the rain.

Libby looked like Robin. He could live with that. He could even live with the notion that he'd never got over Libby, because when she wasn't being a pain in the ass, she was a hell of a woman. He had no problem with the Libby parts of the equation.

It was the Robin parts that made him squirm in his uncomfortable chair as the questions rolled over him.

Had he used Robin to indulge an old memory?

If he had, did that make him as selfish as his old man?

If he was as despicable as his father, what kind of parent would he be over the long haul? The kind who hung in there, or the kind who ran at the first sign of trouble?

And if he was, at his core, the same kind of selfish bastard as the man who had sired him—did that mean that Casey would be better off with Sharon, after all?

LIBBY HAD NEVER BEEN one of those little girls who wanted to be a ballerina when she grew up. They seemed too flighty for her. But the first day of camp made her feel like a dancer as she leaped from one place to the next, always as gracefully and smoothly as possible, and always with a smile.

She had learned long ago how to anticipate tears from either a parent or a child who wasn't quite as ready to say goodbye as expected. She knew when to soothe, when to joke and when to pretend that sudden requests for changes in cabin assignments were easy, welcome and reasonable. She could spot a potential prankster from twenty feet away and she could peg a parent as a source of constant phone calls within the first two minutes of a conversation.

But she was totally unprepared for someone to put the focus on her.

She was in the dining hall, her command base for opening day. Parents and campers rotated through the various arrival stations set up around the perimeter—cabin assignments, T-shirt pickup, discussions with the nurse. The large room hummed with voices, occasionally pierced by a shriek or a camera flash when someone realized that the new owner was not only a former NHL All-Star but the face that had sold a million bottles of body wash. Sam himself circulated through the buzz, shaking hands, posing for pictures and guiding people to the display filled with plans and drawings of the waterfront pavilion project.

Libby had been worried about the display when he proposed it, afraid it would cause people to linger in the building and add to the congestion. But Sam had assured her it would work, and she had to admit he'd been right. New arrivals circulated through the stations, then followed the line of exhibits to the far wall and out the door. If anything, the desire to see the next picture kept things moving better than usual.

Not only that, but the staff members who were escorting families to their cabins told her that instead of lingering to fuss over bunks and storage, many of the kids and parents were dumping their things as quickly as possible so they could head down to the inlet. Sam had arranged to have some backhoes and dump trucks on site for the kids to sit in. The reports she was receiving made her long to ditch the crowded dining hall and head down to the inlet to see the action for herself.

The fact that leaving the hall would give her a break from Sam—who had spent the day watching her with an intensity she would never have expected from him—only made it more difficult to stay at her table.

She was taking advantage of a thirty-second break in the action to sit back, breathe and check out the action at the other stations for potential problems, when a very pregnant woman marched up to her, holding the hand of one of Libby's favorite campers.

"Libby! Hi! How are you? Can you believe it's been a year already?"

"Carrie! Amazing, isn't it?" Libby grinned as if she hadn't had thirty parents express that precise thought already that afternoon. She looked past Carrie to her son. "Hey, Mick. Welcome back. Wow, you got tall!"

Mick gave her a grin and a wave before darting over to the next table to yank on the shirt of one of his old cabinmates. Libby shook her head. Those two had been a deadly combination the previous year. She was afraid to think of what they could do with an extra year of intelligence and plotting on their side.

But she didn't have long to fret about what pranks the boys might be cooking up, for before she knew what was happening, Carrie had leaned in as close as her baby bump would allow.

"So, Libby. Can I just say how delighted I was to hear that you had applied for the job at Uplands Central Schools?"

If it was physically possible for a stomach to drop, Libby was sure hers did just that at those words. "I… How did you… Who told…"

Carrie's grin was reassuring, as was her quick pat to Libby's arm. "Not to worry. I only heard because people who knew that Mick went to camp here asked me about you. But believe me, they know a lot more about you now. You might want to start brushing up on your interview skills, if you know what I mean."

Holy crap. She had sent in the résumé almost on the spur of the moment, a visceral reaction to the discovery

that Sam had a child and all the baggage that went with
it. She'd been certain her application would be simply one
of hundreds. But now… She swallowed hard and glanced
around the room.

She was really going to leave.

Not right this minute. Probably not for the Uplands job,
because who gets the first position they apply for? But she
was really, truly going to leave camp at the end of the summer. The thought left her so numb that all she could do in
response to Carrie's chatter was smile and nod and hope no
one would notice if she were to suddenly curl up in a ball
beneath the picnic table and start rocking.

"Seriously," Carrie continued as though Libby were
hanging on her every word, "you would love it there. Our
principal is a doll, completely behind the teachers, but she
does a great job of pulling in the parents and making sure
no one is left out. The kids—well, you know what they're
like here, so that won't come as a surprise to you. Really a
good bunch. I worked in a couple of other districts before
Uplands and I tell you, it's one of the best I've seen."

Something long buried stirred inside Libby—something
she hadn't felt in years. Not since her last education class,
when she and fellow students could spend hours debating
theory and practice.

"Listen, you're probably overflowing with references,
but one from within the district is always going to count
for more. Feel free to toss my name around at will. I'd love
to see you in our school." Her voice dropped so low that it
was almost impossible to hear her over the constant buzz
from the other tables. "Though I have to say I was amazed
when they told me. I thought you would never leave camp.
Everything's okay, right?"

Unbidden, Libby sought out Sam in the crowd. Yep, there
he was, laughing with a father. The words *Canucks, Bruins*

and *youth* rose above the buzz. Libby shook her head and turned back to Carrie.

"It's just time to move on, you know?"

Carrie glanced around the dining hall. "Yeah, I guess even paradise would get boring after a while. So use my name, keep me posted and good luck. Not that you'll need it. The school would be lucky to get you. I'll make sure they know it."

With a wink she ventured back into the crowd, leaving Libby slightly dazed.

But before she could process her jumble of emotions, the sound of her name pulled her attention up—and then, quickly down again. Down, as in, to the level that would be occupied by a small boy-child toddling through the crowd.

"Bibby!" he shouted, lifting his arms toward her. "Biiiiibby!"

"Casey!" She scooted around the table and picked him up, nuzzling the fluff on top of his head and dropping a loud smack of a kiss on his cheek. "What are you doing here, buddy?"

Her answer came from Sam, not Casey. "Exactly what it looks like he's doing. Hunting through the hall for the pretty girls."

Heat flared in her cheeks, but she did her best to present an unruffled face to Sam. "Everything okay?"

"Sure. It all looks great from my end. You've created order out of chaos."

"No, I meant with Casey." She poked his soft belly through his Overlook shirt, reveling at the sound of his delighted giggle. "What are you doing down here, mister? It's kind of busy for a squirt like you."

"Rock!" He shoved a sweaty hand in her face to display his latest treasure.

"Easy, squirt." Sam patted Casey's back. "Mrs. Collins brought him down to say hi before nap. It's only for a minute."

"Only a minute, huh? Good thing. Otherwise someone might come along and scoop you up and go boing, boing, boing…"

Caught in bouncing the child up and down, Libby let the rest of the room slip out of focus. For a second or two it was just her and Casey, soft and giggly in her embrace, making silly noises and laughing together while the crowd faded to a dull roar and slipped out of focus.

Then she turned and lifted her head and saw Sam. Sam, who was watching them with an expression she couldn't quite name, but which made her twirl away again, fast, before he could see the pink that he had brought to her cheeks.

"Okay, squirt. I'd better give you back to your old dad."

"It's okay." Sam's words were soft. "Another minute won't hurt."

"Oh, but I—"

"Libby?"

She tore her gaze from Casey and glanced at the smiling face of a woman who looked familiar, though for the life of her Libby couldn't remember the name.

"Molly Stevens. It's been a few years. But wow, you've been busy!" She patted Casey's arm. "Hey sweetheart, look at you, all cuddled up with Mommy."

It was physically impossible to feel color draining from a face, but Libby was sure she could sense the downward rush of blood as she processed Molly's meaning, then thrust Casey back at Sam.

"Molly. Hi. Um—no. This isn't— I'm not—"

"Whoops, looks like we scared Libby speechless." Sam slipped smoothly between her halting words, laughing and extending a hand and a smile while effortlessly hoisting

Casey higher on his shoulder. "Hi, there. Sam Catalano, the new owner. This is my son, Casey."

They chatted. Libby nodded and smiled when it seemed appropriate, but the truth was, she was barely aware of the words bouncing around her. There was only one word she kept hearing.

Mommy.

Sam had laughed off her confusion as fear. Little did he know he was only half-right. She was indeed scared, but not of anyone thinking she was Casey's mother.

No, what left her struggling to put two thoughts together was the memory of the first brief second of Molly's assumption. That quick flash when she heard the word *Mommy* and realized it was meant for her, and her whole world had gone warm and cozy and full.

She wasn't scared of being called Casey's mother.

But she was terrified by how absolutely right it had felt.

CHAPTER NINE

FIRST AS A CHILD, then a teen, Libby had lost track of how many times she had come home from school to the sight of Gran shoving their possessions into boxes and bags and being told that it was time to move on again. For a while she had walked around in a perpetual state of nervousness, scared to go to school because she was sure that one of those times, Gran would forget about her the way she always seemed to "forget" to pay the rent. But as she grew, she learned how to wrap that fear inside some emotional cotton batting and tuck it far away to be dealt with later.

That skill served her well now as she took her fear that she was falling too hard for Casey and shoved it to the back of her mind. There was too much else to think about. The first week of camp was always a learning experience for all concerned. Add in a new owner and the constant parade of equipment going to and from the site of the pavilion, and she had plenty of other worries to fill her mind.

Plus something was still up with Sam. He was forever jumping away from the computer as if to block her vision of an email. He had a habit of stuffing mail into his pockets. And more than once, she walked in on him in the middle of what seemed to be a heated discussion on his cell phone. Usually he ended the calls abruptly, tossing the phone onto his desk with a scowl that made her take a step back toward the door, then turning and greeting her as if nothing were out of the ordinary.

It was the same kind of behavior he'd exhibited before he brought Casey to camp, actually. Though at least then he'd been smiling instead of snarling.

Sam Catalano was hiding something.

She took her time, concentrating on the staff and the kids and the day-to-day duties, all mixed with an early rush of pranks, which she suspected could be laid at the feet of one Mick Blasting. But on the Friday of the first week, her chance appeared.

She had just set her dinner tray on the table when an unmistakable "Biiibby!" sounded through the hall. Casey was double-timing it through the rows of picnic tables, dodging kids and trays as his little feet carried him in her direction.

Libby laughed at the child's delight and caught him up in a tight hug, ordering herself not to melt when soft arms went around her neck, but failing miserably. She couldn't think about it then. Later, maybe. Much later, when she no longer had to see Casey on a daily basis.

A moment later another tray landed beside hers. Sam dropped onto the bench, turned so he was straddling it, facing her, and said, in an ominous tone, "We need to talk."

She gave him a quick once-over, searching for clues as to his intent, but all she got for her time was an irritated frown and a blast of male presence so strong it made her blink. She was used to displays of testosterone. That went hand in hand with physical activity, the rivalries that developed among the staff over the course of a season and people wearing shorts.

It was different with Sam. Maybe because he wasn't trying to outposture anyone. He was just being himself, a stronger, more defined version of the boy she'd loved. Wanted. Whatever it had been.

Prelude to Heartbreak, by Sam Catalano. That's what it had been.

"What's the trouble?" She kept her eyes fixed on Casey's grin, blocking out the sight of Sam and of Tanya, seated across the table, who had started doing the dreamy head-on-the-hand thing as soon as he joined them. Damn the man. He was like some human version of the tractor beam in *Star Wars,* sucking weak females ever closer.

"These are meatballs."

"I know." She grabbed his fork, stabbed one of the meatballs in question from his plate and offered it to Casey, who opened wide. "They're delicious, too. Why is that a problem?"

"We were supposed to have meat loaf tonight."

With well over a decade of experience with troublemakers under her belt, Libby could smell problems brewing long before they were formed. It was her own personal status forecaster. Sometimes, one word or one tilt of the head was enough for her to know that the day ahead would be cloudy with a chance of headaches.

There was something in Sam's ridiculous complaint that had her inner alert system lighting up like a Doppler radar map in blizzard season.

"I wanted meat loaf. No one has ever made it the way Cosmo does. I used to dream about it when I was on the road."

"I know. Myra told me she hasn't been able to eat it since she left here. But I still don't see the trouble."

"Look at these." Sam pointed at the offending meatballs, swimming in a pool of brown gravy atop a bed of mashed potatoes. Libby scooped up a spoonful of the potatoes and slipped them into Casey's mouth.

"It's all the same ingredients, Sam. He just shaped them differently. I don't know why you're so upset."

"Have you tasted them?"

"I told you, they were delicious."

"But did they taste like his meat loaf?"

She stopped to consider. "No, I guess not. There was a difference. But—"

"But, Lib, have you ever made meatballs?" Sam pulled Casey's hands down from Libby's hair and filled them with a slice of bread. "They're way more work than meat loaf. All that scooping and rolling. Why would someone choose the more complicated variety when he knows people are hungry for the easy version, especially after I specifically added it back into the menu for tonight?"

He had a point. Not that it mattered in the long run, though Libby had the odd feeling that there was something else at play here, something she was missing. But in Sam's pout she saw an opportunity to glean some information.

"Sam, I have a proposition for you."

On the other side of the table, Tanya blinked. Phoebe, beside her as always, let out a low whistle.

Sam himself just grinned.

Libby shook her head, though she knew her cheeks were burning. "Not that kind of proposition, you doofuses. Sam, I seem to recall asking you to fill out a medical form and emergency contact info sheet."

A muscle twitched in his jaw, nearly hidden behind his five o'clock shadow. "I did."

"Really? Because I looked for it the other day, all through the files, and I couldn't find it anywhere." No need for him to know that she'd been hunting in the hope that she might find a clue as to what he was concealing.

"I did one. Casey, let go of Libby's shirt and have some apple. I filled out the form and left it on your desk."

"Well, the pixies must have broken into the office and stolen it, because I don't have one. So I'll make you a deal. You fill out another one for me, and I'll talk to Cosmo about the great meat-loaf mystery."

Tanya snorted and turned disbelieving eyes on Libby. Great. At this rate, Tanya would soon be dragging Libby to the World Court on accusations of violating the Geneva Convention.

"Hmmm." Sam popped a meatball into his mouth, chewed and made a face of great distress.

"Come on, Catalano. Five minutes of paperwork, and you'll get your meat loaf."

"Your proposal has merit." He stabbed a green bean and stared at it in disgust. Long ago, he used to bribe the kids to eat his beans for him. "But here's the thing. I hate doing paperwork, especially when I've already done it. You, for some strange reason, enjoy talking to Cosmo. I think we need a more even trade."

She rolled her eyes and addressed Casey. "Your father is such a wimp." Glancing up, she heaved a sigh. "Okay. I'm open to negotiation. Name your price."

He sat back on the bench. Ha. She'd caught him by surprise. Point for her.

Then he leaned forward with a wicked gleam in his eye and her stomach sank with the thought that she'd walked into a trap.

"Archery." His smile was terrifyingly satisfied.

Archery. Bows and arrows. The only words, other than *call 911,* that could drive the breath straight out of her body.

"You go out there and shoot some arrows, Lib, and I'll do your paperwork." He paused, then winked the way he had in his commercial. His voice lowered. "Hit a bull's-eye, and I'll talk to Cosmo myself."

Tanya snickered.

"But," Phoebe blurted, "Libby sucks at—"

She slapped her hand over her mouth and shot Libby a glance that was equal parts guilt and apology. Libby simply sighed. Her loveless affair with archery was part of Overlook legend.

Sam, of course, knew it.

She was screwed. Well and truly screwed. But she wasn't backing down yet.

"Fine. I'll see you on the field, Catalano. Tomorrow afternoon during Casey's nap. And a word of warning—if I were you, I wouldn't tempt fate by wearing a shirt with a target printed on the back."

SAM NEEDED LESS than three minutes on the archery range to realize he'd made a serious tactical error.

Of course he had known that Libby loathed archery. Some memories could never be erased, especially when they were formed in adolescence and they included a hot teenage girl in tight shorts jumping up and down on an arrow while chanting phrases that could make a hockey player blush. So yeah, he'd exploited that fact. Not to make her look bad. All he wanted to do was even up the balance of power a bit and have a little fun. Forget about Sharon and lawyers and the way he needed about fifty more hours in each day.

But he'd neglected to focus on a couple of other things. Such as the fact that he had just turned Libby into an underdog.

Libby picked up her bow and promptly dropped it on her foot.

Crap. He was going to look like a mean-spirited grinch, and it would serve him right.

Libby retrieved her bow from the grass, gave herself a shake, then lined up her arrow and lifted the whole precarious assembly to her shoulder. A lone cheer emerged from the small crowd that had gathered around them. Tanya and Phoebe shushed the kids and reminded them to stay back.

"Way back," Libby warned as her arrow skittered down

the string. "Because if I ever get this thing to fly, heaven only knows where it will land."

The kids giggled. Libby shrugged pathetically. Sam closed his eyes and sighed but couldn't drown out the sound of Libby's low muttering as she pulled back.

"You can do this, you can do this, you can do this."

He opened up in time to see her release her hold. The arrow slipped, plunged forward a few pathetic inches and did a spectacular nosedive into the grass.

Sympathetic groans erupted around them.

Mick Blasting—a dangerously dimpled kid who reminded Sam of himself at that age—skittered forward to scoop up the wayward arrow and hand it over.

"I think it's supposed to go that way," he said, pointing to the target-covered bales of hay across the field.

"Thanks, Mick," Libby said dryly. Mick shrugged, gave Sam a long look that was ten points assessment and ninety points scorn, then stepped back, folded his arms and settled in like a self-appointed bodyguard. Sam couldn't help but be amused at Mick's obvious devotion.

The kid had good taste, no doubt about it.

Libby blew her hair out of her eyes, squared her shoulders and tried again. If anything, this attempt was even more pathetic.

A couple of the kids offered a weak applause. Libby seemed to sag for a moment, then pulled herself upright, turned and bowed to the crowd. Mick shook his head and shot Sam a look of pure disgust.

When you screw up, Catalano, you screw up big-time.

Then Libby turned and did the last thing he would have expected. She fitted her arrow into her bow once again, stuck her tongue out at the target and took her position.

If she hadn't been so damned determined, he could have declared himself the winner and walked away. But that was the thing about Libby. She didn't give up until she wrestled whatever was beating her to the ground.

He could continue to make her fight on her own. Or he could man up and do the right thing.

He moved in beside her.

"I'm sorry," he said, pitching his voice for her ears only. "I shouldn't have done this to you."

Something flickered in her eyes. Relief? Surprise? It was gone so fast he didn't have time to name it.

"I think I can get us out of this gracefully. But you'll have to trust me. And, maybe, try to forget who I am for a couple of minutes."

Her stance shifted from merely wary to full alert. It was as if an unseen puppet master had jerked all her strings at once, yanking her upright and ready to spring. He settled one hand on her shoulder, taking care to keep his palm firmly on the material of her T-shirt, avoiding the slightest chance of skin-to-skin contact. That would make her shy away for sure.

"It'll be okay. I promise."

Behind them, Mick snorted. A hint of a smile danced around Libby's mouth at the sound. Sam sucked in a quick breath at the way a simple twist of her lips could make the years fall away.

"Okay, hotshot." She extended the bow. "You've got two minutes."

He pushed the equipment back toward her.

"Not like that. Like this." Before he could stop to analyze, before she could figure out what was happening, he stepped behind her, reaching around to lift her arms into position.

She froze. He followed suit, holding his breath, hoping he hadn't blown it, that she wasn't going to run scared, that he was going to be able to stay focused despite the double whammy of memory and sensation crashing over him.

He was wrapped all around her. And twelve years had disappeared in the space of one step.

Her spine brushed his chest. Her bottom curved against his groin. Her scent rose to meet him, pine forest and fresh-cut grass and that hint of coconut that said she was so much more than just a camp girl. She gulped so hard he felt the vibration, and he had to draw on every bit of discipline he'd ever owned to stop his hand from sliding around her waist to tug her flush against him.

Live the goal, Catalano.

"You okay?" His voice came out a lot huskier than he'd expected. Her shiver ran through him.

"Libby?"

"Fine. Perfect. No problem."

Right. No problem for him, either. Except he was having the damnedest time remembering what he was supposed to be doing, or why all these people were gathered around. Or anything, really, except he was holding Libby again, and she was warm in his arms, and nothing had felt so right in a long, long time.

"How about you?" she asked, and there was a strain to her voice that he would swear hadn't been there before.

"How about me what?"

"Are you okay?"

"Absolutely. Hunky-dory. Never better." Other than not being able to breathe, of course.

"Then should we give this a shot?"

Hell, yeah. That was the best thing he'd heard in—

Oh. Right. She was talking about archery.

His arms tightened around her. She sucked in a breath, and it was as if the air went straight into him, knocking him off-kilter.

"Come on, already." It was Mick. "Shoot or something."

Sam's body voted for the *or something* option, but his

brain reminded him that he'd better start thinking about archery. Fast.

"Here's part of the problem. You have your arrow upside down. See these?" He pointed to a trio of plastic feathers, two green, one red, that circled the shaft.

She nodded.

"They're called fletchings. Keep the red one pointing down toward the ground. Then you fit the bowstring into this little notch on the arrow—" he guided her fingers over the arrow, the string, but all he felt was his skin against hers and the heat shimmering off her "—and then raise it to your shoulder. You ready?"

"Ready," she breathed.

He lifted the bow to her shoulder. His arm brushed the side of her breast on the way past. She flinched. He jerked back, both from the unexpected contact and the spark coursing through him.

"Sorry," he mumbled.

"Let's just shoot this sucker and get out of here."

"Right. Uh, pull back on the bow, more, more, extend that arm...tuck your fist in so it brushes against your ear...not so close, you'll hurt yourself...looks good, how does it feel?"

She cleared her throat. "I think I'm ready."

That made two of them.

"Trust yourself," he said, hoping she wouldn't pick up on his own uncertainty. "I'll help you hold position while you line up with the target, okay? Move slowly, attagirl. Just like that."

Her tight nod sent her braid brushing against his chest. He closed his eyes and let himself simply breathe for a second.

"I think I've got it," she whispered.

"Okay, on three we let go. One...two...three!"

They released the arrow together. It soared through the

air, aiming for the ground. Sam sucked in a fast breath. If it tanked now...

As if it heard his request, the arrow stayed on course, rising as it flew nearer to the bale of hay.

"Come on," Libby whispered.

"Come on, come on," Sam coaxed, squinting to follow the movement, pushing the arrow with his will.

Thwack! The arrow kissed the edge of the paper target.

The kids broke into cheers. Libby leaped into the air. The bow fell to the ground as she jumped round to face him, her arms upraised. Laughing and shouting, Sam threw his arms open to gather her in—

Only to see the joy drain from her face, replaced by confusion and something that looked a hell of a lot like fear.

It was like watching a window close over her eyes.

"Looks like you owe me some paperwork, Catalano." She gave him an exaggerated wink, no doubt for the benefit of the crowd. "But because you helped me out, we'll split the difference and I'll go talk to the big bad cook."

With a finger wave to their audience, she gathered her equipment and headed off, leaving Sam alone and bewildered as he watched her walk away.

SHE HAD TO GET OUT OF HERE.

Libby took advantage of the cheers and excitement to duck away from Sam and make a fast exit from the archery field. She replaced her equipment and hiked up the hill toward the office, but before she hit the steps she remembered that Sam would be there soon for his phone-and-filing shift. There was no way that she was ready to spend an hour alone in the office with him. Not yet.

Damn the man!

She took a hard right and quickstepped to the staff parking lot, scowling at the sight of his sporty silver hatchback with the PUCKY ME license plates. He was everywhere. Even when he wasn't physically present he was still there. It had been the same on the archery field. He stepped up to do his good-guy hero act, and he reached around her, surrounded her, and try as she might, she still couldn't erase the feeling of his chest against her back, his arms sliding along the length of hers. And when his hand had grazed the side of her breast—

She stopped beside her sensible little compact and pressed her hands to her cheeks. She needed space. She needed perspective.

She needed a new job.

CHAPTER TEN

SAM FINALLY CRACKED midway through the second week.

He'd been a model counselor/owner/trainee to that point. He supervised his campers. When he dropped them at activity areas, he hightailed it to the office to see what tricks of the trade Libby was waiting to teach him while forcing himself to block out the memory of her in his arms. He mopped latrines. He sang songs. He patted homesick backs and called parents and jollied Cosmo and filed report after report after report.

In his spare time he talked to lawyers and finished unpacking and hung with his kid. He was busier than he had ever been in his life, and he loved every minute of it. Even when Libby was bossing him around. Even when she juggled everyone and everything so effortlessly, even Casey, that he would have felt inadequate if she hadn't gone out of her way to make sure he was learning.

She might not be in a classroom, but she was still a hell of a teacher.

Nonetheless, he wasn't so dedicated that he was going to miss out on a golden chance that fell into his lap on the third day straight of hazy, hot and humid. Casey was napping, no one had any urgent needs, and for once, Libby hadn't given him a list of chores to do while his kids were occupied. So when it came time to lead his crew to the beach for swim time, he was only too glad to grab his suit and jump in with them.

From his first dive into the mercifully cool waters, he knew it was his best choice of the day. He paddled around while the lifeguards buddied up the kids, then started a game of Marco Polo. He was still splashing and shouting when he felt an unexpected tap on his shoulder.

Whirling in the water, he came face to face with Mick Blasting, also known as The Camper Most Likely to Give a Leader a Heart Attack.

"Hey, Mick, what's up?"

"I have to tell you something." Mick paused to push long red bangs from his eyes. "But you have to promise I won't get in trouble."

"Try me." Keeping a straight face would be a chore.

"I heard that somebody carved swearwords on the bottom of the dive raft."

"Oh, you *heard* that, did you?" Sam let his feet settle on the muddy bottom of the river as he turned to check out the raft. Ancient and wooden, topped with faded green indoor-outdoor carpeting, it bobbed just beyond the roped-off swim area and was officially reserved for the counselors. But for at least as far back as Sam's days, troublemakers had taken great pleasure in swimming out to hide in the open space where the oil drum floats raised it above the water. The fact that this practice was strictly forbidden made it all the more attractive.

"I didn't go out there myself. Really." Mick's eyes were far too wide to be convincing.

"No problem, buddy. I believe you." *Not.* Sam was pretty sure he was swimming into an ambush. But since he'd been in the water the whole time the kids had been there, he doubted there had been time for anyone to rig a booby trap. And if there truly was something under there, it was better found by him than a kid.

"I'm going to take a look," he said. "Make sure no one follows me."

With a deep breath, he dived beneath the line of buoys marking the swim area and struck out for the raft. He hoped this wouldn't take long. The raft was tethered by a chain to a large, flat rock, so even though it was in deep water, it was possible to stand on the stone and rest. But the last time he hid under the raft, twelve years ago, he'd been with Libby. Resting had been the last thing on their minds.

One final dive and he was under. When his feet grazed the pebbly surface of the rock, he knew he was in position. He surfaced slowly. Exhaled.

And almost lost his footing when he came face-to-face with a wide-eyed Libby hiding in the shadows, staring at him with her hands over her mouth as if to hold back a scream.

"Of all the— What the hell are you doing under here?" he whispered.

"Well, I'm certainly not doing my nails."

He bit back an unexpected laugh. The last thing they needed was to draw attention to themselves.

"What are *you* doing here?"

"Mick sent me. Some story about swearwords carved in the wood."

There was just enough light for him to see her eyes roll as she groaned.

"He saw me coming out here. Waved at me and everything."

"Then why didn't I see you?"

"Because you were facing the other way, splashing like a hyperactive seal."

He spared a moment to feel insulted, then decided not to bother. The situation was lending itself to far too many other thoughts to waste brain space on any but the most pressing—such as fighting back memories of how it had felt to hold her against him on the archery field, or wishing for a bit more space under the raft. He could see her head and a couple of inches of creamy neck, but that was all.

"You never told me why you're hiding out under here."

"How very observant of you."

He looked her over again, more closely this time, lingering over the bits of skin he could see. Maybe it was just the shadows, but for the life of him, he didn't see anything that resembled bathing-suit straps.

He grinned. "You're skinny-dipping."

"Are you out of your mind?"

Unfortunately, that seemed to be the case, especially when his overactive imagination filled in the blanks conjured up by the words *Libby* and *skinny-dipping*. It was a darned good thing he was submerged. "Prove it."

She fished around in the water and tugged a thin strap above the surface. "See? Bathing suit."

"Looks mighty skimpy to me. You sure that's not string from the raft?"

"No, it's not, and speaking of the raft, why don't you go up there and leave me alone? Or go tell Mick that his joke wasn't very funny."

"Nah, I'd rather stay down here. You're sure that wasn't a piece of twine?"

"Positive." She raised her hands from the water and inspected them. "Hmmm. Pruney. Maybe *I'll* go up on the raft."

"Sure. Because you know, it's mighty dark under here. You could be holding up anything and I couldn't tell what it was."

"For heaven's sake, Sam, I just said I'd go up top. Would I do that if I was skinny-dipping?"

No, she wouldn't. But he wasn't sure if he was ready

to see long, leggy Libby stretched out on the raft—or to imagine her lying above him while he dog-paddled below.

"Prove it."

"What?"

"Prove that's really your bathing suit."

"No!"

But when he swam closer to her, she didn't shy away. When he held out his palm, reaching for the fabric, she swallowed, but slipped her hand under the water.

She tugged the strap above the surface. He reached. His finger slipped under the thin cord, marveling that such a skinny little thing could hold up breasts that held such a large place in his imagination.

She gulped. "How is Casey—"

"Shh."

The sound of breathing—his? hers?—echoed in the enclosed space. Her eyes glistened in the dim light. He smelled water and wood and something hauntingly Libby, that made him run his finger higher up the minuscule strap. He moved in closer and ran his other finger along the line of her jaw and bent—

She gasped. Jerked back. And then went very, very still.

"Libby?"

"Turn around."

"But what—"

"Turn *around*," and then he saw the hunch of her shoulders, saw a scrap of thin cord floating on the water and understood.

He stepped back on the rock, as much to keep her from seeing his grin as to honor her request. He doubted Libby would be too pleased if she saw his delight at the thought of her unbound.

"Jeez, Lib, I'm sorry. I didn't mean to do anything." At least, not that.

"It's an old suit. I should have known better, but it's my favorite. *Was* my favorite, I mean."

"Did it, like, break, or just come unfastened, or what?"

"I can't tell. It's too hard to see."

"I don't suppose I could—"

"No!"

He stared up through the cracks in the raft, squinting at the stripes of sunlight leaking through. "You can't stay here forever."

"Yes, I can."

"There's going to be kids out there for another twenty minutes. You'll have to come out eventually."

"I think I can— Ow!" A hollow clang echoed around him.

He spun around. "What happened?"

"I bumped my elbow on the oil drum. Turn around."

He bit back his instinctive offer to kiss it and make it better. "Lib, there's not much room to maneuver here, especially when you can't see what you're doing. Let me help."

"I told you to turn around."

He sighed and rotated. "Want me to go get one of the girls?"

"And have everyone know we were under here together? No, thanks."

He bit his tongue to keep from reminding her it had been one of the kids that had sent him over, fully knowing she was there. By this point they had probably organized a pool as to who would come out first and whether or not they looked happy.

"Let me help, Lib. I won't do anything, I promise."

Silence.

"Libby? You don't have a lot of choices here, babe."

He heard a sigh, then a soft splash. "Give me a minute. I just need to— You promise you won't make me regret this?"

"Scouts' honor."

"You were never a Scout."

"True, but it sounds better than hockey-guy honor."

At that she laughed, the sound wrapping around him
and spinning him back to the days when Libby and laughter were synonymous in his mind. When he turned to face
her she was still smiling. It suited her. There was no hint of
the tense look he'd seen on her at other times, like when she
was planning schedules, or the sadness he'd seen sometimes
when she stopped at the top of the hill to look out over the
camp. This was Libby the way she was meant to be, confident and strong despite the desperate way she clung to the
top of her bathing suit.

Better yet, with her hair wet and slicked back, she didn't
look a bit like Robin. Libby's face was longer, the bones
stronger. The similarities he'd seen were strictly coloring
and posture. That had to be it.

"Ready?" he asked.

She nodded and started to move on the slippery rock,
but with her hands occupied it was too painful to watch.

"Stay there." He paddled slowly to her back, close enough
to reach but not to scare her off. He couldn't blow this.

"Do you see the ends?" she asked.

He squinted in the dim light. "I see something. Can you
hand them back to me, or should I reach over your shoulders for them?"

He saw her hands move, then stop. "You'd better do it."

He could do this. Sam pulled himself closer, muttered a
"sorry" when he bumped against her bottom, tried to hold
himself away from her while peering over her shoulders for
the loose bits of fabric.

"Okay, I see one. Hold on." He reached over her right
shoulder and down, congratulating himself when he plucked

the scrap from the water without touching her. He pulled it up and rested it against the naked skin at her neck.

"Hope it doesn't slip." He moved to the left side. "Uh-oh."

"What?"

"I don't see this one. Is it under your, um—" he gulped at the thought of the possible locations "—your hand?"

When she bent her head to check, the skin at her nape called to him. It was all he could do to keep his hands under the water instead of reaching to caress, to stay upright instead of bending to press his lips against that inviting bit of softness.

He had faced down the most aggressive defensemen in the NHL. He'd looked into the eyes of players who had made it their mission to stop him in his tracks, even if that meant colliding with him at top speeds and/or throwing him against unforgiving boards. But none of those experiences had tested his resolve like the sight of Libby's bowed neck.

"It's stuck. I'll have to, um… Close your eyes," she said.

He closed them. But that didn't stop him from picturing the length of cord sheltered in the hollow between her breasts, from imagining how it would feel to slide his hand down there in search of the elusive string and…

Oh, jeez. He was in big, big trouble.

"Here it is." Her words yanked him from his reverie. On the off chance that she was a mind reader, he clapped his would-be-wayward hands to his side, only to pull them back up when he slipped on the rock and started to go under.

"How are you doing?" He took the glorified string in his palm, certain he could feel the warmth from her body flowing through it. "Getting tired?"

"Fine. How about you?"

"Wrinkled, but okay. Give me a second and— Wait, I lost it—hang on, I think I— Damn!"

The string slipped back over her shoulder. He started to

grab it, realized his hand was way too close to a no-touch zone, jerked back and slipped off the rock. Water raced into his open mouth and closed over his head. He came up coughing and sputtering, but still able to hear Libby's giggles.

"Go ahead and laugh," he said darkly when he was able to speak. "You'll get yours."

"Ooh, I'm scared." Another snicker burst free. Either he or she had shifted so they were facing each other again. There was just enough sunlight striping through the boards for him to see that she now clutched her suit with one hand while the other stretched behind her neck, probably holding both ends of her strap in place.

A practical move, to be sure. She couldn't know that, despite the water that reached to her collarbones, the pose rendered her more alluring than anything he'd ever seen on a locker-room calendar.

At least, he didn't think she knew.

He scowled with all the fake anger he could muster. "Turn around. I'm going to fix this thing if it kills me."

She complied, bowed her head, then pulled her fingers away fast as soon as the ties had been transferred back to him. Her suit hand stayed in place while the other trailed through the water, softly splashing. Keeping her balance? Or trying to cover the sound of their breaths, which mingled and mixed before echoing back around them?

"Hey, Sam. You didn't hurt yourself, did you?"

He could swear there was a quiver to her voice that hadn't been there earlier. If he were a gentleman, he would ignore it.

"I stubbed my toe. I think you need to kiss it and make it better."

So much for his gentleman badge.

"I'm not kissing your toe!"

He wasn't sure if the sudden rise of her shoulders was due to his words or the fact that a twist of the reluctant straps had sent his knuckles against her skin.

"Hold still, I've almost— The thing that holds it together broke off. I have to tie it and there's not a lot of extra… So you're not a toe kisser?"

She went very still below his hands. "This is inappropriate. You're my boss."

I'm a lot more than that, toots.

He yanked the knot tight and made sure his hands were well clear of her before he added, "How about neck kissing?"

"No. You never told me how Casey's doing. Are you done yet?"

"Yes. Last time I checked, he was down for a nap. Belly-button kissing?"

She dived underwater. He waited patiently, counting in his head until she reappeared.

"Fifteen seconds. Pitiful. What was your opinion on belly-button kissing?"

"Sam—"

"Elbow kissing?"

"You can go now. Assuming you can walk on your poor stubbed toe."

"Ah, you caught me. My toe is fine. But I think you bit your lip trying to get away from me." He reached across the darkness to lay a finger in the center of that intriguing mouth. "Maybe I need to kiss this and make it better."

"There's nothing wrong with my mouth." But though she continued to tread water, she didn't move away.

"Are you sure? 'Cause you know, it's a good half hour to the hospital. A little preventive medicine might be a good idea."

"Oh, I don't think…"

"That's good," he said, inching himself closer, letting his finger slip across her lips and down her chin. "Don't think."

"But what if— One of us should be out there. You know." Her gulp was audible. "The first rule."

"If they need us, they'll find us," and he let his free hand glide through the water, let it brush against the soft firmness of her shoulder, let it settle there and urge her toward him. His hand slipped lower, gliding along the length of arm.

"I—I…"

"Shh. Quiet." He inched closer, their thighs brushing as he lowered his mouth to hover over hers. "In fact, maybe we'd better make sure neither of us can make any noise at—"

His words were pierced by the sound he'd been dreading most—three long blasts on a whistle. The signal to get out of the water for a head count. Libby jerked back and groaned.

"They counted you, didn't they?" she said.

"Yeah. You, too?"

"Of course. We have to go out there." She sounded about as thrilled as he was at the thought, though he doubted it was for the same reason.

"Stay. I'll go and tell them you can't come out right now."

"No. The suit is okay. I can do this. But thanks."

She smiled then, a real smile that held all the warmth he used to associate with her. His stomach tightened and heat burst through him and to hell with the lifeguards, he wasn't about to let her slip away from him. Not when he felt like he had just got her back.

But as quick as the girl he remembered had appeared, she disappeared again with a shake of her head and a quick sigh. "Let's get this over with," she said, and dived beneath the surface, kicking away from him.

Damn, but it would have been nice to keep her with him for a bit longer.

Sam gave her a few seconds on the off chance no one would put one and one together. Then he churned through the water, keeping his head down as long as possible until biology forced him to come up for air. He scanned the faces of those already on the shore. Most of the kids were too busy whispering among themselves to have noticed them. Mick elbowed the kid next to him, sealing his place on Sam's Most Wanted list.

But it was the counselors and lifeguards that made him want to dive back under again. Awareness, understanding, barely muffled laughter—he saw them all. Just like he could already hear the jokes and innuendos that were undoubtedly going to roll through the camp before nightfall.

It wouldn't be the first time he was the subject of rumor-mongering.

But it was probably the first time he'd ever wished it were true.

CHAPTER ELEVEN

ONE THING BECAME very clear in the days after the Raft Incident, as Sam came to think of those moments: Libby was doing everything in her power to avoid him. It was just like the first days all over again. Except this time, he was pretty sure that it wasn't resentment, anger or plain dislike that was making her turn herself and her schedule inside out to keep him at arm's length. It was, however, a definite kind of discomfort.

And damned if he wasn't feeling it, too.

It didn't help that someone had made up new, raft-centered lyrics to the old "Boy and a Girl in a Little Canoe" camp song and posted a copy on the staff bulletin board. He ripped it down as soon as he saw it, of course. But the words stuck in his memory. The line "he groped her and he tugged, and her suit fell down" seemed to be permanently engraved in his mind. And every time he turned around, someone was singing or humming the tune.

He wasn't the only one who heard it, of course. He and Casey happened to be at the other end of the lunch table when a couple of the guys began whistling it in fabulous harmony, causing Libby to frown, shake her head and ask the waterfront director why everyone was fixating on that song. Phoebe covered her mouth, giggled and shook her head. Beside her, Tanya sighed heavily.

He had to tell Libby. It was only fair. The logical solution would be to wait until they were both in the office and then give her the whole story, but as she was currently setting new speed records for running out of the room whenever he walked in, that didn't seem likely.

Instead, he made a point of walking back to her end of the table after clearing his place. He didn't sneak. Didn't try to hide his movements. Trying to be surreptitious would only make things worse, and no way did he want to bring more embarrassment on Libby's head. While Casey toddled ahead of him, hell-bent on reaching his beloved Bibby, he sauntered down the aisle between the picnic tables, came to a halt behind Libby and rested his foot on the bench beside her.

"What the—" She lifted Casey to her lap before glaring at Sam's work boot, then transferred the glare to him. "Feet on the floor, Catalano."

Instead of complying, he leaned forward to rest his elbow on his knee. No one was going to think he was afraid to get close to her.

"Cosmo needs to talk to us after lunch." He grabbed Casey's hand and wiggled. "Asked us to stick around for a few minutes."

She rolled her eyes and began to rise. "Is this about the meat loaf again? I'll pop in there now and—"

"Not now." Sam deliberately rested one hand on her shoulder and shoved her gently into her seat. There. The whole camp was his witness. He could touch her without turning to a puddle of mush.

Though it was a damned good thing no one could read his mind—or, more accurately, his fingers, which practically snarled a sign-language rebuke when he lifted them from her age-softened T-shirt.

"But if there's a problem—" she began, and he shook his head.

"No problem. He has some ideas about the menu for Backward Day and wants to run them past us. Five, ten minutes, tops, but not until he's done with serving. Does that work for you?"

She gave him an odd look again, one he realized he'd seen from her a handful of times since he came back—the one that he was pretty sure meant, *I know the man is hiding something but I can't figure it out.* He held his breath and tried to send her a telepathic message to do as he asked with no questions.

At last, she nodded. Though maybe that was just the side effect of the little knee bounce she was giving Casey.

"Okay. Twenty minutes should give him enough time. I'll make sure I'm here then."

She snagged her sandwich with the hand that wasn't around Casey's tummy and took a bite. He congratulated himself on a successful covert mission. No one would suspect he was trying to get her alone, least of all her. Now all he needed to do was drop a quick word to Cosmo and—

She set her sandwich back down. A stray shred of lettuce clung to a corner of that mouth he'd been so close to capturing beneath the raft, and damn but he lost his breath again.

From the corner of his eye he caught movement as Phoebe elbowed Tanya. Phoebe grinned. Tanya drooped. And though every instinct in his body urged him to lick Libby's lips clean—or, at the very least, to wipe them with his thumb and then continue tracing the line of her mouth until every crease was forever imprinted in his memory—he settled for snagging a napkin from the table and handing it over, dancing it just out of Casey's grasp.

"Mine!"

"Sorry, squirt. Lib, you've got something here." He touched the matching spot on his own face. She frowned, but dabbed appropriately. He gave a quick nod of approval before reaching for Casey, who continued to lunge for the napkin.

"Come on, Case. It's nap time. See you in twenty," he said to her, and wandered away as nonchalantly as he could manage when he knew at least three pairs of eyes were following his every move.

It was a damned fine thing that he had plenty of experience in dealing with sneaky paparazzi. Because the slimiest reporter on the planet had nothing on the eyes and ears of Camp Overlook.

IT TOOK ABOUT TEN MINUTES to take Casey to the house, hand him over to Mrs. Collins and scoot back through the woods to the rear of the dining hall. By the time he knocked on the back door of the kitchen, Cosmo was slapping a wooden spoon ominously against his thigh.

"Catalano!" the cook growled before the knock had finished vibrating. "What the hell are you planning against Libby, and why are you dragging me into it?"

So much for beating the gossip line. Sam had planned to approach Cosmo as his boss, but since the old man was glaring at him like the fiercest defenseman he'd ever faced on the ice, he opted for a fast change of direction.

"Sorry to disappoint you, Cos, but I'm trying to help."

Cosmo grunted and turned back to the stove. "Hell of a twisted way to help, getting the whole place talking about her behind her back."

"That's why I told her you wanted to talk to us. She knows people are whispering, but she doesn't know about that song. I ripped it down before she could see it. I want to tell her, but she won't come within ten feet of me—"

"Smart girl."

Sam paused, then chose to let it pass. "Anyway, I needed an excuse to get her to stick around long enough to talk."

"And I'm your excuse."

Sam nodded.

Cosmo grunted again and gave the pot a vigorous stir. The scent of spaghetti sauce wafted out toward Sam, reminding him that he'd been so preoccupied with the Libby problem and feeding Casey that he'd barely touched his own lunch.

"Got a better idea," Cosmo said. "You take yourself off someplace and I'll tell Libby why everybody's singing."

"No, thanks," Sam said, though he was pretty sure there was no charity involved in the offer. "I helped cause this, I'll make it better."

Cosmo snorted as he wiped his hands on his apron. "Right. Just like you made everything else better when you bought the place."

"Look, Cosmo, I know you didn't want Myra to sell—"

His words were lost to the dull clang of an oversize bowl being thunked on the counter. "Damn right I didn't."

"For the love of— It's not gonna change. How about you deal and move on?"

Cosmo's shoulders drooped. His jowls shook. For a second he looked like someone had snapped whatever was holding him upright, and that he would drop at any moment.

Holy crap.

Sam started to move forward, thoughts of a heart attack or an apoplectic fit racing through his mind, but Cos shook himself like a giant Saint Bernard and pulled himself upright.

"Here's what you need to deal with, smart-ass. This place shoulda gone to Libby the way My— The way things were intended all along. If you hadn't come in here waving your checkbook, she would never—"

"Myra sold so she could help look after her sister. You know that as well as I do. If it hadn't been me, she would have found somebody else."

The muttered curse as Cosmo turned his back to Sam

was pretty clear evidence of how much he believed that. But Sam was more focused on something else Cosmo had said.

"What do you mean, Myra intended for the camp to go to Libby?"

Cosmo sniffed as he grabbed a bowl of tomatoes from the counter and carried them to the stainless-steel island dominating the kitchen. "Just what I said."

"Yeah, well, for the next minute, pretend you know how to string more than three words together at a time and clue me in, okay?"

Cosmo peered at the knife block in front of him before selecting a blade that Sam was pretty sure had been chosen more for its ability to intimidate than its ability to cut.

"What do you think it means, hotshot?"

Sam was about to reply with an epithet of his own, then stopped. Cosmo wasn't going to offer up any more details, that was clear, and he had a feeling Libby would choose a summer's worth of archery over telling him the truth. He pulled his phone from his pocket and hit the speed dial to Myra.

"Who you calling?"

"Sure as hell not the Ghostbusters."

Cosmo's face twisted. "You're not gonna go disturbing—"

"Sam?" Myra sounded surprised and only slightly wary, which he supposed was a good thing. "How are you?"

"Not to worry, Myra. Everything's fine. I have a quick question. Cosmo here just told me that the camp was supposed to be Libby's, but he won't explain what he meant. Could you clue me in? It's kind of important."

More important than he would have expected, actually. Maybe because he'd screwed things up so badly at first, and if there was something else that could come between him and Libby, he wanted to know before it blew up in his face.

Or maybe because he wanted reassurance that he wasn't the selfish bastard he suddenly felt he had become.

"Sam, I really don't think… That was between me and Libby. If she wanted you to know, I'm sure—"

"Were you planning to leave it to her in your will?"

Silence. The kind of silence that let him know he'd hit pay dirt.

Unbidden, a scene resurrected itself in Sam's memory— Libby and Myra in the office as the news of the sale was broken. Myra had apologized to Libby, saying something about a promise she'd made, and Libby had jumped in to cut her off with a look of pure disdain in his direction.

"She knew, didn't she?"

This time the silence was broken by a soft sigh.

"Okay, Myra. I know you don't want to say anything, and I respect that. I think I have all I need. Thanks." And then, because he couldn't resist getting back at Cosmo somehow, he added a quick "Cosmo sends his love" before ending the call.

Cosmo went as white as his apron, whirled away from Sam and commenced whacking a knife through a pile of tomatoes. Sam barely noticed. The implications of his discovery hit him like an elbow to the stomach. He had bought Libby's future out from under her.

No wonder she had been so furious.

And now he was helping destroy her reputation. Not on purpose, of course, and not by himself. But he sure as hell hadn't taken the high road with his approach beneath the raft.

He had to make it up to her somehow.

The only question was, how was he supposed to help make things up to her and prove there was nothing between them when, every time he saw her, he wanted nothing more than to drag her back beneath the raft and finish what he'd started?

LIBBY FORCED HERSELF to take her time leaving the dining hall. She toyed with her sandwich and nibbled a couple of carrot sticks and did her level best to ignore the grin playing around Phoebe's mouth.

On the other hand, Tanya's woeful expression was just too junior high to be ignored. And ignore it Libby had done, for at least a week now, maybe two. But it was becoming apparent that Tanya had developed a crush on Sam that wasn't going to wear itself out without a little help.

She pushed back from the table and scooped up her plate. On her way she gave Phoebe a quick tap on the shoulder and nodded toward the door. The girl raised an eyebrow but nodded.

Two minutes later, they were both outside beneath the sugar maple that provided both shade and an excellent spot from which to see everyone exiting the hall, thus earning it the camp name of the Sneaky Tree.

"What's up, oh great and powerful one?" Phoebe's words were light and airy, but there was a keen mind beneath that head of beaded braids.

"I'm worried about Tanya. This infatuation with Sam is getting ridiculous."

A quick grin crossed Phoebe's round face. "Jealous?"

What?

Libby wasn't sure whether to be embarrassed or enraged, so after a moment of stupefaction she decided it best to simply ignore the comment and move on. "Look, I know everyone falls for everyone else over the summers, but she's veering into obsession territory. I've never seen her like this, and I'm afraid she's going to do something she'll regret."

Phoebe crossed her arms and leaned back against the tree trunk. "You think she's going to throw herself at the Most Valuable Boss?"

"You're her friend. You tell me."

Phoebe wound one of her braids around her finger. "I don't think so. You know Tanya. She's a drama queen from way back. She's all about the buildup and the excitement, but not so great at the follow-through. Remember a couple of years ago when she found that bald spot in her hair?"

"Oh, crap. I managed to forget that one." Libby shuddered at the memory of the way the girl had collapsed on the office sofa, sobbing out her need to see a doctor right away! Now! Because, oh, dear God, her hair was falling out! By the handful!

She narrowed her eyes at Phoebe. "You know, we never did find out how that hair removal cream ended up on her head."

"You think I did that? To my best friend? Just because she was flipping out over some idiot boy back home and she maybe needed a reality check? Nah. I would never pull a stunt like that."

"Right. From now on, as long as you and I share a cabin, I'm sleeping with a guard dog."

"I thought you already had your own personal defenseman for that job."

It took a moment for the implication to sink in. "Phoebe, I'm sure you all had a lovely time wondering what happened beneath the raft, but here's a message for you and everyone else on the staff. There is nothing between me and Sam. Nothing. Furthermore, there never will be."

"That's not how Cosmo tells it."

Cosmo. The one person who had been around even longer than she had. Of course she should have expected him to talk. "Cosmo is remembering back to a time long ago, in the proverbial galaxy far, far away, when Sam and I were as silly as—as—as Tanya is now."

"Long ago, huh?" Phoebe pursed her lips and whistled the opening notes of "A Boy and a Girl in a Little Canoe."

"Okay, that's enough. I've had it up to here with everyone fixating on that song. What's the story?"

"Oh, come on, Libby. You must have seen it."

"Seen what?"

Phoebe's grin faded in wattage, though not in width. "You really don't know?"

"Clueless. And you know how much I hate not knowing what's going on in my own camp."

"I thought it was Sam's camp," Phoebe said, then took a step back at Libby's glare. "Okay. Yesterday morning, somebody put a note up on the staff bulletin board with a new version of that song. But instead of the little canoe, it was a boy and a girl and a hideaway raft."

"Holy—"

"It wasn't me. I swear."

"You know," Libby said slowly, "I don't really care who did it. And I'm not surprised. If I saw two adults emerging from the raft together, I'd be making jokes, too."

"I think there's a hell of a *but* on the horizon."

"A *but*…no. It's an *aha*. Like that explains why Tanya has been shooting daggers at me the last couple of days." Another incident shifted in her memory. "And those valentine hearts I found on the office door yesterday."

"Hearts?"

"With lace and everything. I thought one of the little girls must have made it in the craft hut, but now I think someone else was behind it."

Phoebe groaned. "You're gonna tell us we have too much free time and find more chores for us to do now, aren't you?"

"Hmm. That's a good idea. I hadn't been thinking along

those lines, but now that you mention it, maybe I should have all the counselors help haul those rocks you want moved from the waterfront."

"I have a better idea. Why don't you just move into Myra's old house with Sam so we can all stop wondering?"

Libby came as close as she ever had to telling a staff member exactly what she could do with her suggestion, but sanity intervened in the nick of time. It was good that Phoebe was saying these things, she reminded herself, because how else would she know about them? And wasn't it a testament to the trust Phoebe had in her that she felt comfortable enough to say such things to Libby without fear of reprisal?

Forget those tabloids Dani wrote for. For real intrigue and slander, all anyone had to do was listen in on a conversation between any two Overlook counselors.

"Make you a deal," she said tightly. "You drop a few hints to Tanya that she's a bit old to be making puppy-dog eyes at the boss, and I will let you both keep your days off for the rest of the summer. How's that sound to you?"

"Simple. I like it." If Phoebe's head nodded any faster, it could spin into its own galaxy.

"Good. See you later." Libby patted Phoebe's shoulder and headed back into the dining hall. On the way she passed Tanya, who subjected her to a wide-eyed tragic glare before lifting her chin and sailing dramatically toward the craft hut.

Great. Just great. Libby debated stopping her for about half a second, then decided against it. Tanya wasn't about to listen to her. The message would be far more effective coming from Phoebe. Besides, the girl was merely a symptom.

It was time to deal with the cause.

SAM WAS PREPARED for Libby to get pissed off when she realized he'd tricked her into talking to him alone. But when

she walked in with her eyes blazing, he felt as discombobu-
lated as he had when Cosmo already knew about his plan.
Was the whole freakin' world a step ahead of him today?

"Problem?" he asked, when she drew close to the table
he'd staked out in the back corner. Whatever was behind
her glower, he hoped to hell it wasn't him.

"Yeah. A couple of them." She paused in front of the table
as if debating. Then, to his surprise, she boosted herself up
beside him, resting her feet on the bench below.

"Well, well, well, Miss Kovak. Do you know how many
campers would howl in delight if they saw you parking your
heinie on the tabletop?"

"Right now I'm more concerned with other places they
think I've been parking it. Though I guess it's the staff
more than the kids."

He looked at her, at those lush lips pursed somewhat
with her apparent disapproval, and wondered what would
happen if he were to trap her chin in his hand and slide his
other arm across her back and—

He wanted to kiss her. Some parts of him wouldn't mind
doing a whole lot more than that, to be honest, but his upper
brain still had a stake in this, so he would settle for kissing, at least for the moment. He'd been so close beneath the
raft.... So cold-shower, still-haunting-his-dreams close...

But there was more at stake here than just a kiss. Or two.
She was working her magic on him again, and he owed
her big-time, and he had no business whatsoever thinking
about kissing anyone who was his employee. Especially
when every time he looked at her with Casey, the doubts
started up again.

"So what's up with Cosmo?" She glanced toward the
kitchen.

"Uh—actually, Lib, I kind of made that up to get you to
talk to me. See, there was this song—"

"The one on the bulletin board? About you and me? Yes. I know."

Point for Libby.

"Oh. Well, I wanted to tell you, but I didn't think you would appreciate hearing about it with a dozen or so other folks hanging around, but since you've been kind of avoiding me, I—"

Her shoulders drooped as she let out a long sigh. "And here I thought I was being so subtle."

"Sorry."

"It's okay. You're right. I have been running away. Not because I'm scared of being with you," she added, pulling herself upright and sending him a sideways glance that had him sitting straighter, too. She did it so well that he almost believed her. "But I knew there would be—speculation— about us after the raft. I thought that if we were never alone together, that might nip the talk in the bud. Guess I was wrong."

This definitely wasn't the time to tell her that if conditions were different and he wasn't so damned unsure, they'd be giving folks more material to discuss, not less.

She leaned back on the table, bracing her hands behind her. Casual. Relaxed. No way could she know that sitting like that made certain parts of her anatomy curve into prominence in both her profile and his imagination.

Could she?

He shifted a bit farther down the table and kept his gaze firmly focused on the massive stone fireplace.

"Avoiding you didn't do anything except possibly make us look guiltier," she said. "And it was kind of inconvenient."

"True."

"So, I guess we should return to regular, everyday life. If we carry on as normal and show people that nothing's going on, well, that should stop the talk faster than if we go to great lengths to disprove it. And," she added thoughtfully, "it might help with the Tanya problem."

"What Tanya problem?"

The glance she shot his way was pure *oh, please*.

"You honestly expect me to believe you don't know she has a crush on you?"

Ah, crap. "I had a feeling. Hoped I was wrong."

"Yeah, well, even you get it right on occasion." She softened the words with a friendly pat on his knee. "Don't let it go to your head."

As if she realized what she'd done, she froze, blanched and jerked her hand back. Not soon enough, though. Not before his pulse jumped and his breath caught and he leaned forward, ready to grab her hand and wrist and anything else she would allow, doubts be damned.

"I'd better—" she began, and scooted partway off the table.

But he couldn't let her go. Not yet. Instead, he blurted out the first words that came to mind.

"I know you told Myra you would stay on for the summer, but Lib, I want you to think about keeping the job for real."

She stopped with her bum firmly on the bench, then tilted her face up to him. Which would have been encouraging if she hadn't pushed herself backward at the same time, increasing the distance between them.

"Hang on. How did we get from people spreading rumors to talking about Tanya to talking about my job?"

He shrugged and stuck as close to the truth as possible. "I don't know. It's been on my mind for a while now, and this seemed like a good time to say it."

"But I..." She reached out and rubbed one finger along a scar in the wooden planks, then flattened her palm over it. "I don't know," she said without meeting his gaze. "Can I think it over?"

He shouldn't be unhappy that she hadn't jumped at his offer. It wasn't as if he'd given her any warning.

"Sure. Take all the time you need. It's yours as long as you want it, Lib."

She seemed on the verge of asking something else, given the way she glanced up at him, but then his phone buzzed. He grabbed it from his pocket and checked the display.

Sharon.

He cursed softly and shoved the phone back into the depths, hoping Libby hadn't seen the name. But when he looked her way, she had twisted away from him again to examine the fireplace on the far wall. He wondered if she was pondering the thought tickling the back of his mind: What would happen between them if she stayed?

"It does mean a lot to me," she said softly. "The camp, that is."

He nodded and waited, forcing patience he didn't feel. There was more coming. He was sure of it.

"Can I—" She twisted round, facing him, another hint of pink rising in her cheeks. "May I ask you something personal?"

Casey. "Depends what it is."

"Do you miss playing hockey?"

It was so far from what he'd been expecting that all he could do was repeat the question like an overgrown parrot. "Do I miss hockey?"

She nodded and leaned forward as if to soak up his every word.

"I— Well, yeah. Sure. Not all the time, and not the way I thought I would." Back when he thought he'd retire when he was ready, not when life had twisted to hurry the process along.

"I'm glad I'm not missing out on Casey's life anymore," he said slowly. "I don't miss being on the road all the time, or waking up hurting so bad that I didn't know if I could get out of bed. But yeah. I miss the guys. And the fans. And—"

"And what?" she asked softly.

"And— I don't know. There were times, out on the ice, when the game was going right and I was skating full-out, and the crowd was on our side…. It was like— I don't know. Like I was flying. Sailing away from everything. Just…flying." He shrugged. "Does that make any sense?"

"I think so." She gave a sad little grin. "Though I wouldn't know for sure, since I've never flown."

He looked at her then, letting himself drink in the sight of her full lips and her wondering eyes and the curves that started at her neck and moved down, teasing him, tempting him, and thought, *Ah, Libby, there are so many ways to fly….*

CHAPTER TWELVE

IT WAS THE FIRST THURSDAY of the second session, and Sam was in a whistling kind of mood as he walked away from the campfire. One hand cradled a sleepy Casey against his shoulder, the other ruffled young Mick's hair, and his heart was full of "Kum Ba Yah." Three weeks down, and he finally felt as though he was getting a handle on this new way of life. Not completely. Hell, no. And he developed a serious case of the jitters every time he thought about next week's home visit from the social worker.

But overall, life was good. Casey was in love with Mrs. Collins, and had settled into his new routine and new home so completely that Sam was cautiously optimistic he really had done the right thing for his little boy. He himself had found his own rhythm at camp, Sharon hadn't called in a couple of days and Libby—

Okay, so Libby was still keeping distance between them. Not enough to make it appear she was avoiding him, but he could feel it all the same. It wasn't an angry kind of distance, though. More like she was watching him. Waiting for…something.

Though maybe that was just him, studying her for similarities to Robin, doing a little cheer every time he spotted a difference—of which there were plenty. Robin might have reminded him of the Libby of his youth, but the adult Libby had evolved in ways he could never have anticipated. The physical resemblance was undeniable, true. But he was starting to see that even if some surface similarities had drawn him to Robin in the first place, their relationship had developed so slowly and stayed so mellow that he knew it was nothing like what he'd had with Libby back in the day. He and Robin had shared a solid friendship with convenient benefits. It had never been that easy with Libby.

The thing was, Sam would never have achieved the things he had if he'd been drawn to the easy path.

He tipped his head back and looked up at the sky, drinking in the stars crowding the blackness from the clear night. The moon was full and smiling. Maybe he could convince Libby to sit on his front porch for a while and talk over her future at the camp. And if, along the way, they ended up as close as they'd been beneath the raft, well...

"Hey, Sam." Mick's voice cut through both the darkness and his thoughts. "What was that?" He pointed to the sky.

Sam squinted in the direction of the boy's finger, searching the sparkles. "I don't see anything, buddy."

"Something moved. Up there. It almost looked like a firecracker. Look, there's another one."

A long-buried memory rose to the surface. "It's probably shooting stars. Maybe a meteor shower. I know there's one every summer, but I can't remember what it's called. Or when it actually—"

A high-pitched scream ripped through the night. There was nothing playful about it. Nor was it a child's shriek when something went bump in the night.

It was the scream of a grown woman.

Sam shoved Casey into Mick's arms, ignoring the sleepy wail, and pushed Mick toward the buildings. "Go to the dining hall," he ordered the boy. "Take Casey. Get in there and stay put."

"But—"

"*Now*, Mick!"

Sam watched only long enough to ensure the boy was running in the right direction, then raced flat out toward the source of the screams, pushing through a crowd of counselors herding kids to safety. The closer he got to the source of the commotion, the harder his heart thumped, and not from exertion. The scream had come from Libby's cabin.

Please let her be okay. God, please let her be okay....

He was almost there when a second wave of uneasiness reached him. This one had nothing to do with his hearing.

"Oh, crap!" He yanked his T-shirt up over his nose and mouth as the unmistakable stench of skunk rolled over him.

Trying to breathe through his mouth, he pushed his way through the wall of campers. He shouted a few instructions for everyone to get to the dining hall and close the windows. He doubted that anyone heard him. Nor did he really care. He was simply marking time until he found—

Libby.

She walked slowly away from her cabin, her arms around a sobbing Tanya's shoulders. The relief when he spotted her left Sam momentarily unable to move. He felt almost lightheaded, but then, that was probably just the skunk. After a couple of breaths that were too deep for comfort, he hurried to join them.

"Send a critter off the deep end, Tanya?" He patted her arm, firm and bracing, but couldn't stop his other hand from settling at the center of Libby's back. He wasn't trying anything. He just had to touch her. To make sure she was fine.

"Tanya got a little surprise when she walked into our cabin," Libby said. "So did the skunk that was hanging around the door."

"By your cabin? Why would it be hanging out there?"

"I have no idea." Libby sounded unutterably weary, but still she urged Tanya forward. The only indication that she was bothered by the smell was the tears running down her cheeks.

"Is it still around?"

Tanya hiccuped. "No. It took off into the woods. Oh, Sam, it was awful!"

With no warning, she lurched out of Libby's embrace and into his. His arms closed around her automatically. Being Brynn's brother had given him plenty of experience with hysterical females. He patted her back and made "there, there" noises on autopilot while wishing Libby was the one throwing herself at him—and from a very different kind of need.

Unfortunately, the lady in question was currently frowning at him as if he were personally responsible for the perfume in the air.

"Here." She grasped Tanya's arm and pulled her away from him, though not with the tenderness he would have expected. "I'll take care of Tanya. Why don't you close the cabin windows? We can try to keep some of the smell outside."

She wanted him to get closer to that stench? Sam groaned inside even as he sprinted forward. The sooner he dealt with the windows, the sooner he could get away from the cabin and into the shower. Or would he need a tub of tomato juice?

He wrestled with the heavy wooden shutters as fast as possible, rewarding himself when the stench grew too bad by imagining him and Libby lathering each other head to toe with fluffy suds that smelled sweet and covered little.

By the time he finished, Libby had guided Tanya out of the wooded cabin area and onto the open space by the flagpole. Dim light spilled out of the adjacent dining hall. Tanya sat on the grass, still sniffling to Phoebe and one of the other counselors. Libby and her clipboard were issuing orders by flashlight.

In other words, everyone was doing exactly what he would have predicted.

"All set," he reported when he reached Libby. "But we'll have to scrub it out tomorrow."

"There's a lot of things we'll have to do tomorrow, but it's too late and too dark to even think of them. Right now we need to figure out places for us to sleep."

A suggestive comment now would be a very bad idea. "There's what, six of you in there?"

"Right. There's two bunks open in the oldest girls' cabin. Phoebe and Tanya can go there. One with the twelve-year-old girls, we'll send Hannah there."

"I'll bunk in the infirmary," said the nurse.

"Great. That's three, right?"

"Four," he said. "And I know you won't like this, but since it's just for tonight, there's two sofas in my living room."

She rubbed her hand over her eyes and turned to the last counselor. "In that case, Katie, you go with Tanya. Phoebe, you and I will take the sofas."

"Wait." Tanya pushed to her feet. There was just enough light from the dining hall and Libby's flashlight to see the panic on her face. "Look, the kids are going to be upset tonight because of this, and I'm not, you know, up to looking after anyone else. I'll take a sofa, and Phoebe can hang with Katie."

"Sounds reasona— *Oof.*" Sam's breath whooshed out as Libby's elbow caught him in the stomach. He would have asked her what the hell that was about, but she jumped in to talk before he quite got his breath back.

"Call me heartless, Tanya, but I think the best thing for you tonight would be to help someone else. It will keep you from dwelling on your own distress."

"But I—"

"Besides, Phoebe is a third-degree black belt, so we don't have to worry about Sam behaving inappropriately with her. Not that he would, but tomorrow morning when I get a dozen phone calls from parents complaining about the mixed-gender sleeping arrangements, I want every possible argument on my side. I'm sure you can understand."

Ah. The Tanya-crush thing. Of course.

For a moment Tanya seemed ready to protest. She hovered nearby but when Libby turned her back to her, she huffed out an exasperated breath.

"Fine," she said in a tight voice. "But I need a shower first. And I can't sleep in these, and all my stuff—" She gestured toward the path, the cabin.

"Don't worry about it," Sam said. "I'm sure between me and the other guys, we can come up with extra T-shirts and things you could use for tonight. You, too," he added, looking significantly at Libby.

"That bad?"

The stench could easily replace tear gas, but he wasn't about to tell her. "You'll probably feel better."

"Okay." She must be tired, for all the determination she was pushing at Tanya seemed to disappear when she talked to him. It was almost like—like she trusted him.

Sam took off toward the dining hall with a smile on his lips. The camp smelled to high heaven and Tanya seemed ready to spit bullets, but Libby had let him help. She almost, maybe, perhaps, trusted him.

It was kind of like seeing a shooting star.

HE WAS SLEEPING right above her.

For what had to be the forty-third time that night, Libby yawned and wriggled to turn from her back onto her stomach—no easy feat when lying on a sofa. She punched her pillow and shifted her legs and tried to forget that Sam was right upstairs, tried to resist the lure to roll onto her back and stare up at the ceiling and imagine him stretched out above her.

She wasn't having much luck.

Sleeping—rather, *trying* to sleep here—had been one of her worst ideas yet. But the thought of a real shower in a real house with real privacy had been her undoing. Phoebe hadn't been exposed to the smell, so she had sacked out while Libby lathered and rinsed and repeated until she was sure she had drained every ounce from Sam's hot water tank. Then and only then did she dry herself with a velvety towel and slip into the oversize hockey jersey and boxers that he had left out for her.

Thank God Sam had been nowhere in sight when she tiptoed out of the bathroom. A fast glance in the mirror had showed her that the jersey clung to her in a way she was pretty sure it had never fit Sam. Bad enough that she was spending the night trying to banish the thought of how the silky fabric would have felt against Sam's skin. There was no need for both of them to lie awake all night, wondering…

Oh, jeez. She punched the pillow, shifted onto her side and curled up tight.

THE DULL SMACK OF FIST against pillow drifted up the stairs and through the open door of Sam's bedroom. He pulled his own pillow over his head and tried to block out Libby's restless rustling. But he did take perverse pleasure in knowing she was having just as much trouble with this arrangement as he was. There would be hell to pay tomorrow when the kids were faced with two sleep-deprived leaders, but for the moment, he smiled grimly at the knowledge that he wasn't alone in this agony.

And *agony* was about the only way to describe it. He'd kept his eyes down and his head turned when he ushered

Libby into the bathroom, then made sure his door was her-
metically sealed until he heard her creep down the stairs. He
knew he'd been too tired for the test of strength he would
have faced if he'd seen her in his faded old Ice Cats gear.

Too bad he had a vivid imagination.

All through his own shower he had pictured, too clearly,
the way his shirt would hang on her; the way the neck would
gape, offering a hint of her warm, firm shoulders; the way
the fabric would drape over her breasts; the way it would
hit at her upper thigh, so all a man had to do was wrap his
hands in the worn fabric and hike it up a couple of inches
and then, God, then...

He rolled onto his stomach and groaned into the pillow.
From downstairs, he heard her stir again. He should close
the door. He would. Except the batteries in Casey's baby
monitor had died an hour ago, and he wasn't going to risk
sleeping through the little guy's morning cries. Not that
there was much chance of that with the way his night was
going, but still....

A sigh of pure frustration echoed through the night. He
wondered if she was lying on her back. If the bed and boards
between them were to disappear right now—if some twist
of fate sent him free-falling through the air until he landed
on her—would they be face-to-face? Would she shift to accommodate him, slide her arms around him, open to him?

This wasn't going to work.

He sat up and shoved his feet into flannel-lined slippers. He would go downstairs. Grab some batteries from
the kitchen. Come back up and fix the frickin' monitor
and close his door against all those nocturnal sounds that
seemed to be on a direct path to his groin.

Though how he was supposed to walk past the living
room, see Libby warm and restless on his sofa, and then
keep going, was beyond him.

With a deep breath and a prayer for strength, he started down the stairs.

A creak from the upper step made Libby jerk and look toward the hall. There was just enough illumination from the night-light at the bottom of the stairs for her to follow Sam's descent. One foot, two feet…calves, thighs, the lower edge of his boxer shorts. She should be considerate and close her eyes, but she was too busy absorbing the sight of the muscles she'd felt when he tangled against her beneath the raft.

She gulped. Why on earth didn't they make night-lights a bit dimmer? Or, maybe better, a few watts brighter?

His feet hit the ground floor. She lingered over the sight of his stomach and his chest, naked above his shorts. She'd seen his unclothed chest many times, had felt the firmness of his pecs when he brushed against her under the raft. But there was something about seeing him like this, in the silence broken only by Phoebe's soft snuffling, in the darkness that seemed to obliterate the rest of the world, that made catching a glimpse of him all the more tantalizing.

Sam Catalano had grown into one hell of a man.

His feet changed direction. He was turning toward the kitchen. Libby wasn't sure what she wanted to happen, but she did know she didn't want him to walk away. Not yet.

"Sam?"

Her whisper hung in the darkness before he turned back toward her. She propped herself up on her elbow to watch him cross the space to where she waited.

"What's up?" he whispered as he crouched beside her.

"Thanks for your help tonight. It was…nice…knowing you were there. To help, I mean." She allowed herself a small sigh. "I'm, um, not really used to that. You know?"

"I know." His hand hovered near her cheek. She fought the urge to press against it.

Silence filled the space between them, cut only by

Phoebe's sudden snort from the other side of the room. His grin flashed bright in the darkness. She bit down on her lip to hold back the giggles.

"So. You didn't want Tanya up here tonight, huh?"

"It seemed the most prudent course, all things considered."

"You think she planted a skunk in her cabin to get close to me?" His leer was pure testosterone. "That's kind of hard to believe, even for someone as awesome as *moi*."

She would slug him, except her palm might misinterpret the signal and turn it into a caress. Instead, she fisted her hands around her blanket and pushed herself upright. "I know it sounds ridiculous, but it was too convenient. Know what I mean? Something is making my antenna beep."

"Hmmm."

He must have said all he'd planned to say, because he put his hands on his knee as if to stand. But she wasn't ready for him to leave. Not yet. Not when the darkness and the false intimacy made it so much easier to give voice to her thoughts.

"Sam...I know about your parents."

"Son of a— Did Brynn tell you?"

"No. I mean, she said something at the barbecue that made me wonder, but don't blame her, okay? She didn't give me any details. I found those on my own."

Silence.

She rushed on, desperate to have it over now that she'd begun. "I read about your mom being sick and your dad leaving." She leaned closer. "That was why you walked away from me back then, wasn't it."

He froze, his face blank in the bits of moonlight reaching through the windows. With slow, deliberate movements, he rose from his spot on the floor.

Don't leave. Don't go. I need the truth.

As if he'd heard her, he stood only enough to reach the sofa. She pulled her legs up to give him room to perch on the edge, elbows on his knees, all his energy seeming to be centered on his clasped hands.

"Mom was supposed to pick us up from camp," he said slowly. "Me, Brynn and Trent. But instead of her, it was— our father. We asked him what was up but he brushed it off. 'Nothing,' he said. Mom lost a crown and had to go to the dentist. It sounded legit to me. I had other things on my mind."

She palmed her cheeks. Could he feel the heat of her blush? She could well imagine some of those *other things* that had been filling his thoughts.

"So we drove home, and Mom wasn't there, but hey. The dentist. The old man sent Brynn and Trent over to the neighbor's place to get Lukie. While they were gone, he sat me down and told me what was really going on."

Even the shadows couldn't soften the sudden tightening of his shoulders. "It was cancer, Lib. Bad. She'd been in the hospital for two weeks already but wouldn't let us know. She didn't want to spoil our fun."

Her hand slipped from her knees to his back as she leaned forward, aching to embrace the scared kid he had been. "Oh, Sam. I'm so sorry."

"Yeah, well, that was just the intro, you know? Because after spilling that all over me, our so-called father told me he was leaving."

Oh, dear God. She had hoped it wasn't true, hoped like hell the coach's memory was mistaken or that there had been some time between his mother's illness and his father's desertion, or...

She didn't realize she had moved until she rested her head against the side of his shoulder. She tried to pull back from the heat, but his hand came up as if reaching for her. So what could she do but slip her palm into his?

"Good old Dad. Said he was no good in a crisis, that he would just make things worse if he stuck around. We'd be better off without him, he said. He was just waiting for us to come home so we could look after Lukie." His muscles bunched beneath her hand. "The selfish son of a bitch left without even saying goodbye to the others."

"I am so, so sorry. If I had known..."

"You had your own problems. Neither of us was in any shape to help the other."

"Maybe not," she said softly. "And I do understand, Sam. But...I would have liked the chance."

There was a moment, as if he was weighing his answer, before he said, "When I said there were things I regretted... that was the biggest."

Sense told her she should let him go now. Between what he'd said and what he hadn't, she was swimming in a sea of emotions that needed time and processing and distance. Add in her worries over what he was still hiding, and the smartest move she could make would be to let him get up and do whatever he had come downstairs to do.

But she needed sleep. She needed to know a little comfort after a rotten night. She needed to know that five, ten years from now, when she thought back to this moment, she wouldn't curse herself for being chicken.

Most of all, she needed to touch Sam.

So she reached up, sliding her hand over his. She flattened her palm over the cords in his arm and let it slide high, higher, urging him closer to her. Her fingers brushed the hair at the nape of his neck and he rested his hand gently on her waist and she smiled, not just with her mouth, but with everything in her, because it felt so damned good to lean toward him and know what was going to happen and know, really know, that it was the only thing she could possibly do. And that even if she had a choice, she wouldn't want it to turn out any other way.

I refuse to regret this, she thought, and then her lips brushed his.

CHAPTER THIRTEEN

THE FIRST TOUCH WAS SOFT, tentative, a physical question awaiting a response. Libby closed her eyes and let herself sink into the kiss, into the feel of Sam's lips against hers, into the warmth of his touch and the shape of his mouth. He was the same but not, yet a part of her recognized him at once as the *something* she'd been searching for in all the kisses she'd shared with other men in the past twelve years.

It's Sam, a voice whispered in her head. *Of course.*

She'd been waiting for him and she didn't even know it.

He ended it first, easing away to rest his forehead against hers. "Hey." The word was warm against her cheek. "Guess I should have come downstairs a while ago."

Silly man. Didn't he know that there was a time to talk and a time to put that mouth to far better uses?

This time the question mark was gone. This kiss was one that demanded attention, the kind that made a girl sit up and say, *Hot* damn, *where have you been all my life?* It was the kind of kiss that evolved, that spiraled and swirled as it grew hotter and harder, the kind that made her wind her arms around his neck and arch herself up and ache for the feel of Sam against her, the weight of Sam over her, the heat of Sam inside her.

This was supposed to leave her relaxed enough to sleep?

She couldn't stop kissing him. She couldn't. Even when her mouth slipped away from his she kissed him, tasting the salt of his skin, caressing the stubble on his cheeks, press-

ing her lips into his hair to muffle her gasp when his mouth
scraped against her neck and his tongue traced her and she
remembered, oh, how she remembered....

"Twelve years," he whispered against her skin. The vibration shuddered through her.

"Worth the wait."

She could feel his smile on her neck before he spoke.
"You gonna make me wait another twelve?"

"Mister," she said, shifting to be even closer, "you
couldn't last another twelve seconds."

"You want to bet?"

No. "Sure."

"Okay. Here's the deal." His fingers were in her hair,
playing against her scalp. "If I make it twelve full seconds,
you kiss me again. If I don't..."

"If you don't?" She arched against him, needing more
of his touch.

"Then I guess I have to kiss you."

This was bad. This was so, so bad. "One Mississippi,"
she whispered into the night. "Two Mississippi, three Mis-
siss—"

The word was swallowed by his mouth on hers, plead-
ing, demanding, and she gave him everything he asked
and more. If the first kiss had been a question and the second the answer, this one was the promise of what could be.
This kiss was hot and liquid, and when he moved and his
fingers brushed the side of her breast she moaned into his
mouth, willing him to leave his hand exactly where it was.
She could never get close enough to him. Never.

Until she realized that Phoebe wasn't snoring anymore.

The silence barely registered at first. Her mind was filled
to overflowing with the slam of her pulse and the ragged
catch of Sam's breaths. But there was something unnatu-
ral about it. Something she couldn't ignore, no matter how

much she longed to simply lose herself in Sam. Something...
watchful.

She pulled back, raising a hand to stop Sam from following. His eyes narrowed. They stayed silent, frozen, listening.

Nothing.

Finally Sam leaned closer to whisper, "You think she
woke up?"

"Probably."

"You think she'll talk?"

"No." She reconsidered. "But if anyone asks her anything, she probably won't deny it."

"I, uh, think maybe I'd better go to the kitchen. Get whatever the hell it was I came down here for and head back upstairs." There was a huskiness in his voice she'd never heard
before, and damn, she loved the sound of it.

"That's probably a good idea."

He stroked her cheek. "Don't suppose you want to come
with me." His finger trailed lower. "After Phoebe is sound
asleep."

Want to? Oh, yes, more than she'd wanted anything in
a long, long time. But it was a big step between a kiss and
a trip upstairs, and as much as her body said *go for it,* her
damnable common sense had started to kick in as her tem-
perature dropped.

"Sorry."

"I must be psychic. I knew you'd say that."

"Then you know I really, really mean it about being
sorry."

"Not as much as I am, sweetcheeks." With a quick, silent
kiss to her nose, he moved away from her. "Never thought
I'd be grateful to a skunk."

"Me, either. Sweet dreams, Sam."

"I doubt they'll be sweet."

Libby knew the feeling.

"See you in the morning," he said, and padded away.

Libby watched until he left the room, then pulled her pillow over her head so she wouldn't hear him when he climbed the stairs. There was no telling where her body might lead if she listened to his footsteps. The only certainty was that if she followed him now, there'd be no stopping.

SAM COULDN'T REMEMBER the last time he'd snagged so little sleep yet still woken up feeling like the world was full of rainbows and unicorns.

His good mood stayed intact even after discovering that Libby and Phoebe were long gone. It kept him smiling through the adventures in diaper wrestling that Casey seemed intent on winning. It had him whistling as he headed down the hill and into the kitchen to check on the tomato juice supply.

And that, of course, was where his grin met its match.

Cosmo greeted him with a glare. "You got a hell of a nerve, lover boy."

Oh, hell. So much for Phoebe not talking.

"You're the soul of tact, you know that, Cosmo?"

"Tact my ass. I told you to stay away from Libby."

It would feel so damned good to point out that the lady in question had been the one initiating things, but no way in hell was he sharing that little tidbit. Time for an abrupt change of topic.

"How much tomato juice do we have?"

"None, and it won't work in a cabin. Gotta use vinegar and coffee grounds. I already put some in there and opened the windows."

Now, that was definitely not the response he'd been expecting. "You didn't have to do that. Thanks."

"Some of us sleep downwind of there." Cosmo fixed

Sam with the evil eye. "You know. Sleep. That thing most people do in the middle of the night."

"You were always too fast for me, Cos."

"And you were always a troublemaking little twit, so we're square. Leastaways on that."

Sam could see where this conversation was going. He figured he had three choices: walk away, let Cosmo get things out of his system or take the old "the best defense is a good offense" route.

Time for Cosmo to get a taste of his own medicine.

"Tell me something, Cos. Why do you keep coming back here?"

"You trying to get rid of me?"

"Not yet. Let's just say I'm curious. You've been working here every summer for as long as I can remember."

"So? Maybe I need the money."

"I sign your checks. You're not making that much."

"Lucky I'm independently wealthy."

"Avoiding the question, Cos?"

Cosmo's grunt was so deep, it could have been scraped from the bottom of his barrel chest.

Sam grabbed an apple from the bowl on the counter. "See, here's the thing. You always had that grumpy old man thing going for you, but never this bad. I have a feeling something's eating you, and call it ego, but I don't think it's just me being here."

He was totally talking out of the side of his ass but something—maybe the way Cosmo seemed to be hanging on his every word even while he cracked three eggs at a time—told him he was zeroing in on a truth Cosmo would prefer remained unsaid.

"So what's the deal? You don't want the job, you hate me or you keep coming back because there's something here you love?" Sam squinted into the light, carefully assessing the sudden shake to Cosmo's hand, the way he fumbled an egg and let the shell slip to the counter.

Incidents from the past few weeks spun and settled into a pattern. Cosmo's over-the-top belligerence...his refusal to make Myra's favorite meat loaf...the way he stumbled over Myra's name and changed the topic whenever some-one else mentioned her...

Well, damn. He hadn't seen that one coming.

"Or should that be, some*one* else?" Sam asked, a bit more gently. "Someone who *used* to be here?"

Cosmo stood with his hand hovering over the bowl. For just the briefest second, Sam read the sheer agony on the older man's face. Cosmo looked like a giant Saint Bernard who'd just lost every friend he'd ever had in the world.

Then he tossed the shells into the sink and pointed to-ward the door. "I don't have time for this horseshit. Out."

No way. "You have a thing for Myra."

Cosmo's laugh sounded far too forced to be convincing. "Look who's talking. A guy who can get his face on a ce-real box but still lets some gal lead him around by his—"

"Libby isn't leading me anywhere, mister." At least, no-where he wasn't headed already.

"Not even under the raft?"

"Nothing happened. You tell Myra you have the hots for her?"

Cosmo shook his head in disgust. "You had a beauti-ful woman hidden away with you and you expect us to be-lieve you didn't do anything about it? Even you aren't that pathetic."

"You spent thirty-some summers with a woman and never told her you want her? That's textbook pathetic."

"Maybe you oughta use some of that body-wash stuff on your hair. You know, to get rid of the crap that's working its way into your head."

"Maybe you oughta call Myra and tell her you miss her before you drive the rest of us round the bend."

From the way Cosmo shrugged, too casual, too careless, Sam knew he'd suggested a course that Cosmo had already considered at great length. Considered and rejected.

Which meant he was hurting.

Which meant Sam's camp was suffering.

But more than that—Sam was shocked to realize that he was hurting for Cosmo.

Sam tossed his apple from hand to hand. Maybe it was because he himself had just been treated to a hell of a belated welcome back by Libby, but he hated to see Cosmo this miserable. Despite everything, he liked the man. He liked the way Cosmo always looked out for Casey and slipped him extra treats. He liked how protective Cosmo was of Libby. He liked the way Cosmo treated him just the same as he had all those years ago.

The guy was a pain in the ass, but he was a loyal, reliable pain, and that went a long way with Sam.

"You know," he said slowly, "every time I've talked to Myra, she's asked about you."

No response.

"And when we were negotiating the sale, she made sure you would have a job here as long as you wanted. You and Libby. You were the only two she pointed out specifically."

Cosmo pulled a whisk from a drawer and commenced a brutal attack on the bowl of eggs.

"And call me a fool, but I seem to recall Myra hanging out in the kitchen a whole lot back in the day. Way more than I've ever needed to be here, or Libby, either. Makes me wonder if Myra might have been looking for something more than cooking tips."

Cosmo hefted his bulk away from the work island and

ambled toward the refrigerator, where he stopped and looked back over his shoulder. "You're right. You are a fool."

"Yeah, well, here's the thing about fools. Something I learned back in school." Sam gave the apple a quick shirt polish before admiring its gleam. "The old fools—you know, the court jesters—they had two jobs. The first was to make the king laugh. The second was to call things the way they saw them. You know. To tell the truth that nobody wanted to hear."

He bit into his apple and sneaked a peek at Cosmo while the juice dribbled down his chin.

"I'm just talking about what I see, Cos. And the way I see it, you have two choices. You can keep on making yourself and Myra and everyone around you miserable." He backhanded the juice from his chin while heading for the door, where he paused to salute Cosmo with the upraised apple. "You can be as pathetic as you want for as long as you want."

Cosmo's lips clamped together as if he were forcing himself not to ask about the alternative. Lucky for him, Sam was going to offer it anyway.

"You can be miserable. Or you can man up, speak up and live the goal."

SAM WAS STILL SHAKING his head when he walked into Libby's cabin. As he'd expected, she was already there, looking around the area near the door. As he hadn't expected, the scent had already faded from tear inducing to nose wrinkling.

She hadn't noticed him yet, bent over as she was, peering intently at the area around the door. Looking for—what? Footprints? She had said something seemed off, but in all honesty, he wasn't sure how Tanya could have engineered a skunk spraying on cue, even if she had wanted to.

On the other hand, Libby looked mighty cute bent over

like that with her shorts riding up the back of her firm legs and one very fine badonk-a-donk beckoning to him. Memories of the night before filled his head and heated his body. It might have been nothing more than some kisses and a little groping, but it was the most action he'd seen in longer than he cared to remember. Add in the fact that it had been luscious Libby in his arms, and he couldn't be blamed for having wicked thoughts about grabbing her around the waist and hauling her into the deserted cabin for some further indulgence.

"Morning," he called, before temptation could undermine his better sense. "I take it the CSI team has finished their investigation?"

She straightened slowly, turning with a self-conscious smile and a slight blush that told him her thoughts were probably mirroring his. That certainly didn't go far toward keeping his intentions honorable.

On the other hand, there was nothing dishonorable about a good-morning kiss or two.

He moved in closer. Her eyes widened. She took a deep breath and raised a hand.

"Hang on. We need to talk."

Talking had its points. Look what it had led to the night before. But he had a feeling Libby wouldn't be quite as pliant in the light of day.

Course, he would never know if he didn't try.

"You're right. Absolutely."

Ha. She hadn't expected him to agree.

"But this is probably the kind of discussion that needs privacy," he went on. "No one's going to venture into that cabin with the smell and all. What do you say we—"

"Nice try, Catalano." Her words were stern and her clipboard was tight against her breasts—lucky damned hunk of wood—but the rolling of her eyes told him she wasn't nearly as immune to his charms as she would like him to believe.

"Two things. First, the easy one. I don't think there was a real skunk anywhere near here last night."

"You want to tell that one to my nose? 'Cause it's having a hard time finding the ground between what you're saying and what it smelled last night."

"But that's the thing. You smelled a skunk last night, right away."

"Still not seeing where you're going with this, Lib." Though he was mighty happy to watch her mouth purse while she was thinking.

"When a skunk first sprays, it doesn't smell like what you expect. It's more of a burnt rubber, electrical kind of scent. That characteristic skunk smell comes later." She frowned. "I was here less than a minute after Tanya screamed. It already smelled like skunk. That's just not right."

"Maybe it's not right, but how—"

"Fake scent."

He blinked. "Excuse me?"

"They make it for hunters. You know, to mask their own odor while they're in the woods. Goes on strong but it fades faster than the real thing, which would explain why it's not so bad today." She sighed. "You're a guy. You used to live around here. Do you mean to say you never went into a hunting supply store and looked around?"

"Nope. I didn't have time for that, and all my friends were hockey players, so they were in the same boat. But how did you learn about this?"

Her cheeks pinked up adorably. "Oh, a friend," she said, far too casually.

Logically, he knew that she hadn't spent the past dozen years twiddling her thumbs waiting for him, but watching her mention this "friend" brought out his inner caveman to a degree he would never have anticipated. She was his, dammit. *His.* The thought of someone else laying claim to those lips hit him in the gut strong enough to make his breath hitch.

He turned to inspect the wall of the cabin. Better to focus on the daddy longlegs crawling up the side than to keep looking at Libby when he felt this confused.

"So you think Tanya got hold of some of that stuff and sprayed it around to make the cabin uninhabitable."

"Bingo."

He risked a peek in her direction. "She doesn't strike me as the sort to hang around hunting supply stores."

"She wouldn't have to. Her, um, her uncle owns one."

Again with the forced casualness. The way she suddenly wouldn't meet his eye heightened his suspicions.

"And would this uncle be the same reason you know about this stuff?"

"I don't think that's pertinent."

The hell it wasn't.

"How well do you know him?"

"That's none of your business."

His stomach dropped. *None of your business* was code for *I slept with him but I don't want to talk about it.* At least he was pretty sure that was what it meant.

She had a past. She had a life outside him. He, who had broken her heart and then brought a child into the world in their years apart, had no right to be bothered by the thought of her having other relationships.

But he was anyway.

"I wasn't asking because I wanted to know about your love life," he lied. "I just wondered if you would feel comfortable giving him a call and asking if he had done any special orders for his niece."

"I could," she said thoughtfully, and he had to fight back

the urge to grab her then and there and kiss her until she was incapable of remembering that guy's phone number, place of work or even his name. "But, you know, that part isn't so important. What really matters is why she would have done it."

"The supposed crush."

"Sam, you walk into the room and her IQ drops by about thirty points. I don't think we can call it a *supposed* crush anymore."

He raised his hands in mock surrender. "Not doing anything to encourage it, I swear."

"I know you're not."

Damn, the world was a brighter place when Libby believed in him.

"I had Phoebe talk to her, but I guess that wasn't enough."

"I have an idea." He moved in closer. "The whole camp thinks there's something between me and you already. How about if we—"

"No." The word was crisp, clear and far too certain for his ego.

She must have realized that she'd been too decisive, for she closed the gap between them and placed a hand on his arm. "Look, Sam. I'm not going to lie. I had a very nice time with you last night, and yes, you are very tempting. But I can't… Things are really uncertain now. I have to figure out what's happening next. What's best for me. I need a clear head to do that, and I might regret telling you this, but you have a tendency to mess up my logic, you know?"

She peeked up at him almost bashfully. His gut contracted with want.

"Running around and convincing everyone that we have a real relationship might be a good strategy for dealing with Tanya, but it's not something I can do. It would be too

easy to confuse make-believe with reality, and I can't....
I just can't."

"What if it wasn't all make-believe?" The words were
out before he could think better of them, his hoarse whisper hanging in the air like a magnet that could either pull
him and Libby together or push them apart depending on
which way it flipped.

Her eyes were big but filled with regret as she answered,
"That would make it even harder."

"It wouldn't have to—"

"Sam. Please." She turned away, but not before he saw
the death grip she had on the clipboard. "I understand what
happened when we were kids. But there are still things that
you...no, things that I need to decide. So for right now I
need to keep it light."

"Friends." Good thing she couldn't see the way his hands
fisted when he said the word.

She nodded, then turned back with a grateful smile. "I
would like that very much."

It wasn't enough. He wasn't sure what the hell was growing between him and Libby, but while it undoubtedly included friendship, he was pretty sure there was a lot more
to it than that.

He didn't want to encourage her. Didn't want to fall for
anyone, not now when so much of his own life was still settling into place. But he also knew that he and Libby had a
shot at something wonderful, and he wasn't ready to give
up on that. Not yet.

She had said last night that she would have liked the
chance to help him when things fell apart with his family.
Maybe, if he opened up a little to her—not about the most
intense stuff, but if he asked for her help on some other
things—maybe that would be a way to pull her closer with-

out scaring either of them off. A trial run at a different kind of intimacy.

He closed his eyes for a second and pictured it. Him and Libby, sitting on his porch on that cushioned swing Brynn had bought to replace the bum-bruising chairs, talking about… About what? Not the custody suit. Not the camp, either. But there was a hell of a lot more throwing him for a curve these days.

"Can friends give each other some advice?"

She blinked, regarded him with puzzlement for a second, then nodded slowly. "Sure. Why not?" A flash of her old mischief lit her face as she added, "Heck, we both know I love bossing you around anyway, so why not make it official?"

"Well, then, friend. I have a question for you." He lowered himself to the slate step and patted the space beside him. She eyed him with all the skepticism he would expect, then sat primly on the far end, leaving a good six inches of stone between them. He made sure she didn't see his grin.

"It's about Casey. He sure seems to me like he's settling in okay, but the kid's been through the wringer lately, what with losing his mom and coming to live with me and then moving not once, but twice." He was pleased with how easy it had been to gloss over the whole Sharon aspect. "I think he's doing a great job of handling it, but you know more about kids than I do. Does anything seem off to you?"

She lowered the clipboard to her upraised knees and tapped her finger against the papers. "It's been a long time since I took developmental psych, but he certainly seems to be on target for most things. Since kids usually regress when there's a major upset in their lives, that's an encouraging sign."

"Regress?"

"You know. If they were, say, potty trained, they would

start having accidents again. Or in Casey's case, maybe he would start needing a bottle again after being weaned from it. Things like that."

"He did that. When he first came to me. Sha— His day-care provider told me he was down to a couple of bottles a day at that point, but after he moved in with me, boom, it was like he couldn't get enough of them. Brynn said she felt like she was running a dairy for a while there."

"And now he's off them again?"

"Other than one at bedtime, yeah. And the pediatrician told me to cut that out once he's had a few more weeks here."

"Sounds good. Other than that, he seems to be making friends with everyone, but he definitely turns to you as his source of comfort, so I'd say he's pretty securely attached to you."

"To you, too."

Oops. He hadn't intended to mention that. But Libby was already staring hard at her papers, drawing absently on them with her fingers.

"I noticed." She flashed him a quick grin. "He's not alone in that."

And now he was jealous of his own kid. He thought that wasn't supposed to happen for another twenty years or so.

"I have wondered if it might be better for me to spend less time with him. In case, you know." She returned her focus to the papers. "I don't want to be the source of another loss. He's had enough of those already."

Then don't go. But he couldn't say that to her. He'd taken enough from her already. He would not, could not, impinge on her freedom by imposing his wishes on her. He would not be that selfish.

"If it's up to me, I say, don't worry about that. He needs all the great people he can get right now. If you leave, yeah. It will be hard. But he'll have me and Mrs. Collins, and he'll start going to a playgroup in the fall, just a couple of days a week, but enough to give him a new focus. He's going to have people come and go his whole life. I want him to learn that it's okay. The last thing I want is for people to be on eggshells around him, to get him thinking he can't handle it or that he shouldn't get involved with folks because it will hurt too much when it's time to say goodbye. That's no way to live."

He'd been thinking only of Casey when he spoke, talking freely as he realized Libby was the first one he'd really discussed his son with since Brynn left. Sure, he and the pediatrician and Mrs. Collins had lots of conversations about Casey. But it was different with Libby. Freer. Safer. Kind of like how it used to be with Robin, when they each knew that no one else in the world would ever care about their little boy the way they both did.

But in his relaxation, he hadn't realized that his words of living in fear of loss could apply to Libby, as well.

That is, he was clueless until he saw the way she pulled herself upright, sitting straighter and stiffer on the hard step while small patches of red formed in her cheeks.

"Okay. That came out the wrong way. I wasn't talking about you, Lib. Honestly."

"I never thought you were."

Bull. But he'd bungled the moment, and he wasn't going to make it worse by trying to explain himself.

"Actually," he said, "I was kind of thinking about Cosmo. Did you know he has a thing for Myra?"

"What?"

Well, that certainly got her thoughts turning in a different direction.

"You have got to be out of your ever-loving tree."

"I don't think so." He told her about his run-in with Cosmo, about the hints he'd picked up over the past weeks, about the way Cosmo couldn't make a convincing case against Sam's theory. When he was done, Libby looked at him with—whoa. Was that respect in her eyes?

"You know, I almost hate to admit it, but I think you're right. I would never have believed it, but it all fits. Why didn't I see it?"

"Maybe because you're too close. Sometimes it takes a fresh eye, you know?"

"Well, you certainly have the 'fresh' part down," she said cheekily, and he gave thanks that she was still able to tease him.

He grabbed a stick from the ground and twirled it between his palms. "The big question is, do you think Myra feels the same way?"

"Hmmm." She slumped back against the door, staring into the sky. He took advantage of the moment to drink in her face in profile, relaxed and happy, the way he always wanted her to look.

"Myra always asks about him," she said slowly. "And there's something there in her voice. She's always given him liberties that none of the other staff had, and she was constantly finding reasons to talk to him when it wasn't really necessary. I thought it was just, you know, they'd been friends forever, even before he came to work here."

"Really?"

"Oh, yeah. All their lives, from what I've heard. So I assumed she was just talking to him about people they knew, or bitching to him about me. Like he was her safety valve."

"Makes sense."

"But when I take a step back… She had lots of other friends, but never like Cosmo. Not just because he was here and handy, either, but she always laughed more with him than with anyone else. Laughing with someone, having little private jokes, inventing excuses to be together—those are all pretty good signs that there's something there."

"Agreed." He leaned back beside her, focusing on her bit of sky. "So what do we do about it?"

"Absolutely nothing."

"Oh, come on. We can't let them walk around miserable for the rest of their days. Myra needs some happiness, and if Cosmo doesn't get over himself soon, I might have to use his head for shooting practice."

Libby laughed but shook her head. "Sorry. I don't inter-fere in matters of the heart. You already pointed out some stuff to Cosmo, and I have a feeling that leaving here has brought some things home to Myra, as well. The rest is up to them."

"Where's the fun in that?"

She giggled and turned her head to face him. "Sorry, Catalano. You'll have to find your own fun."

Her breath caught, and he realized that her mind must have flown off in the same direction as his. He stared at her, at the sudden confusion in her features, and promises be damned, he wanted nothing in the world more than to lean across the space between them and kiss her. Not from lust this time—okay, maybe a bit—but because it was the best way he knew to bring the smile back to her face.

But he had promised not to push. God help him, he would abide by it.

But God help him again, he hoped Libby didn't take too much longer to figure out what she planned to do.

Because doing the right thing was becoming more dif-ficult by the minute.

CHAPTER FOURTEEN

As soon as Libby walked into the crowded dining hall, she knew that Phoebe had talked. The smirking counselors and the thunderclouds that Cosmo kept aiming toward Sam were her first clues. Phoebe's refusal to meet her eyes was her second tip. And when Tanya walked past with a load of trays, stopped in front of Libby, then turned suddenly so a cup of orange juice and a bowl of cold oatmeal "accidentally" flew off the trays and all over Libby's shirt, well, it didn't take a master detective to put all the pieces together.

"Oh!" Tanya gasped, her eyes big and undeceiving. "Oh, Libby, I'm so sorry. I thought I heard someone calling my name, and I didn't know you were there. Oh, my gosh. Let me help."

Libby accepted a napkin from Mick, who was hovering by her elbow, and removed herself from Tanya's reach. She dabbed at the mess all over her shirt and decided then and there that she'd had enough. Enough of Tanya's attitude. Enough drama. Enough of trying to deny that—whether she wanted it or not—there was something growing between her and Sam.

She'd meant what she said down at the cabin. She wasn't about to indulge in public displays of affection on the off chance that it would bring a halt to Tanya's infatuation. For one thing, it wasn't appropriate. For another, she doubted it would do anything besides make Tanya even more determined. The girl was a pain-in-the-ass drama queen but she wasn't one to give up easily. More important, she was still a good counselor and the kids adored her. Libby would have to suck it up.

But that didn't mean that Libby was going to roll over and play dead.

"Not to worry," she said briskly while she dabbed. "It's not the first time I've had food dumped on my lap, Tanya. Why, I remember once in high school, your uncle Rick dropped a whole plate of spaghetti on me. That was a serious mess."

She forced a laugh for the benefit of the wide-eyed kids surrounding them.

"How is he, by the way? It's been a while, but you know, some people you just never forget. I remember being so amazed when he told me about some of the tricks hunters use for staying hidden from animals when they're out in the woods."

This time there was nothing fake about the sudden widening of Tanya's eyes. She recovered quickly with a nonchalant shrug.

"He's okay, I guess. I haven't seen him in a while."

"Really."

"Ages and ages."

"That's too bad. Your family always struck me as being so close. You know. Folks who would do anything for each other."

Tanya's cheeks flared, and for a moment, a little of her bravado slipped. She rearranged a bowl on her tray. "Well, things change."

"Yes, they do. And those changes can happen when you least expect them."

Confident that her message had been received loud and clear, Libby smiled sweetly at Tanya and moved on. Problem one, dealt with. Problem two was next.

She worked her way to the front of the room and raised her hand in the "quiet" sign. Within a minute, all her good little campers had stopped talking and were watching her with varying degrees of curiosity. Except, of course, for those who were still busy inhaling Cosmo's apple-spice oatmeal.

"I have some announcements."

From the corner of her eye she saw Sam slide into the building and lean up against the door. An unexpected but not entirely unwelcome hit of pleasure ran through her. She did know how to pick them. Not that she was ready to pick Sam for anything, except possibly a few more twists to her memories, but still. A girl had a right to stand back and sigh once in a while, didn't she?

"First, thank you all for dealing with last night's events so quickly and appropriately. Campers, you did a great job of staying calm, and counselors, you can be very proud of how well you cared for your kids. Great job all around. I am so proud of all of you."

She waited for the applause to die down before launching into the usual morning reminders and birthdays. At last she came to the real item on her agenda.

"Last night, after things calmed down, Sam and I were talking, and I had an idea."

A few snickers, a few coughs, a smothered laugh. Yep. Exactly what she'd expected, and exactly why she was up here facing them head-on. Hiding and pretending weren't going to stop the rumor mill. The best she could do now was to deflect it in the direction she wanted it to go.

"Next week, we'll kick off the Tour de Camp. For those of you who are new, that's when we run a series of competitions, with the cabins competing against each other. On the last Friday we'll have a big camp-wide final competition. Well, I decided that this year, we should establish a new tradition. From now on, the winners of the Tour de Camp will have their names inscribed on a trophy that will be housed in that beautiful new pavilion down by the water."

Applause, laughter and whistles sounded through the hall, but she paid little attention to them, focused as she was on Sam—the way he jerked, the smile spreading across his face as he gave a thumbs-up to her suggestion.

She made a mock bow, joked about making Sam pay for the trophy and dismissed them to their activities. The hall emptied slowly until there remained only her and Sam.

"You should be with your group," she reminded him as she met him at the door.

"Alex can handle them for five minutes. I wanted to check in with you." He gestured toward her shirt. "I don't know much about fashion, but I'd bet oatmeal isn't the hot new accessory."

"Don't worry. I'm going to change before the office starts smelling like apples and cinnamon."

"There are worse things," he said quietly, and she could see by the rigid set to his shoulders that he was barely holding back his anger. She placed her hand on his arm without thinking, but once she realized what she'd done, she refused to back away. She might be trying to resist Sam, but even friends could offer some physical reassurance.

"It's okay. I'll live."

"Things have gone too far. She needs to be out of here."

"Sam, take a breath. We can't prove anything."

"What if it hadn't been oatmeal that got you, huh? What if a knife had gone flying?"

His protectiveness was so over-the-top that she wanted to roll her eyes, but at the same time, she couldn't. Maybe because it felt more comforting than she would have expected to have someone looking out for her for a change.

"It was cereal, Sam. I'm okay."

"She's on probation."

"For what? Assault with a deadly grain?"

His grin was reluctant but still real enough to ease some of her concern. "Okay. Nothing official. But she's on— whatever they called it in *Animal House*. Secret probation."

"Double secret probation," she corrected him with a laugh—then faltered when she realized that at some point, she had moved even closer to him. Her hand had slipped higher up his arm and her toes all but touched his, and his mouth, oh, his mouth was close enough that she would barely have to give in to temptation to kiss him.

"Well." She stepped back, once, twice, hands clasped behind her back, not meeting his gaze. "I'd better get to work."

She grabbed the clipboard from the table—when had she let go of it?—and hurried out the door before she could do something foolish like abandon her best intentions. Kissing Sam in the dark after a lousy night, for the sake of old times and new peace, had been one thing. Yielding in the middle of the day when her common sense was wide-awake was entirely different.

Damn the man. He was the most infuriating blend of appeal and secretiveness that she had ever met. If only he would talk to her. Really talk. The discussion of Casey had been a big step but he was still holding back, still hiding things.

She wouldn't play that game. No matter how much fun it might be at the time, there was no way to win.

THE NEXT FEW DAYS seemed to fly for Sam, a blur of activities with the kids, increased lessons from Libby and evenings of toting Casey to campfire before tucking him into bed each night. In between there were calls with the lawyers and overseeing the work on the pavilion and doing what he could to prepare for the home visit from the social worker scheduled for Friday morning. It was a hell of a juggling act, and he had to admit he was getting tired in a way he'd never known before. Not just physically—he could handle that after years of training—but in his brain.

His emotions were getting sick of the roller-coaster thing, too. The custody suit would soon be behind him—but what if it didn't turn out the way he hoped? Libby was handing more and more of the camp over to him—but what if he messed up when she wasn't around? She was friendly and easy with him, joking in a way that almost reminded him of the old days—but there was a line still between them, an elephant that had plopped itself into the middle of every conversation, every glance, every breath they shared in the same room.

Kissing her had changed things. The memories were stronger now and the tantalizing nearness of her was even more enticing than it had been before. He knew what he was missing now. Knowing ratcheted up his desire by about a thousand times.

Worst of all, it was well into August and she still hadn't given him an answer about what would happen in September.

He tried to focus on the positive. Cosmo hadn't turned into Mr. Congeniality, but he had stopped barking at everything that breathed. Tanya was still mooning over him, but she was keeping her distance. He was getting more and more confident about the camp policies and procedures, and his kids were getting excited about the Tour de Camp.

Still, he was in a kind of subdued mood when Casey had his chat time with Jody and Andy Thursday night. Instead of busying himself with paperwork or a book, he sat on the edge of the bed and watched Casey, staying out of the conversation but paying close attention to what was happening. Casey had missed those kids so badly, and it showed in those first calls. Things were easier now. No more tears, for which Sam was grateful. But as he listened and watched, he could see something he hadn't anticipated.

The cousins were drifting apart.

Sure, he had known they wouldn't be as close as they had been when Casey was part of their everyday lives. But tonight, he could see that Jody and Andy were going through the motions. Their attention wandered. They were relying on old games and jokes to talk to Casey, and more than once he heard Sharon in the background reminding them that they needed to stop asking her about tomorrow and focus on Casey.

Well, hell. He didn't want Casey devastated with each contact, but he didn't want the kids to become strangers, either. They were all scheduled to see each other in September when he and Casey returned to Nova Scotia for the hearing, but the more he saw, the more he realized that September was too damned far away.

Maybe he could talk to Libby about it....

No. He shot the idea away as fast as it had appeared. Talking to her about Casey the other day had been good. It had been almost a relief to share his worries with someone else. But that had been small potatoes. This—the whole custody thing—this was too close, too scary, to share with someone who might not even be in his life at the end of the month.

But he could imagine what Libby would say if she knew. Once he put it that way to himself, the answer was clear.

When the call was winding down, he crawled across the bed to get his face in the camera. "Hi, guys!" He waved, pulling Casey's hand away from the microphone.

They perked up right away, which only affirmed his decision. For a minute or two he answered their questions about the camp and asked them about their summer. Then he rolled Casey over to the side and said, "Hey, I want to talk to your mom for a minute. Is she handy?"

"Sure. Mom! Uncle Sam needs to talk to you!"

In the background he heard Sharon's questions, her reluctant "Tell him I'll be right there." He smoothed Casey's hair and tickled his belly and waited for Sharon to seat herself in front of her camera.

"I'm in a hurry, Sam. Jody has a swimming lesson, and we have to leave in five minutes."

"I only need half of that. Are the kids out of earshot?"

She frowned, as if bracing herself for bad news, but called to the kids to go to the bathroom and gather their swim things. "Okay. I bought you two minutes. Talk fast."

"It's nothing big, but I didn't want to say it in front of them and upset any apple carts. I'm thinking September might be too long to wait for the kids to get together. Would they like to come for a visit before then?"

"A visit? To your camp?"

For once, he seemed to have pierced Sharon's usual calm and collected attitude. With the mask of resentment stripped away she almost reminded him of Robin. Libby was still head and shoulders above her in that department, but in that second, he could see the resemblance.

It hurt. But it also made it easier for him to say what he wanted to say.

"Yeah. Here. My treat. I know you guys are busy, so it wouldn't have to be long, just a few days, but I think they would have fun here. There's sure enough for them to do."

Too late, he realized that it might have been a good idea to check with Libby before he floated this idea. He was still mastering the fine art of group sizes and adult-to-child ratios, and he wasn't as up on their enrollment for the third session as she was.

He wouldn't mention having the kids take part in any

camp activities until he checked with her. She would help him see if Jody and Andy could participate in groups, or if he would have to plan their use of the facilities around that of the campers. But there would be a way to handle that, he was sure. She would help him figure it out.

"I... This is quite a surprise." Sharon had never sounded so uncertain in all the time he'd known her. "I don't know.... It's such a long drive, and I don't want them to fly alone...."

He gritted his teeth and pushed out the words he knew he had to say. "I wouldn't want them to fly alone, either. The invitation is for you, too."

Sharon sat back in her chair. She stared at him, first in surprise, then with suspicion.

"Why?"

It was a fair enough question. "I think they're drifting apart. I don't want that any more than you do. I can't get away until camp is over, so this is the logical answer."

And, he realized, it could work in his favor, as well. If he got Sharon up here, got her to see how great this place was and how Casey was thriving here...well, it would be silly to think she might drop the suit. She was too invested in it at this point. But maybe she wouldn't fight as hard. And maybe, once it was over and his right to keep his son with him had been established, once and for all, maybe it would be easier to build a new working relationship with her if she felt in her heart that Casey was happy and healthy and safe.

She would always be Casey's aunt. She would always be in his life, and long-term, Sam wanted her to be there. She loved Casey and she could share more of Robin with him than he himself ever could.

They would have to work these things out after the hearing. Why not start now?

"I don't know." Sharon spoke slowly, but to her credit, she seemed to be giving the idea serious consideration. "We have a lot going on this month already, and I don't have the calendar in front of me. But I… This is so sudden, I can't…"

A sharp rapping on Sam's front door gave him an easy exit. "Look, someone's at my door, and I know I caught you by surprise. Take a couple of days to think it over and let me know. There's no hidden agenda here, Sharon. I just want what's best for Casey and his cousins, same as you."

She gave a quick nod and said goodbye as he ended the call, gathered Casey and booted it down the stairs while yelling that he was on his way. She hadn't seemed overly enthusiastic about the offer, but he couldn't blame her. He was kind of blown away himself.

His equilibrium took another direct hit when he opened the door to find Cosmo standing before him, taut and barely recognizable in a neatly pressed shirt with an overnight bag at his feet.

"Cos?"

"I'm taking tomorrow off. Won't be back until lunch-time Saturday. Don't worry, I prepped everything I could and lined up folks to do what else is needed. You won't have any trouble."

Sam could feel his jaw sagging but had no time to do any-thing about it before Casey lurched forward, reaching for his buddy. Cosmo's face softened as he reached for the child.

"Have fun while I'm gone, kid. Make your old man mis-erable for me."

Sam found his voice as Cosmo gently set Casey on the floor before hefting his bag.

"Uh…is everything okay?"

"Fine and dandy."

"You gonna tell me where you're going?"

"Nope."

Cosmo turned his back on Sam and headed for the dark-ness beyond the circle of light spilling out of the house.

Taking a wild chance, Sam called, "Say hi to Myra for me, will you?"

Just like that, Cosmo stopped and stiffened. Not long. Just enough to tell Sam that his suspicions had been dead-on.

In one of the fastest recoveries Sam had ever seen, Cosmo headed back into the night. "See ya Saturday."

"Yeah. See you." Under his breath, he added a swift and sincere "Good luck."

And then he grabbed the walkie-talkie at his hip. He couldn't wait to spill the news to Libby.

BRIGHT AND EARLY the next morning, Sam dropped his kids at the games field, hung around long enough to be sure that everyone was behaving and the counselors had the situation under control, then loped up to the office. Libby was headed into town for a meeting. The social worker was due a bit after that. He hadn't been this nervous since the first time Robin had left him alone with Casey while she ran to the store.

Half a dozen people stopped him on his way, but he had made sure to give himself extra time to allow for such occurrences. By the time he burst through the door he was kind of puffed that he had dealt with them all, known the answers to their questions and still arrived with five minutes to spare. Enough time to broach the subject of Sharon and her kids visiting camp, not enough to have to go into details.

He bounded up the steps, waltzed into the office and allowed himself a glow of pride when he saw Libby's pleasant surprise. He'd made her smile like that. Yeah. Him. And if he was going to be dragged through hell once the social worker arrived, the least he could do was keep the smile on Libby's face and earn himself a few minutes of heaven.

"You're early."

"Just call me Mr. Reliable."

She rolled her eyes. "Well, then, maybe I'll stop telling you to show up ten minutes before I really need you."

Her smile softened the words, and he took them in the joking vein he knew they were intended. Camp wasn't the only thing he was mastering. He had almost earned a degree in Libby Kovak 101.

So he felt very secure in offering her his biggest leer and saying, "Do you mean we have time to kill before you have to leave?"

Her blush was as adorable as he had anticipated. "Forget it, mister. Hands on the table and all body parts to yourself."

"Fine." He heaved an overly dramatic sigh before leaning over her shoulder. "Did you miss me?"

"No."

"Oh, come on. Just a little?"

She made a great show of checking the clock. "My, look how late it is. I really need to hit the road."

"Sure. You do that. Because we both know you're just running away to keep from throwing yourself at me."

The deepening of the roses in her cheeks told him he wasn't as far off as she would like him to believe.

She shook her head and started to rise, but he grabbed her arm before she could make her escape. "One quick thing."

"I am not kissing you. I don't care how quick you say it will be."

"Did I say anything about kissing? Did I even hint at it? No. Seems to me you're the one who keeps bringing it up." He shook his head. "You know, I think we've stumbled across a case of the lady protesting too much."

"Uh-huh. You keep telling yourself that, pal." She softened the words with a saucy smile before adding, "Here's something to fill the time. Lesson one." She pointed to the open file drawer. "My shins are going to be permanently scarred from tripping over that. How about we practice closing it?"

He kicked it, too hard, and pain radiated up his leg. "Ow!"

She leveled an amused glace in his direction. "You broke how many bones playing hockey, and you're whining over a stubbed toe?"

"Hey, I earned those breaks fair and square. Not like this. I could swear I closed that sucker." He wiggled his toes inside his sneaker, then grinned. "Besides, when I got hurt playing hockey, I had therapy. And massages. Those really helped. How would you like to—"

"No massages." She winked. "But you do get points for trying."

He'd take points. Full frontal body contact would be better, but points would eventually have to add up to something mind-blowing. Wouldn't they?

Distracted by thoughts of Libby's hands sliding over him, rubbing hot peppermint-scented cream into every aching muscle—and he was developing more aches by the second—it took him a moment to remember what he needed to discuss with her.

"Listen." He boosted himself up on her desk and leaned forward so he was at her eye level. He spared himself a breath of soaking in the nearness of her, then gave himself a shake and pressed on. "Casey has an aunt. Robin's sister. She has two kids, really great ones, and when Casey was with Robin, he was with them every day. They miss him. He misses them, and last night when he was talking to them, I kind of invited them to visit. They haven't said yes yet," he added as her eyes widened. "And I didn't say anything about having them take part in camp stuff. But I wanted to talk to you about the possibility."

"You wanted to check with me before you made definite plans?"

"Yep."

"Well." She leaned back, arms crossed, but eyeing him in a way that made him think he'd just earned a bunch more points. "Well, well. It seems you can be taught after all."

"Yeah?" Silly to feel as though someone had turned on a light inside him, but it would be even sillier to pretend he wasn't getting a glow from her praise. Or maybe that was just the head rush he was getting from inhaling her coconut shampoo.

"It certainly looks that way."

He leaned closer, lowering his voice. "Do I get a gold star, teacher?"

Her eyebrows arched and a smile played on her lips, pulling him even closer. "I seem to be all out of stars."

"Not fair. I was a good student. I deserve a reward."

"Yes, you do," she murmured, and her hand came up to his chest. He leaned in, aiming for that mouth, fully intent on claiming it once again.

He was so focused that when she pushed against his chest and sent her chair flying backward, he stumbled off the desk and almost did a face-plant on the floor.

Her laughter wrapped round him as he straightened up.

"I hope you're proud of yourself," he said with mock severity.

"Immensely." She snorted before dissolving into giggles.

This was the Libby he remembered, the one who could tease and laugh and make his world right with a smile. He'd missed her.

And that, he realized with a start, was what had drawn him to Robin. It wasn't the fact that she bore a resemblance to Libby, though as Brynn had pointed out, lots of people did seem to favor a physical type. But what had attracted him to Robin was the same thing that had pulled him to Libby all those years ago—the confidence, the humor, the determination.

He had a type, all right—strong women who took what life handed them and made it their own, laughing all the way. The same traits he admired most in his mother and Brynn.

There was nothing wrong with that. Nothing at all. Even better, he was pretty sure there was nothing selfish about admiring the same qualities in two women who shared a certain physical similarity.

"Hey. Sam, are you okay?"

He shook his head at Libby's sudden concern, then realized he was sending the wrong message. "Fine. Not to worry. I just— You know how all of a sudden things can come clear when they never were before?"

"Sometimes." She drew in a small breath. "You want to tell me more?"

Sam had never pretended to have all the answers when it came to women, but even he knew that telling Libby he had just figured out why he'd had the hots for both her and Robin was probably not going to earn him any more points. He pulled himself away from the desk and headed for the door.

"Another time. I should get back to my group."

Her eyes clouded, as if his words had pulled a screen between them. For a second he wondered if he'd hurt her again. But her voice was cheerful as she said, "Of course. Can't have you neglecting your duties. Don't want to lose your job."

She was still teasing, still smiling, but the sparkle had fled from her eyes.

Dammit. It wouldn't help to tell her the truth, at least not now when she had to run and there wasn't time for long ex-

planations, but there had to be some way to help her. Surely
there was something he could say to ease her mind.

But before he could wrap his brain around the right approach, she was out of the chair, reaching for her purse and
the clipboard he'd come to hate.

"I'd better hit the road. See you when I get back."

He watched her go with an ache in his gut. Partly because, with her gone, there was no one to distract him from
the upcoming visit. But mostly he hurt because he'd hurt
her. Again. All because he was afraid to tell her the truth.
All the positive spin in the world couldn't change that fact:
he was afraid.

And he was sick of it.

So he was scared. Who wouldn't be? But the cold hard
truth was that keeping silent wasn't going to do a damned
thing to change the outcome of the court case. The only
thing he was impacting was his relationship with Libby,
and sure as hell not for the better.

He'd killed their chances once, when he was young and
stupid enough to think that keeping silent would give him
some kind of power over his fears. He wasn't that naive anymore. Nor did he think that he would ever be lucky enough
to get a third chance if he blew this one.

Dammit to hell and back. If Cosmo could find the
strength to speak up, then so could Sam.

CHAPTER FIFTEEN

LIBBY TURNED OFF the highway to navigate her car around the bumps and through the ruts leading to the staff parking lot and realized she was humming. Come to think of it, she'd been doing a lot of that lately. Since that night on the sofa with Sam, to be precise.

Was it the smartest thing she had ever done? No. Did she regret it? Nope. Her only regret was that he was still holding back. Maybe he was waiting to see if she would be around after summer's end. She could understand that. It was a lot more pleasant than indulging other thoughts, such as the possibility that he simply didn't want or was incapable of being honest with her.

It would be so much easier to think clearly if she didn't keep remembering how his seduction techniques had improved over the years.

Her good mood had carried her through the frustration of driving into town only to learn that the person she was scheduled to meet with had come down with a bug and had to go home, just after she had left the camp and couldn't be reached. She'd had a long drive for no reason and she didn't really care. She ran into the bakery and treated herself to a decadent cinnamon roll and the best iced coffee she had ever had, bar none, then sipped and nibbled her way back to camp.

And, of course, she wondered about Sam. A lot.

She parked the car, but Carrie Underwood was singing

about a cowboy Casanova so she lingered a moment, belting out the words while digging her phone from her purse for a quick look. Not a lot of messages. Two from her ill-fated meeting—aha, they *had* tried to contact her—one from Sam, a couple from parents who called so often that she recognized their numbers and one that she didn't recognize but set her heart racing when she listened to the voice mail.

It was the Uplands Central school district. And as she learned when she returned the call, they wanted her to come in for an interview.

She sat for another minute after hanging up, staring at a truck rumbling by en route to the pavilion but barely processing the sight.

And realized she was…surprised.

Not that she'd been invited for an interview. After her conversation with Mick's mother, she'd kind of expected that. No, what left her dazed and staring into space was the fact that she was—well—excited. She was already anticipating questions and formulating her answers and, holy moly, picturing a classroom in her mind. With her at the front of it.

But how could she be excited about teaching when, not two months earlier, she'd planned to spend the rest of her life at camp?

The answer came to her in a flash, much like the way the sunlight glittered that moment, bouncing off the rearview mirror of another car pulling onto the lot. It was because a teaching job was her way to get the camp back. Of course. She'd forgotten for a moment, which made no sense, though her current Sam-induced hormonal rush could be responsible. She would teach in the school year and work at the camp in the summers and save her money so she could somehow buy the camp when Sam eventually packed it in.

If she was a bit excited about the prospect of teaching, well, that was a bonus. Especially since she no longer believed that Sam would leave as easily as she had once thought.

In fact, if she were being honest, she kind of hoped he would stick around for a—

"Excuse me."

Libby jerked out of the la-la land she'd let herself drift into and realized there was a woman standing by the open window of her car. She gave a little jerk and fumbled for her keys.

"Just a moment," she said, and gathered her trash, phone, purse and clipboard while raising the windows. The stranger waited patiently. Something about her made Libby's teeth ache. She seemed too poised, too confident, too...

Juggling her various bits and pieces, Libby struggled out of the car while trying to figure out why the woman had her on edge.

Please, let it be more than just pettiness because she's slim and gorgeous and I'm back in the Emergency Bloat skirt.

The other woman watched Libby with an air of amusement, but simply said, "I'm Elise Farne, here to see Sam Catalano. Could you tell me where to find him?"

This woman was too *alert,* Libby realized. She was too watchful, too observant. In her sleek brown pants and mustard-colored shirt, she made Libby think of a lioness, all tawny and golden and ready to pounce.

"He should be with the kids right now. I'm Libby Kovak, the assistant director. Perhaps I can help you?"

"I'm not here about camp business, thank you. How can I let Mr. Catalano know that I'm here?"

The easiest thing to do would be to take this—whatever—to the office and page Sam over the walkie-talkie, but everything in Libby rebelled at the thought. Not until she had a better idea who the woman was and why she was here.

"He's probably at the craft hut with his group. But he didn't mention anything to me about an appointment this morning, so I might need you to—"

"I assure you, he's expecting me. I spoke to him just yesterday to confirm our meeting. So if you could let him know that I'm here…"

"I'll walk you there myself."

There were times when a decade-plus of talking to kids, staff and parents came in handy. It meant that Libby had a full arsenal of tricks up her sleeve when she needed to extract information from someone determined to keep it from her. Usually she preferred to wait until the other person was ready to open up anyway, but this was one of those cases when waiting simply wasn't an option.

Unfortunately, the woman gracefully navigating the ruts and gravel—in heels, no less—made Libby's interrogative efforts look like a kid trying to wheedle the location of a Christmas gift from a tight-lipped parent. By the time they rounded the corner, Libby had learned nothing more than the fact that the woman had driven in from Brockville and that the ride was indeed pleasant on such a lovely day.

As if the woman's evasiveness weren't enough, as they rounded the corner to the craft hut Libby realized that Sam had set up this meeting for a time when he knew she would be off the premises—in other words, a time when he was supposed to be one hundred percent focused on the camp. Scheduling a private meeting for himself at this time veered on a violation of the rule that said one of them had to be fully available at all times.

The excitement that had carried her through the past few days drained away with every step. All she felt now was confused and disappointed and angry. And tired. So very, very tired.

Then she saw Sam hightailing it away from the craft hut. Tanya stumbled behind him.

And though she hadn't believed it possible, the morning slid even further downhill.

IF HE DIDN'T PUT DISTANCE between himself and Tanya right now, he was either going to fire her or drop her in the middle of the woods without a compass. Maybe both.

It had been such a good morning once he made his decision to speak up. At snack time there was food Casey would actually eat, Mrs. Collins hadn't batted an eye when he'd told her to call him when a woman showed up at the door, and Mick's father had called with the welcome news that Mick had a new baby sister. Sam had handed the phone to Mick and grinned like a fool at the boy's excitement. When the call ended, the craft hut erupted with slaps on the back and high fives and fist bumps. In the excitement, Sam had slipped out the back door to call the kitchen and request a special cake for Mick at dinner.

But the moment he ended the call and turned to go back in the building, he found himself face-to-face with Tanya.

Literally face-to-face.

"Sam." She grabbed his shirt and twirled it around her hand before he could back away. "I need you."

Please, God, let her mean anything except that.

"Tanya—"

"No. Please. Let me talk, I… Sam, you have to know how I feel about you. That night, after the skunk—and it really was a skunk, you have to believe me—just knowing you were there made all the difference in the world to me. I need to be alone with you." She shimmied closer so her breasts brushed his chest. He sucked in his breath to avoid the contact but she pressed closer. "Let me come to you tonight," she whispered, rising on tiptoe to bring her mouth closer to his. "After lights-out. Let me show you exactly what you mean to me."

She leaned in closer. Her hair tickled his nose. She was going for the kill—er, the kiss.

But while Sam was still trying to get a handle on running a camp and being a father, there was one thing he knew how to do very well. He knew how to move.

She tipped her head back and angled her mouth and in that moment, when she was so focused on getting herself in position, he slumped to one side, throwing her off balance. She stumbled. Her grip weakened. He ducked, spinning away from her, reaching back in time to grab her arm so she wouldn't do a face-plant.

Tears swam in her eyes as she stared at him, open-mouthed.

"Never again, Tanya. Got it?"

Harsh, maybe, but he was in no mood to let her down gently. She had brought this on herself. "Try anything like that again and you'll be off the grounds faster than you can blink."

"But I—"

"No buts, Tanya. Let it go now and I'll forget this ever happened. Push it, and you'll be on instant probation. Or worse."

She clamped her mouth shut. Good. He would have been a lot more reassured if not for the anger he saw flashing in her eyes.

It was gone almost too fast to register, replaced by tears and sorrow, but it sent a shiver through him that the August heat couldn't ease.

He turned and headed around the building, choosing to go the long way rather than brush past her to go through the back door. He heard the gasp behind him, heard the sniffle of tears, but he didn't buy it for a minute.

Tanya was up to something. And the sooner he could talk to Libby about it, the—

He rounded the building and stopped so fast he almost gave himself whiplash. There stood Libby, looking more pissed off than he had seen her since those first awkward days in the office. Beside her stood a woman who had to be the social worker, here to do his home study.

Ah, crap.

Then, because life wasn't sufficiently screwed up, Tanya called out, "Sam, please, you have to give me a chance. Just one more—"

She stopped in midwail. Sam's muscles tightened as he watched Libby's glance flit from him to Tanya and back again. The social worker could have been watching a Ping-Pong tournament, that's how fast her head was bobbing between the three of them.

He took a deep breath, praying for some profound insight that would enable him to turn this around, but Libby beat him to the punch.

"Sam, this is Ms. Farne. She says you're expecting her. Tanya, I need you to deliver Sam's kids to lunch and then meet me in the office."

Anyone who didn't know her would see nothing but her smile, hear nothing but the brisk efficiency in her voice. But Sam heard an iceberg bigger than the one that had done a number on the *Titanic*.

"Give me one second to wrap things up," he said to the social worker before grabbing Libby by the arm and pulling her around the corner.

"I can explain everything," he said.

"I sincerely doubt it."

"I will. Tonight. Just let me get through this. Let's get through the day, and tonight, when we can have more than five minutes without an interruption, I'll tell you all of it."

"Oh, I see. Would that be tonight, when you finally decide to come clean? Or tonight, after you've had a whole day to concoct some story?"

"Libby, no. It's not anything like you're thinking."

"I had no idea that you could read my mind, Sam. Which, come to think of it, you obviously can't. Because if you could, you would know that the only thing I'm thinking about right now is that I have a camp to run. You know. That camp you were supposed to be looking after until you got too busy with everything else."

She turned her back on him and marched up the hill with a tightness to her step that let him know it might be possible to have messed things up worse than he already had—but somehow, he doubted it.

ONE HOUR AFTER DELIVERING Sam over to the mysterious woman, Libby picked up her glass of iced coffee and wondered what would happen if she were to spike it.

Tanya had shown up as ordered, but—surprise, surprise—refused to elaborate on anything. When questioned about the scene with Sam, all she would say was that it was personal.

Libby was so damned tired of having people use that line on her.

But much as she longed to find an excuse to fire the girl on the spot, she knew she couldn't. Tanya's work with the kids was as fabulous as ever. And while there were rules in the staff handbook about harassment, it didn't appear that Tanya had crossed that line yet, at least not judging by what she had seen.

All Libby could do was give the girl a severe warning, which engendered less response than a weather forecast. She sent Tanya on her way and stared out the window and wondered what the hell she was going to say to Sam when he showed up.

Because she knew that the moment he disposed of who-ever this woman was, he would be trotting down to the of-fice. He might offer an explanation. He might invoke the "it's personal" line.

And she couldn't say which prospect frightened her more.

She wasn't going to stay there, waiting for him. She'd waited enough over the past dozen years. Making sure her walkie-talkie was secure on her belt, she headed for the one place at camp where she could be pretty sure Sam would never think to look for her: the pavilion.

As she walked down the hill, automatically checking in with counselors and kids on her way, Libby replayed the weeks since Sam walked into the office. The secrets. The laughter. The moments alone in the dark, when for a brief period everything seemed to work. The flutters in her stom-ach all week when she relived his kisses. The excitement that had gripped her after the request for an interview, and then the crash when the mystery woman appeared and she realized Sam was hiding even more from her than she'd thought.

Playing it all together, piece by piece, made it impossible to dodge the truth any longer. And the truth she saw was a frightening prospect indeed.

She was falling in love with Sam all over again.

She came out of the woods and into the clearing. The pavilion rose from the ground like a tree from the forest floor, graceful and strong and dappled green and brown and gray. Her breath caught at the way the structure seemed to grow from the river on one side and the trees on the other. The ground was still churned up and the fireplace was only half-complete, but it still looked aged. Settled. She walked into the largest section and let it surround her.

What was it Sam had said when she asked what would happen to the pavilion if she left the camp? That the work would stop on it immediately. That if she were to leave, it would stay unfinished. Abandoned. A permanent reminder of what could have been.

"You idiot," she whispered to the half-finished structure. "You stupid, silly, forgetful, total dumb-ass idiotic—"

"Practicing your speech to me, Lib?"

She jerked and whirled around.

"How did you know I was here?"

"I saw you walking this way and followed you." He moved swiftly into the space, dodging toolboxes to stand before her. He clutched a baseball cap in his hand and it gave him an earnest, almost shy look. She longed to tug it away from him and demand an explanation and then kiss him until there were no brain cells left to carry on a conversation.

And that scared her most of all.

"We need to talk," she said.

He nodded and stepped toward her. She stepped back.

"That woman—" he began, but she raised a hand to stop him.

"Let me go first. It will simplify things all around."

"Lib—"

"Please, Sam. Just let me say it."

He opened his mouth.

"Please."

He shook his head but clamped his lips tight. She pulled in a deep breath, wishing she could get everything out before she had to inhale again, knowing that was impossible.

"First, let me assure you that Ms. Farne never said a thing to me other than her name. Whatever it was that you were trying to keep secret, well, it's safe."

"I wanted—"

She raised a forefinger. "At first, when she showed up, I was curious, you know? No. Wait. More than that. I was worried. She looked so official and she was being so secretive and I felt this need to—I don't know. To protect you. I was worried she posed some threat to you or Casey, and—"

"Dammit, Lib, would you shut up and listen to me?" He flicked the baseball cap to the ground, sending it skidding like a forgotten Frisbee. "She's a social worker, okay? A goddamned social worker. And I had to play nice with her because Robin's sister is trying to take Casey away from me."

Libby stepped back. Her hands flew to her face then clawed at the air as if trying to turn the clock back to the instant before Sam spoke. But one look at the bleakness in his eyes told her that there could be no pretending.

He needed her. No matter what he had done, he needed her to keep it together for him.

She twisted her hands together. "Tell me."

"That's it. There's nothing else to say. Sharon wants Casey. She thinks she can give him a better home than I can. She's fighting me for custody."

"But you're his father. You love him."

"So does she."

Questions poured through her, one on top of the other, layered with realizations as the whole summer did a fast rewind through a new filter. So much made sense now. So much still left her grasping for answers.

"This doesn't— Has she ever seen you with him? Because seriously, how could anyone watch you with him for more than five minutes and not know that you belong together?"

He gave her a hint of a grin. "Thanks."

"What's going to happen?"

He leaned back against a half-finished pillar, lowering

himself slowly to the dusty stone floor. "We go to court in September. My lawyer says I'll win." He sounded unutterably weary as he added, "Of course, with what I'm paying her, it's not likely she'd say anything else."

Libby knelt beside him, placing a tentative hand on his arm. "How can I help?"

He shrugged and stared up at the rafters. "You have any moral objection to kidnapping?"

"I have a feeling Brynn would be the best bet for that job."

"You have a point."

His hand settled over hers. She knew what he expected—that she would flip her hand over to meet his, palm to palm. That she would curl her fingers through his and lean forward and kiss him and promise him she would be there for him. She knew it was what he wanted, what he needed, because every kind and decent instinct in her was urging her to do just that.

But there was a wall between them, and she couldn't push through. A wall he had built. One secret at a time.

His thumb rubbed the back of hers.

She slipped her hand slowly, gently from beneath his.

He searched her face, eyes filled with confusion. "Lib?"

"September isn't very far away. I'm sure you're going to need to spend more time on this as your court date gets closer. I can cover for you. Meetings, filling in with your group, whatever. Casey belongs with you. Anything I can do to help make that happen, just say the word."

And she would. She loved Casey too much to let him be batted around by life the way she had been. He was happy here, here with the father who adored him. Whatever she could do to make sure his life stayed stable, she would do it.

But that was as far as she could go.

"Lib." There was an edge of fear to his voice that she

had never heard before. "Look. I know what you're thinking, that I should have told you before this. The thing is—"

She shook her head, silencing him with her palm over
his mouth. "Don't. Please."

His eyes widened. She let her hand slip away—slowly,
giving herself the briefest chance to touch him one last
time—and pushed herself upright.

"I can't do it, Sam."

He lunged to his feet. "What do you mean, you can't do
it? Lib, I— Look, I know I screwed up, but I—"

"You hid this from me, Sam. Deliberately, and with great
thought. Just like you did when you left me. Just like you
did about Casey. And if I hadn't caught you with that social
worker, you would have kept on hiding it." She pushed the
words out even though her heart was breaking at his guilty
flinch. "You don't trust me, Sam. I could understand it at
the beginning of the summer, but now?"

She pressed her fingers to her mouth to hold back the
words her heart wanted her to say, of forgiveness and understanding and reassurance. She couldn't do that. To say those
things would land her straight in his arms and then his bed
and then—what? A lifetime of hovering around the camp,
wanting him and watching him while he kept his secrets?

Rule number one in Libby's survival handbook: look
after yourself first. No one else is going to do it.

"I will do whatever I can to help you win this court fight,
Sam, but that's it. No more."

"God, Libby. I didn't— I never meant to hurt you. I swear
I didn't—"

"I know you didn't. And that makes it worse, you know?"
She swallowed back the tears. "Because all I can think is
that keeping secrets is your default mode. You don't mean
to do it, but you do. And I can't do this anymore."

"Lib. No." He stepped forward, hands out, reaching for

her as if to stop her, but she moved back before he could get to her. Away from his words. Away from his secrets. Away from the hurt.

"There's two weeks left of camp, Sam. I believe that's the customary amount of notice that employers request."

"Libby—"

"It's too late, Sam." She swallowed hard. "I quit."

CHAPTER SIXTEEN

IN THE DAYS FOLLOWING her resignation, the truth became starkly clear to Libby: her Overlook days were coming to an end. A complete and total end.

She couldn't come back next summer. Not after what she'd said. Not with the way she couldn't trust her stupid idiot heart around Sam. As for the man himself, he wasn't going to be leaving anytime soon. It was time she accepted the truth and moved on.

No matter that she had no idea who she was if she wasn't the assistant director of Camp Overlook.

It caught her at the most unexpected times. She stepped out of the office and saw the greens and blues spread beneath her and got a lump in her throat. Cosmo walked out of the kitchen in an apron that proclaimed himself A Hunk-a-Hunk of Burning Chef and she laughed until she cried. And each night at campfire, she had to fake singing the words to "Taps." To do more than that would risk breaking down in front of everyone. The kids. The staff. Casey.

Sam.

But she couldn't think about Sam. Couldn't let herself dwell on the hurt or the disappointment or, worst of all, the way he had kissed her that night.

It would be better when camp was over, when every breath and sight and sound wasn't a reminder of all she was losing. She forced herself to think of the future. She remembered how much she had enjoyed talking to Mick's mom about teaching, and she focused on that heady feeling when she'd been called for an interview. And three days after resigning, she drove to the Uplands Central district office to talk with the hiring committee.

The school was small but vital. The interview itself was far more enjoyable than she would ever have predicted. The enthusiasm she thought she would have to fake came easily, no doubt because the more she heard, the more she wanted to learn. She handled all questions with ease, save one, and had plenty of points of her own. All things considered, she pulled out of the parking lot feeling optimistic and more energized than she'd been since resigning.

Well—at least about teaching.

Thinking about the interview made her remember Dani and her résumé suggestions, which in turn reminded her that Aidan had been scheduled for his tonsillectomy two days earlier. On an impulse she pulled into the first grocery store she saw and cruised the aisles in search of treats that might appeal to a very small boy with a very sore throat. She added a lightweight toy plane to her collection of pudding cups and applesauce in tubes and headed for Dani's place.

But her plan to spend a few minutes, drop her gifts and head back out came to a shrieking halt when Dani answered the door. Her eyes were red. Her cheeks were puffy. And from the amount of wrinkles marring her oversize T-shirt and nothing else—Libby was pretty certain Dani hadn't made it out of her pajamas in at least a day.

"Dani? Are you okay?"

Tears spilled out of Dani's glazed eyes. She wore no makeup. Libby sucked in a breath. Dani had practically been born wearing blush and eyeliner. Something was seriously wrong in Dani's world when she answered the door without at least a touch of lipstick.

"Aidan is miserable. He hurts so much, poor baby, and

he doesn't know…and he won't eat because it hurts, but he has to…. The other boys are tired of being cooped up here in the house and they're driving me crazy. I haven't been able to sleep for three nights. I can't remember the last time I had a shower. And I… Oh, Libby, I lost my job!"

Libby was in no position to give anyone employment advice, but she absolutely knew how to take charge of a situation that was in jeopardy of falling apart. Within a matter of minutes she sent Dani to bed,.bribed the older boys to put away the groceries and clean the house with a promise of outrageous payment and settled herself in a rocking chair in the backyard with little Aidan. Silent tears rolled down his cheeks, so much like his mother's that it was like seeing double.

"Shhhh, sweetie. Shhhhh."

With the aid of some spoon gymnastics and a great deal of distraction, she got some applesauce and a few sips of iced juice down his poor little throat. It wasn't much, but at least she felt she'd staved off dehydration and starvation for a while.

The next thing she knew, he was asleep on her shoulder. Reluctant to disturb him and with nothing immediate pressing on her, she sank lower in the chair and shifted so his face was no longer in direct sunlight. The other boys raced around the backyard, and Libby rocked and hummed and tried to avoid thinking about the one interview question she'd fumbled. The one that asked her where she saw herself in five years.

The one that had made her picture, suddenly and all too clearly, an older Casey running around the camp while she and Sam stole kisses in between chasing a curly-locked toddler.

The one that left her feeling as raw and aching as poor

Aidan's throat. And the one, she knew, that was going to cause wounds that would take a lot longer to heal.

ON THE LAST WEDNESDAY of camp, Sam took Casey down to the just-finished pavilion and wondered how the hell he had blown things so badly.

Not with the camp itself, which was drawing to a close as quickly and effortlessly as a newly sharpened skate on freshly groomed ice. Nor was the problem with Casey or the custody suit. He wasn't looking forward to the hearing, now less than a month away, but he was going to be damned ecstatic to have it behind him. Soon it would be fall and the legal worries would be over and he and Casey would be able to settle into a quieter routine.

The pavilion was done. Tanya had stopped crying when she looked at him. Sharon had thanked him for the invitation to visit, but said, with what sounded like true regret, that they couldn't fit it in before school. And just that morning, Cosmo had very stiffly handed in his resignation. It seemed he was moving. The fact that he wouldn't say where he was going told Sam all he needed to know, and for a moment, he'd been happier than he had in days, especially when he heard Cosmo humming as he walked away. Cosmo and Myra. It still blew his mind, but thank God someone had finally got things right.

Yep, everything was just hunky-dory. Everything and everyone.

Everyone except Libby.

She was polite. She took over his group in late afternoons, freeing him to be in the house when Casey woke after his nap. She made sure she passed on everything she thought he might need to know, and with the impending end of the camp, there was a lot.

But when he tried to talk to her, she shoved paperwork

in his face. She stopped playing with Casey. She stopped
laughing. She did her job and kept everything running and it
was killing him, because he could see she was dying inside.

All because of him.

"Dada!"

Casey peeked out from the giant stone fireplace that
dominated the center wall of the pavilion. The delight
on his face made Sam grin. The pavilion had turned out
perfectly—stone pillars, wood roof, open to the woods on
one side and the water on the other. It was everything he
had hoped. Everything Libby had wanted.

No. It was everything he had *thought* she wanted. But it
seemed he didn't know her as well as he believed.

He looked around the pavilion again, at the open sides,
and shook his head at how blind he'd been. Openness. That's
all she had wanted from him. But like an idiot, he had
closed himself off, hiding away his fears and worries long
past the point where it was needed. And what did he have
to show for it? A pavilion that was going to remind him of
her every time he walked into it. A camp that was going to
echo without her.

What had she said that first day? He had said he would
build the pavilion at the inlet, the spot they claimed as their
own all those years ago, and she had looked him in the eye
and said she didn't visit that area anymore. Now he knew
why.

So much for living the goal.

His cell phone rang, yanking him away from his self-
imposed misery. He pulled it from his pocket and checked
the number. His lawyer.

"Hey, Marilyn, what's up?"

"We have a complication."

His feet dug into the ground as he twisted to check on
Casey. Reflex. It made no sense and he knew it, but some-

how, if he could keep Casey in his sights while talking, it made him feel more certain that all would be well.

"What is it?"

"Don't panic," she said, the words a dead giveaway to him that his esteemed counsel was childless. No one who had ever been a parent could hear that there was a complication with a custody suit without jumping straight to panic mode.

"It's really not that bad," she assured him. And once he heard the explanation, he had to admit, it could have been worse.

There was a scheduling problem. Sharon's lawyer needed to have unexpected but necessary surgery and would be out of work for a couple of months. The judge assigned to their case had an opening Friday afternoon and had offered to move their case up so it wouldn't have to drag on.

"The problem," she continued, "is that I have another case then, and I'm sorry, Sam, but I have to honor that first commitment. So you have two choices."

"Tell me," he said, watching Casey grab a rock from the ground and whack it against the stones of the pillars.

"Option one, we take the earlier date and my associate handles the case. He's very good, and since this really is nothing more than a desperation suit on Sharon's part, it shouldn't make a difference."

"And option two?"

"We wait until Sharon's lawyer comes back and tackle it then."

One corner of his brain automatically noted that Casey was doing his best to throw the rock for Finnegan, but the dog refused to budge. The rest was already flying through logistics and scenarios.

"Why doesn't Sharon just find a new lawyer?"

Marilyn sighed. "Her guy is a solo practitioner. He has

no backup. And honestly, Sam, things are so stacked in your favor that I'm sure it took Sharon a long time to find someone willing to take the case in the first place. Unless someone were to walk in with proof that you're neglecting Casey to run some kind of prostitution ring up there, you will be fine. So what do you want to do?"

What did he want to do?

He looked out past the pavilion to the river. He knew what he wanted to do. He wanted to say he'd call back, then find Libby and talk it all over with her. By the time he looked things over with her, he would have a clearer head, a new perspective and a hell of a lot less adrenaline prickling through him.

She wouldn't listen for him, and he couldn't blame her. But for Casey, she would.

"Let me—" he began, but Marilyn interrupted.

"Hang on, Sam. Joe just told me if you want him to do it, he'll need to meet with you first thing tomorrow morning. Someone else needs that time if you don't take it, so I'm sorry, but Joe needs an answer right away."

Tomorrow morning? But he would have to leave—crap—tonight. He would miss the last two full days. Worse, he would lose two full days in which he might pull off a miracle and make Libby change her mind.

"Sam?"

But who was he kidding? She was going. She was going, and nothing he could do or say would change that. All that would change would be the amount of time he had this custody issue hanging over his head, tarnishing his life with his son.

He sighed and dragged his gaze away from the river and back to Casey.

Live the goal.

"Sorry, Marilyn." He gripped the phone tight. "Ask Joe what time he needs me. I'll be there."

LIBBY ENDED HER CALL and set the phone gently on the desk, leaned back in her chair, raised her fists straight up and let out a glorious "Woohoo!" Then, because there was still excitement pushing to get out of her, she stood and did a little dance in the middle of the office floor, ending with a hip thrust and a loud "uh-*huh,*" that seemed to bounce back around her.

She had a second interview. More than that, for the first time in days, she had some hope. Not just for a job, though of course that had been on her mind, but that life could still be full and worthwhile even if she wasn't at Overlook.

Even if she wasn't with Sam.

She still wasn't sure how she would get through her good-byes to the camp, but there was a core of excitement in her that seemed to grow every time she thought about being in a classroom. Maybe this could be a good move for her. Maybe having a new job—if she got it—would make it easier to leave. Maybe it was long past time to resurrect those dreams that had been sidetracked, first by others, and then by her powerful attachment to the camp.

She wouldn't think about her attachment to Sam and Casey. She wouldn't think about the icy fear that stole her breath every time she remembered the custody suit. Not now.

No, now, just for this moment, she would think about what she should wear to the interview. And how she would have to shuffle her schedule to make room for it. Luckily it was tomorrow, not Friday, when camp would be in full insanity mode for the Tour de Camp. She would simply need to double up on the paperwork she had planned for the morning, and run into town after lights-out to grab something appropriate and tell Sam that she would be gone for a while and—

The door squeaked open just then, and the devil himself walked in. She gave a little jump and tried to will away the traitorous jolt of pleasure that insisted on flaring up whenever he walked into the room. There was still something inside her that whispered *finally* whenever she saw him again.

"Close the door, please."

He kept walking. And her stupid heart kept jumping.

Soon, she thought. *Soon. I'll be gone and I'll have new people and places in my life and I won't have to go through this a dozen times a day, won't have to look and him and wonder and—*

"Libby, I'm sorry, but I have to leave tonight."

Her runaway thoughts came to an abrupt halt. "Excuse me?"

"I have to be in Nova Scotia tomorrow. Casey and I. We're flying out tonight."

"But you—wait—Nova Scotia?" She reached for the back of her chair as the implication of his grim expression hit her. "The custody suit?"

He nodded.

"What happened?"

No sooner were the words out of her mouth than she realized how foolish it had been to ask. This was Sam, the king of the secret keepers. His whole family could have been kidnapped at gunpoint and unless someone was forcing him, he would never—

"It's okay. Everything's okay."

She blinked. "It is?"

"Yeah. Don't panic. It's just damned inconvenient."

Reassured somewhat, she loosened her death grip on the chair and sat down. She longed to press for details, to give voice to the *who* and *when* and *why* tumbling through her head, but she held back. Sam had made his choice. He had opted for silence in all but the most essential moments.

So would she.

She reached for her clipboard. "Okay. So what do you need, and when will you be back?"

"Friday night." He gave his head a little shake, then looked at her, really focusing, for the first time since entering the room. "I know the timing sucks, Lib, and believe me, this isn't the way I wanted things to happen. But I have to go."

Then it hit her.

"But I have an interview."

"What?"

She nodded, small and slow, afraid that if she made her movements too big they would attract attention and some malevolent fates would yank away this fleeting chance at some sort of happiness. "Tomorrow afternoon. Four o'clock. They just called."

"Okay. Well. That's great, I guess."

"But, Sam, don't you see? If you're going to be gone from tonight until Friday night—I can't go. One of us has to be here at all times."

"Oh." He ran a hand through his hair. "Can't you reschedule?"

"Can't you?"

Silence.

Rule number two: don't let your happiness show.

God, she was such an idiot.

"Look," he said heavily, "where's the interview? I can call them and tell them the situation if you want. They can probably—"

There was a fast knock at the door, followed immediately by Phoebe poking her head into the room. "Yo, Libby,

I have that report you— Whoops. Bad timing." She backed away. "Sorry."

"Wait," Sam said, never taking his eyes off Libby. "Come up to my place in half an hour," he said softly. "I need to talk to you. About what happened."

Rule number one: no one else is going to put you—

No. No, as much as her instincts told her to walk away, now, to look out for herself and go to her interview and stop delaying her inevitable departure, she couldn't do it. This was Casey they were talking about. Casey's life with Sam. That had to come first.

She nodded. He nodded. And then, with another fast glance at Phoebe, he crossed the room, framed her face with his hands and planted a fast kiss on her forehead.

"Thank you," he said, and left.

She looked at Phoebe. Phoebe looked at her.

"Damn." Phoebe whistled. "When he decides to turn it on, he doesn't hold back, does he?"

SAM RACED THROUGH his preparations at top speed. His first call, made as he tossed Casey's things into a suitcase, was to Brynn. The plan all along had been for her to come with him during the custody hearing, to take Casey on a visit to Sharon and then be in charge of him while Sam was sweating bullets in front of the judge. Godsend that she was, she was able to rearrange her schedule. She would meet him late that night.

Then came the call to Sharon, who, he had to admit, seemed almost as rattled as he was. She jumped at the chance to see Casey the next day. After they agreed on a time and she had offered her stiff thanks at his willingness to reschedule, he felt he had to say something more.

"Listen, Sharon." He kept his voice as gentle as possible, all things considered. "We don't have to do this. You know

the judge is going to side with me. There's no reason why
he wouldn't. Why don't you and I bury the hatchet, draw
up our own agreement about when Casey can visit you and
move on? You know that's how it's going to end anyway.
Why don't we cut out the middle man and do what's best
for Casey?"

Her prolonged silence had him pausing in the middle of
grabbing the current favorite blankie while cautious hope
had him pressing the phone tight against his ear.

Then she spoke again.

"You know, Robin almost decided to marry you. You
know why she didn't?" She hurried on without waiting for
him to give his version. "Because she said you could charm
words out of a monk who took a vow of silence, and if she
said yes, she would never know if it was because it was the
right thing or because it was what you wanted."

He closed his eyes. *Damn, Rob, I'm so sorry.*

"I'm not giving in, Sam, no matter how badly you want
me to make things easy for you. Casey deserves the chance
to grow up in a regular family with people who will be there
for him and give him a stable, settled life. I'll see your sister tomorrow and see you in court on Friday."

With that, she hung up, leaving him clutching the phone
and hoping his so-called charm would have better results
with Libby.

He had Casey's clothes, bears, blankets and toiletries
packed and had retreated to his own room when there came
a soft knock at the door.

Libby.

"You said you—" she began, and then she looked at him,
really looked, and some of the stiffness melted away as she
let loose with a small giggle. He tilted his head, not sure
what was so funny until he realized he had a shirt draped

over each shoulder, another in each hand and a tie dangling from each elbow.

"Sorry. I, uh, can never figure out which shirt goes with which tie."

For a second he saw a spark of the old Libby in her eyes. "I hope you're not asking me for fashion advice." She tugged on her Overlook tee. "Because I have to tell you, there are at least six counselors who could do a better job of that than I can. Two of them are guys, so if that's what you—"

"The court date's been moved up. It's happening on Friday."

He hadn't planned to say it so abruptly. But time was short, and he needed—God, how he needed—to share it all with her. It scared the crap out of him. He shouldn't need her this much. But the thought of not telling her, of not hearing her perspective and her gentle assurance that all would be okay—well, that frightened him even more.

She inhaled once, wide-eyed and ragged, then gave a short nod.

"Can you give me any details?"

He did. The whole story this time, not just the bare facts he'd limited himself to at the pavilion, but all of it. He started with Robin's move, through Sharon's time as Robin's child-care provider, then the double shock of Robin's death and Sharon's challenge.

"I understand why she's doing it," he said. "Casey's the last bit of Robin she has left. I get that she's holding on for all the wrong reasons. But Casey is as much mine as Robin's."

Libby's eyes widened, and she seemed to turn inward for a second, as if he'd hit a nerve, but he couldn't stop to analyze it now. By the time he finished explaining the change of hearing dates he was sitting on the bed with Libby perched beside him, twisted to face him, and—hang on—how had he ended up holding her hand?

Not that he was complaining. Especially since she hadn't seemed to notice yet. The warmth of her hand against his was more comforting than any lawyer's words of assurance, no matter how well informed they might be.

"So I have to go," he said. "I don't want to and the timing sucks and I'm so, so sorry, Lib, but I—"

"Let me guess," she said with a hint of sorrow. "You have no choice."

He hated the hurt in her voice, the way her shoulders hunched forward as if to ward away unexpected blows. How often had she had those words tossed at her in her life? Would it be better or worse if she knew he really did have a choice, but she was paying the price for it?

She must have noticed their clasped hands, for she pulled back abruptly and jerked herself off the bed.

"Why didn't you tell me before?" She wrapped her arms around herself and stared out the window. "Why all the secrecy, Sam?"

"Because I was scared."

She glanced back at him, fast, then continued her study of the scene outside his window. Her unspoken, "And?" filled the room.

"I wasn't sure if I was doing the right thing for Casey. I was scared about the lawsuit. I wasn't— I still don't know if I'm a good enough father to pull this off. On top of everything, I came back here and saw you, saw that Robin reminded me of you, and I got all twisted around wondering if—"

She continued to stare out the window but he saw the way her arms tightened as if they'd been jerked, the way her head kind of snapped back. "I finally figured out how stupid that one was," he hurried on. He couldn't lose her now. "But the rest… God, Lib, I don't know. After my dad left, I remember being so damned scared, all the time. But I couldn't let it show, you know? Everyone else was already falling apart, over Mom and Dad and everything. They needed someone to be the brave one. I figured it had to be me."

She turned toward him at last, her eyes filled with compassion, and it was like something had been set free inside him.

"Acting like I wasn't afraid made me feel a little braver, you know? And it helped everyone else. After a while I got used to it. It was just what I had to do."

"Default mode," she whispered, and he shrugged. It was as good an explanation as any.

She left the window then and he held his breath as she came closer, her eyes soft and her lips pressed together as if to hold back things she didn't want to say. When she stopped in from of him, he had to fight to keep from pulling her tight. He wanted to feel her heat against him. He was sure that if he was holding her, nothing could ever go wrong again. But it had to come from her.

"I wish you had told me sooner," she said softly. "It might have... Well. It makes things easier to understand. I'm glad you told me."

Yeah, he was just a prince among men.

"And for the record, you are a fabulous father. Not just because you adore Casey, but because you walk the walk, too. You rearranged your whole life to give him stability. You're trying to find a way to include Sharon in his life even though she's challenging you. Heck, you took on that danged dog even though you're allergic. You may be an idiot about almost everything else, but I've seen a lot of parents over the years, and believe me, you are one of the best."

He felt like someone had just released a tie that had been pulled too tight around his neck. She wasn't saying that to reassure him. Her line about his idiocy proved that. But that made the rest easier to believe.

She glanced around the room. Her cheeks pinked and he suddenly realized what a domestic little scene this must be. One man, one woman, a bedroom and a pile of clothing. It happened all over the world every day. Usually between husbands and wives.

Which should have scared the crap out of him, but it didn't.

She turned away then, scooping one of the ties from the bed and rolling it into a neat ball before pressing it into his hands.

"Wear this one," she said. "The green stripe is the color of the pine trees here. Every time you look at it, you'll remember...you'll think of home."

No. Every time he looked at it, he would remember her.

She closed her hands over his. "You have to go."

"Yeah." But the only move he made was in her direction.

She stepped back fast, neatly eluding him. "I'd better get down to dinner. Good luck. Keep us posted, okay?"

Before he could give her an answer, she had slipped around him and out the door.

He went to the window and waited for her to appear, watching as she walked slowly down the hill, moving carefully, as if she'd never walked that way before. Every once in a while she lifted a hand to her face. Wiping away tears?

Ah, dammit to hell and back. In all his need to confess, to open up to her, to draw from her strength, he had never once asked about her interview. So much for telling himself he wasn't cut from the same cloth as his father.

No wonder she had looked so alone, so resigned when she was standing at the window. She hadn't just been hurting for him. She'd been hurting for herself.

She had expected this, he realized. She had come up there knowing he was going to pour out his woes and she was going to get the short end of the stick.

What was it she had called his need to put on a brave face? Default mode? For the first time, he realized that Libby had one, too. But hers was one of expectation—that something was hovering on the horizon, and not in a good way.

That it had only been a matter of time before some selfish bastard messed up her world all over again.

CHAPTER SEVENTEEN

"ANY OTHER QUESTIONS?"

Sam considered the man front of him—Joe, the very smart, very perceptive fill-in lawyer. Joe, who had just buzzed through months of preparation in slightly less than one billable hour.

The truth was that Sam had a boatload of questions, but none of them had anything to do with the hearing or his chances of keeping Casey. No, he was busy wondering things like *Why couldn't we have done this on the phone? Or for an hour before the hearing? Why did you drag me down here and make me hurt Libby yet again for something that could have been handled—*

But there was no point in berating either the lawyer or himself. There could have been complications or questions to be addressed. If he hadn't met with Joe in person, if they had gone into court cold and something happened, he would never have forgiven himself.

He had done what he had to do for Casey. For himself. But as he rose and shook the other man's hand, he couldn't help but think that once again, Libby had paid the price for other people's problems. That look in her eyes...

He piloted the rental car through the streets to the hotel where Brynn and Casey waited for him. The meeting had passed so quickly that he would lay good money Casey would still be asleep when he got back.

Sure enough, when he let himself into the room, Brynn

sat propped up on the ugly olive-green sofa with books stacked on the floor beside her and a notepad resting against her upraised knees.

"That was fast."

He shrugged out of his suit jacket and tossed it over the back of a chair that was almost as ugly as the sofa. "Tell me about it. I even stopped and bought you doughnuts."

"Doughnuts?" Brynn sat up straighter, her brown eyes shining. "You always were my favorite big brother."

"That's 'cause I'm your only big brother, twerp."

"Details, details. Shut up and feed me."

Sam handed over the box and dropped to the sofa, blocking out the excited little cries coming from Brynn until he couldn't ignore them any longer.

"Enough. You're creeping me out with those sounds. Just eat one already."

She pulled a chocolate glazed from the box and settled back in her previous position, eyeing him over the half-glasses she wore when she wanted to appear wise. "Did everything go okay?"

"Fine. It all looks good. Tomorrow afternoon we go in, we prove I'm Casey's dad, we show them the report from the social worker that says there is no reason why I should not have custody and we walk out with everything settled at last."

"So you should be a happy man."

"I'll be happy once this is over," he said with a yank on his tie, and then he stopped as the pattern in the silk caught his attention. The green stripe. The color of the pine trees.

Every time you look at it, you'll remember...you'll think of home.

Just like that, he knew what he had to do.

"Brynn," he said slowly, clutching the tie in his fist, "how

many doughnuts would it take to convince you to look after
Casey by yourself until tomorrow morning?"

CLIMBING UP THE HILL after a final check of the canoe paddles, Libby glanced at her watch as she'd been doing all day,
saw the time—a little past three—and pressed her lips together. She should have been on the road to her interview.
Instead, she was here. And for the first time ever, camp felt
like it was in the way.

She'd long ago given up on trying to figure out whether
she should be sad or angry, and why. Instead, she was wrestling with both. Sadness, of course, for the end of camp
and the loss of an opportunity that had been hers just long
enough to make her see how much she wanted it. For there
was no other chance for an interview. She had called, but
the only times available were today and Friday.

And so, of course, she was angry. At Sam and Sharon
and lawyers and interviewers and most of all, at her own
stupid damned self.

For a moment she had toyed with the idea of going to
the interview anyway. She could. What could Sam do, fire
her? But to go behind his back, to leave the camp leader-
less out of anger and hurt—it felt wrong. It wouldn't work.
The bad karma fairies would get her for sure.

She wiped her forehead and scowled at her clipboard.
At least when she'd had to rearrange her life for Gran and
Myra, she had been able to console herself—or maybe talk
herself into believing—that it was all part of the give-and-
take of love. But with Sam...

No. She wasn't going there. No way would she let herself
think that she could have done something as foolish as that.

But as she crested the hill, she did a two-step of surprise.
The office door was wide-open.

Her first, instinctive thought—*close the door, Sam*—was

immediately replaced by something bubbling inside her like a spring gushing to the surface. It couldn't be…

But sure enough, as soon as her dumbfounded brain remembered to fire off a signal to *move, dammit,* there was a flurry of movement and Sam came tumbling down the steps. Two at a time, in a hurry, just like always.

But the rush of joy she felt—ah, that was new. So new and unexpected that she couldn't move again, could only stand in the middle of the path while her hands flew to her mouth and her clipboard fell to the ground and she couldn't keep from making odd little squeaking sounds of disbelief.

"Hey!" He jogged toward her. Still in a suit, she saw through eyes gone all watery. With the tie she'd picked out dangling loose around his neck. "Didn't you get my message?"

She shook her head, hoping to clear away some of the confetti that had taken over her brain. "I've been out on the grounds for a couple of hours."

She filled her lungs with breath and with him, the scent and the solidity of him, and even though she knew nothing was wrong—she could see that in his eyes—she had to ask, "Everything's okay, right? The lawyer and—"

"It's fine. All fine. But I was done by nine-thirty and all I could think was that I couldn't spend the day stuck in a hotel in Lunenburg when I should be here doing my job so you could go to your interview."

"But I canceled that. I called and told them I couldn't—"

"Yeah, well, I called them from the airport. They filled the four o'clock but once I explained what happened, they said they could see you at five." He reached out and tugged on the neckline of her Overlook shirt. "Time to get into your interview clothes and go to the ball, Cinderella."

She nodded, but the movement just seemed to send her thoughts flying completely out of her head. He came back.

He rearranged everything and spent Lord knew how much money on plane tickets and knocked himself out to get here on time…all for her.

He had done it for her. He had put her first. In the middle of the biggest fight of his life, when he had every right to be focused on nothing but his son and the struggle that lay before him, he thought of her.

"Oh, Sam." And as she threw her arms around him and gave him a brief but absolutely heartfelt kiss, for once she didn't care who might see her happiness or what it all meant. He had come back. For her.

She loved him.

And for that moment, nothing else mattered.

LIBBY MISSED THE OPENING songs of campfire, but slipped into the circle in time for the Overlook Fashion Show, complete with half a dozen of the male staff in high fashion drag. Thank heaven. She never would have forgiven herself if she had missed Cosmo's Julia Child imitation, or the sight of Sam mincing down the log-bordered runway with a pink boa tossed around his shoulders and something that looked suspiciously like two of Cosmo's aprons doing an imitation of a skirt.

The kids howled and the counselors rolled, and she had to force herself to stay in her seat when all she wanted to do was pull him away from the crowd and tell him about her interview. All of it. No more pretending that what she knew wasn't real. No more holding back. As soon as campfire was over, she would steal him away to herself and put her new plan into action—a plan that began with getting him out of those aprons and into her embrace.

But in the meantime, she sang songs and linked arms with kids on either side of her while they swayed back and forth, and counted the minutes until they would be done.

When they stood for "Taps," she caught Sam's eye and tugged on her ear, the way she used to do all those years ago. Surely he would remember their old signal to meet at the inlet.

Judging from the smile he gave her—the kind usually seen on Christmas morning, on receiving a present that had been longed for but never expected—he remembered very well.

AN HOUR LATER, Libby finished her last bunk check, checked the latrines one final time to make sure no one had covered the seats with plastic wrap, and popped her head into Mick's cabin to remind his counselor that he had a history of "sleepwalking" on the last few nights.

With all her ducks in a row, she headed back to her cabin, where she slipped out of her shorts and into jeans, making sure she grabbed the box she'd picked up from the pharmacy while she was in town. She was leaving nothing to chance tonight.

Phoebe wandered in and dropped on her bunk as Libby pulled a sweatshirt over her head.

"Uh, hello. Earth to Libby. You're supposed to be getting into your pajamas, not your work clothes."

"No rest for the wicked," she said lightly as she tugged the hoodie into place. Would it look too obvious if she combed her hair?

Phoebe stretched out on the bunk, propped her head on her bent arm and gave Libby a college student version of the Glare of Death. "You seriously expect me to swallow that line?"

Libby allowed a small smile to escape as she met Phoebe's gaze. "Keep at it. You almost have it down. Another year, maybe two and you'll be glaring with the best of them."

"Nice try, Kovak, but you're not distracting me. And if you think for one minute that I'm going to believe you're heading up to the office, you might as well say hello to Santa Claus and the Easter Bunny on your way."

Damn. Phoebe wasn't supposed to turn all Libby's tricks back on her.

"I have some things to finish." The heck with it. She grabbed her brush and tugged it through her hair. It wasn't as if she was going to fool Phoebe anyway.

"Finish as in finish that kiss I heard you planted on Sam this afternoon?"

Anticipation shivered down her spine, but Libby kept her voice light. "Phoebe, Phoebe, Phoebe. It's my second-to-last night here. Surely I'm allowed to write up some notes and then, oh, sit on the dock and watch the sunrise?"

"Sure you are. If that's how you want to spend it, you go right ahead." Phoebe winked. "Me, I'd be running up the hill as fast as I could to throw myself at that fine specimen of manhood waiting at the top, but you know, that's just me. If you want to go dabble your feet in the river all night, that's what you can do." She winked. "At least that's what I'll tell anyone who asks."

"Come here." Libby grabbed Phoebe's hand, yanked her to her feet and pulled her into a long hug. "I'm going to miss you."

"Me, too." Phoebe's voice was thick, and she sniffed as she pulled back. "But I'm coming back next year. Sam asked me to be assistant director if you aren't here."

"He did?" Libby laughed in sheer delight. "How perfect!"

"Yeah, well, I figured even if you aren't working here, you'll still be around to help me out. 'Cause the way Sam was looking at you at campfire, I wouldn't lay money on this being your last *night* at Overlook, if you know what I mean."

PHOEBE'S WORDS ECHOED in Libby's head as she switched on her flashlight and navigated the path to the river, pulling her hood up against a gentle rain. With every step she felt a little lighter, a little brighter. By the time she reached the water she was sure she must be glowing enough to illuminate the whole camp.

There were probably a whole lot of pranksters who were glad she couldn't. But tonight, she didn't care.

She stopped at the branch in the path that led to the inlet and the pavilion, swallowed and smoothed her shirt the way she had the day she first met Casey. So much had changed since then. But none of the changes could compare to the fact that in the middle of facing down the biggest challenge of his life, Sam had come back. For her.

No one had ever done that before. No one had ever put her first. There were no words to let him know how much this meant to her.

But she was pretty sure there were a few actions that could get the message across.

She walked down the path as quickly as her flashlight would allow. As she drew closer to the pavilion she could see a light bobbing between the trees, and realized he had made it there first. Come to think of it, other than the afternoon when she quit, she couldn't remember a time when she had walked down this path without knowing he was waiting at the other end.

She hoped he always would be.

She hadn't visited the pavilion since that bleak afternoon, and she couldn't see much in the deep black of the cloudy night. As she drew closer she could barely make out bits and pieces of the finished structure. Her flashlight played over a stonework pillar, then over silver wind chimes swaying in the breeze, their muted tinkle a glittery welcome.

She stopped at the edge and waited. Sam's light had disappeared. She couldn't see him but she could sense his presence, close and welcome in the dark.

"You made it." His voice came from her left, and she turned to it, aiming her light near where she thought his feet might be. His chuckle reached through the blackness. His hand closed over her wrist then slipped down to her flashlight. She let it go without protest, even when he switched it off and the darkness closed around them.

Her eyes adjusted quickly, but the night was too deep to allow her to see anything more than the solid black of his bulk directly in front of her. With her vision hijacked, all she knew was the soft tune of the chimes and the softer patter of rain on the roof, the slight hitch to Sam's breathing and the scent of wood smoke that clung to him.

She would never be able to walk past a campfire again without remembering this moment.

She ached to touch and be touched but there were things she had to say first. Lord knew that once she started she wouldn't want to stop to talk. So she inched closer and swayed in his direction. And then, because she needed to know just a little of him, she let her hands bump forward until they found his.

"Hope you weren't waiting long."

"Just a couple of minutes. It's okay. I hear you have a miserable boss."

"The worst." She slid her fingers over the skin on his hand, lingering over each ridge and valley.

"So how was the interview?"

"It was…" She bounced a little in her shoes, just remembering. "I couldn't believe how great it felt. It was like we were in perfect sync all along. They loved my experience with parents. They asked lots of questions about integrating everyday science and nature into the curriculum, and that was straight from what we do here…and the whole time, I kept thinking, this was what I wanted back then. *This* was what I planned to do, to be with the kids, hands-on. I kind of lost that along the way."

"More like you had it stolen from you."

His knee bumped against her thigh. Sheer hot want jolted through her. She closed her eyes and breathed deeply to remind herself of the things she needed to say. As much as she wanted him, she also didn't want anything hovering between them.

This was their fresh start, the clean slate Sam had asked for when he first showed up in the office. She wouldn't let anything mar it.

"Here's the thing. I didn't exactly… I could have pushed myself, you know? But when I finished the degree, I promised myself a year off, just to enjoy life without classes and homework and racing back and forth. Then Myra had surgery, Gran got sick, and then Myra told me she was leaving the camp to me and I…I told myself that this was right, that it was what I wanted. Because I love this place, and I still do. Nothing about that has changed."

"But…"

She nodded. "But when you were talking about Sharon yesterday, you said something about her holding on to Casey for all the wrong reasons, and I—well—I did the same thing. This place was supposed to be a way station. I let it be the final destination. And that would be okay if I'd gone out and tried other things and knew I wanted this because it was right, but—"

"But you were holding on to it because it was all you knew."

His forehead rested against hers. She breathed him in, all smoke and wood, and forcibly reminded her jumping hormones that they'd waited twelve years and they could damn well wait another five minutes.

Maybe.

"You know you can come back here anytime." His whisper caressed her cheek. "Say the word and you have a job. Or say a different word and you can just come over and spend the day." His fingers slipped free of one of her hands. A moment later they were in her hair, caressing, tugging. "Or the night." His lips brushed the side of her neck, making her knot her hands in his shirt to supplement the strength leaching out of her knees. "Or both."

If that didn't sound like perfection, she didn't know what would.

"I'll still have summers." Her hands flattened over his chest and slid slowly higher to rest on the firmness of his shoulders.

"Too far away." The hand that wasn't caressing the back of her neck slid down her rib cage, a steady path of pleasure that made her wriggle forward to press her hips against his.

"And there's weekends," she whispered into his ear while he circled her waist and tugged her flush against him.

"Still too far."

"Mmm, I think you might be onto something." Was there a pillar behind her? She hoped so, because staying upright without support was becoming a waste of energy that could be spent in much more delightful ways. Like sliding her hands over the smooth curve of the bum she'd been eyeing all summer. Like nudging her hips closer to his to feel him pressing against her, feel him wanting her the way she wanted him.

Like arching her back away from the pillar when his hands slipped beneath her shirt and his skin was hot against hers at last…

Like yanking on his shirt because she needed more of him and his strength and his heat…

Like clinging to his shoulders while he shoved her bra

high and palmed her breast and she wanted to tell him she needed him, right then, right there, but there was so much need and so much wonder and so much urgency taking her over that there was no room left for words.

Until he froze, cursed beneath his breath and stepped back.

"What's wrong?"

"I have to tell you something. Something I did. I was going to tell you first thing, then you started talking and then I got distracted and— Shit."

"Your timing sucks."

"Tell me about it."

She breathed in, blinked into the night and forced herself to concentrate on the hard push of the stones behind her back instead of all the other things she wanted to feel pressing against her front.

"I didn't... Lib, I had a choice. I didn't have to do the hearing tomorrow. They gave me the choice of now or in a couple of months, and I—"

"You went for Option A."

"And almost cost you the chance at this job."

"True," she said, and gave a flickering consideration to the fact that she might not feel quite so generous if she was fully clothed. "But did you know I had the interview when you made the choice?"

"No."

"Was I speaking to you when you made the choice?"

"No, but—"

"Were you trying to hurt me, or were you trying to do what was best for your kid by putting an end to an incredibly stressful situation?"

"Yeah, but even after I knew about your interview, I still didn't offer to change things or help you or—"

She stopped his silly protests with a kiss.

"You're distracting me again." The words were warm against her lips.

"Blaming me?"

"Hell, no, but—"

"Sam." She reached deep inside for her best no-nonsense teacher voice. "Listen to me and listen good, because I am not wasting any more time on this. Casey is your son. It's your job to do what's best for him. If I were in your shoes, I would have made the exact same choice."

He didn't protest, but he wasn't kissing her, either, and that was so wrong she could hardly breathe. She had to fix this. Fast.

"I had a choice, too, you know. I could have said the hell with you and the camp and gone to the interview anyway."

"You wouldn't have, though. You're not that selfish."

"Trust me, Sam, I can be very selfish when I put my mind to it." She slipped her hands around his waist and tugged him closer to help drive her message home. "But I made the choice that was right for me. So did you. Sometimes that's a problem. Sometimes it's just life."

"I don't—"

"Stop. Now. You took care of your child and then you came back. That's more than enough for me." She nipped at his lower lip. "But if you're really feeling guilty, maybe you'd better start apologizing, hmmm?"

He growled low in his throat and his mouth took hers and she was sandwiched between him and the pillar and it was a damned good thing because her knees were buckling and her blood was pounding and all she could do was push herself against him and pull him tighter and harder and closer.

"There's an air mattress about two steps behind me," he whispered, and the rest of the world disappeared.

So did her clothes.

And much to her delight, Libby discovered that there

were times when Sam did indeed know when to slow down...and when he knew to go numbingly, blissfully, shooting-star fast.

CHAPTER EIGHTEEN

AN HOUR OR FOUR LATER—who could tell?—Sam stared into the darkness and thought about lines.

Not the lines decorating the blanket he had pulled up over Libby as she dozed beside him, although he had taken a minute to admire the way the green and yellow stripes molded against her dips and curves in the soft glow of his flashlight.

No, the lines in his mind were red and blue, painted on ice. The lines of the game. Red across the middle of the rink. Blue dividing the areas between that red center and the goals. Cross the blue line ahead of the puck, you're offside. Penalty. Send the puck flying across too many lines at the wrong time, another penalty.

Those lines had been so burned into him over his years of play that he hadn't needed to look to know where they were. He just knew. He could feel it within him as he skated. They were the markers that shaped his game and guided his movements.

But now—now, he was pretty sure he was balanced on a line that was growing narrower and skinnier all the time. He couldn't see it, but he sure as hell could feel it. It was the line between *You're amazing and I want you now,* and *I love you and I want you forever.*

He'd been at this point before, with Robin, but that line had been much wider, and nothing had pushed him over. He'd tried. He'd hoped it would happen, because he had wanted to be part of his kid's life, not an absentee jerk like his own father, but the last push, the magic—it never happened.

But with Libby...

He tightened his grip around her waist and closed his eyes. Libby was part of him in a way Robin had never been. When he was with her, he had the same feeling he used to have when he was skating full tilt down the ice and the crowd was with him and the puck was calling him. Like he was flying.

Libby might be leaving the camp, but she wasn't leaving his life. He was going to hold tight to her and keep flying while the line he was balancing on got skinnier and skinnier, until he finally toppled over it.

Because if he wasn't in love already, he was definitely on the verge.

IT WAS STILL O-DARK-HUNDRED when Sam stumbled through airport security in search of coffee. Waking up to Libby had made him lose track of time. When he finally hauled himself out of the blankets, he'd barely had time for a shower before jumping into the car and making the hour and a half drive to the airport.

But if he didn't get some caffeine into his bloodstream soon, he was going to pass out right there in the terminal and sleep through his flight announcement. If not for Casey waiting for him at the other end, he wouldn't care in the least.

He hauled his blissed-out behind to the coffee bar and parked himself in the back of the line of folks in similar states of zombie-dom. He checked the clock and wondered what Libby was doing. Then he remembered what Libby had been doing not so long ago. While that was a very fine thought indeed, it probably wasn't one he should have while out in public, so he distracted himself by examining the counter to see if there was anything worth eating.

Chocolate, chocolate, a bag of mixed nuts, some cardboard masquerading as a pastry. He grabbed the nuts and shuffled forward, searching farther down the counter in case there might be something edible hiding in the rows. But as he looked past the obscenely bright packaging his attention was caught, not by real food, but by something that looked a hell of a lot like his name.

His name, on a tabloid headline.

Panic jerked him to full wakefulness. He dodged out of line, mumbled an apology to the half-asleep man standing in front of the rack of papers and returned to his place while scanning the article. Some mix of prayers and disbelief churned in his gut as his eyes jumped from one damning phrase to the next.

Children's camp...secretive silences...appointments with unnamed doctors...lurking beneath a raft...mysterious visitors...playing in the craft room with the kids while leaving the running of the program to his assistant Libby K—

"Libby?"

His breath flew out of his lungs in a giant *oof,* the way it used to when he'd been checked from behind. The way it had when Sharon told him she was filing for custody.

He lurched out of line, grabbed a bill from his wallet and cut in front of the woman at the register to toss it on the counter.

"Hey!" she protested, and "Dude," said the cashier. He shot a quick look at the bill—crap, he'd grabbed a twenty instead of a five—and then at the woman he'd cut off, with a baby strapped to her chest and a toddler by the hand. A toddler who looked to be Casey's age.

"Sorry," he muttered to the woman. He jerked his thumb toward her and told the cashier, "My treat. Keep the change."

An astonished "Dude, wow" echoed in the background as he walked to an empty space along a wall of windows and read the article from start to nauseating finish. His whole summer was laid out before him, twisted and spiked to make him sound like some sort of playboy at best and a pervert at worst.

He'd had worse written about him. He was no Brad Pitt, but between the commercial and the starlets he had sometimes taken to charity events, he'd landed in the tabloids a time or two. But he'd never hit the front page before, and he sure as hell had never been publicly slandered on the morning of his custody—

Oh, God. The hearing. He had to… What the hell was he supposed to do now?

He pressed his hands to his forehead and forced himself to breathe, slow and deep, even while his feet itched with the message to *run, now!*

Focus.

He could handle this. It was as if he was back on the ice, down one player while the other team trash-talked their way through a power play. As long as he stayed calm and focused, he would be okay.

Live the goal.

The first step was to make as many calls as he could before it was time to board his plane, starting with his lawyer.

While Joe was less than excited about the content of the article or the hour of the call, he assured Sam that no judge worth his or her salt would let a tabloid article influence the final decision.

"The worst that can happen is the other side will use this to buy some more time, maybe ask for a more extensive home study. But I doubt that's going to happen. And if it did, once it was proven that these allegations are untrue—"

"Damn straight they're untrue." Sam pressed the phone to his ear as he paced along the wall of windows.

"Then there's nothing to worry about. You're Casey's biological father. No one is going to take him away from you." Joe's voice turned speculative. "Do you think Sharon might be behind this?"

Sam considered the idea, then just as swiftly dismissed it. "I don't think so. She's desperate, but she's never resorted to anything dirty, and she's basically a decent person. Besides, there's too much that's based on real events. Sharon couldn't have known about those things."

"Unless she had someone working with her. Like, who's the one that's mentioned in here? Your assistant, Libby—"

"No!" Sam barked the word with such force that Joe could probably hear it in his office without benefit of the phone. Libby would never do something like this. He knew it.

"You sure?" Joe asked. "Even by accident? Sometimes reporters can be sneaky and weasel information out of a source without that person ever realizing what's up."

Sam paused in his pacing. Could that have happened? Could someone have got to Libby, *his* Libby, and used her this way?

"In any case," Joe continued, "we'll figure out the details once the custody suit is behind us. Right now, just get on that plane and breathe easy. I'll do damage control from this end. Everything will be okay. Trust me."

Sam grunted at the thought of trusting a lawyer and ended the call. He rubbed at the pounding in his head, then inhaled deeply. It would be okay. A few more hours and it would be over and he could breathe freely again without this band of panic around his chest.

In the meantime, he had to call Libby. She needed—no, *he* needed—to tell her there was a problem. Needed to let her know that somehow, someway, she had been sucked into this. Needed, more than anything, to hear her voice telling him it would all work out, that the legal types knew their stuff, that at the end of the night she would be waiting for him and Casey and it would be just like they were a—

The *bing* of his phone cut off the thought. He frowned at both the display—his manager—and the fact that pre-boarding had started. This was going to have to be quick.

"Hey, Taylor," he said with a sigh, not the least surprised that she was already aware of the problem. Sometimes he thought she had Google Alerts poised to wake her if it turned up anything with his name involved.

Ten long minutes later, Taylor had been calmed and his flight had been called. He shuffled through the line while speed dialing the camp office, then looked at the clock and realized, crap, Libby would be at breakfast. He called the kitchen and braced himself.

"What?"

"Cos, it's me," he said as he handed his boarding pass to the gate attendant. "I need to talk to Libby."

"She's eating."

"I figured she would be eating, okay? That's why I called the kitchen. Could you get her please? It's urgent."

Cosmo sniffed. "Urgent? You want to talk urgent? I got a hundred and fifty hungry mouths to feed, Libby's floating around here wearing the kind of grin that makes me think I oughta be takin' you out back for a proper talking-to and my so-called boss has pulled a disappearing act. *That's* urgent, mister."

"Of all the— Dammit, Cosmo, listen up. I'm getting on a plane. Some idiot splashed lies about me all over a tabloid. And on top of all that, I have to go convince a judge that those lies really *are* lies and he shouldn't take away my kid. Now will you get Libby for me or does your last pay-check go to your obedience training?"

Stunned silence on the line echoed that which Sam realized had settled all around him. Stuck in the middle of the airbridge, waiting to board the actual plane, he was surrounded by a half dozen faces watching him in various shades of worry, confusion and curiosity. Another half dozen were either pretending not to notice or grabbing for their cell phones, undoubtedly to record the Cold Ice man in a very different kind of lather.

He sighed. "Sorry," he said both to Cosmo and all those around him. "Bad morning."

The other passengers nodded almost in unison. Cosmo, however, seemed to be falling over himself.

"Geezum crow, Sam, I'm sorry. You know I didn't—Hell. Son, are you okay?"

Sam wasn't sure what was more astonishing—the fact that Cosmo had apologized, or that he'd called him *son*. Now there was something to ponder during the flight.

"It's okay. Just please get Libby."

"Already on it. Libby!"

Sam winced and yanked the phone from his ear as Cosmo let loose with a bellow that seemed to echo through the walkway. He offered the people around him a sheepish grin. They were probably already alerting the flight attendants that it would be a good thing to make sure there was extra security on the plane.

He held his breath and bumped his way to his seat. Phone cradled beneath his ear, he shoved his bag into the overhead bin and dropped into his seat just as he heard Libby's worried "Sam?"

It was as if someone had pulled a plug from a leaf blower or a jackhammer he'd been holding. That was how fast the sound of her voice settled him.

"Lib. Babe. I—"

The canned announcement that it was time to discontinue the use of all electronic devices rolled over his words.

"Sam, what's happening? Cosmo said—"

"I got to the airport and there was this tabloid. This trash. And it said—"

He was pretty sure he heard Libby saying a word he never once expected to hear from her lips. At least not when there were kids within potential earshot.

"Lib? Your name was in it. Do you—"

"It's not what you think, Sam, I swear. I—"

A flight attendant stopped beside his seat. "Sir, I need you to put that away now and fasten your seat belt."

"Wait," he said, to both Libby and the attendant. "You knew about this?" The panic-band around his chest pulled tight and cold.

"Sir! Did you hear me?"

"I...I might. I have this neighbor...I didn't think she would..."

"Sir, either the phone goes or you're off this plane. Do you understand?"

"Call back as soon as you can," Libby said, and ended the connection just as the flight attendant seemed ready to blow his whistle.

"Wait! No!"

"Yes," said the attendant before bustling up the aisle to close the cabin door.

With three languages full of curses flying through his head, Sam shoved the phone into the seat pouch in front of him before wrestling his belt into position and snapping it around his hips. Then he let his head drop back against the seat, closed his eyes and prepared for an hour of torturing himself by imagining what, exactly, Libby had told someone.

LIBBY STARED AT THE PHONE and let loose with a string of words that made Cosmo step back and blink.

"Where'd you learn to talk like that?"

"I've spent almost two decades listening to you," she snapped. "Where do you think I learned it?"

Cosmo tugged on the strap of his apron. "How bad is it?"

She shook her head. If she tried to tell him the details she would end up thinking—of Casey, of Sam, of what could happen when the judge saw whatever lies Dani had put in that article, because it had to have been Dani, there was no other way—and then she would freeze, just freeze, and be unable to think of how to help. Later, maybe…when she faced Dani and squeezed the truth out of her and tried to find a way through this…then, she could freeze and fall and shatter. But not now.

Now she had to fix what she might have helped create.

Rule number two: don't let your happiness show.

She pressed her fingers to her eyes and allowed herself one deep, centering breath before heading for the door.

"I'll be in the office," she said over her shoulder. "I have to make some calls. Can you handle the main phone for a while?"

"Sure."

She took two steps toward the kitchen exit before Cosmo's hand landed on her arm. "Hang on there, missy. I got one last question."

"What?" She bounced on her toes, needing to be out of here, on her way to the office, to hunt down Dani, to help Sam.

"Are you doing this because you messed up something, or because you've been damned fool enough to fall for Catalano again?"

Her first instinct was to deny, pretend, hide. But this

was Cosmo. When push came to shove, he was like the father she'd never known. The concern in his eyes was real.

Hiding her feelings hadn't done such a great job for her thus far. Maybe it was time to be honest.

"Maybe a little of both," she said softly.

He sighed. "I figured." He patted her shoulder awkwardly. "Whatever you did, I know you wouldn't have done it on purpose. If he doesn't believe that, he ain't worth your time. But I got a feeling he's just as damned a fool for you as you are for him."

She managed a grin, then impulsively reached up and hugged him—quick, before he could dissolve into a panic attack. "Thanks," she whispered. "For everything."

He nodded, his gaze firmly fixed on a spot on his apron, but she could see the faint wash of pink in his cheeks. "You'd best get going," he said gruffly. "Sounds like you got a busy day ahead."

She ventured back into the wall of noise that was the dining hall, where she caught Phoebe's eye and pointed to the door. Two minutes later they were both outside, back beneath the Sneaky Tree.

"I know what you're thinking," Phoebe said as she joined Libby beneath the shade, "but I have no idea where she is. She said she was running to the bathroom, but that was a good half hour ago."

"What?" Preoccupied with thoughts of Sam, focused on asking Phoebe to handle any problems for the next hour or so, Libby was left dizzy by Phoebe's unexpected words. "Hold on. What are you talking about? Someone's missing?"

"Not a kid," Phoebe was quick to say. "Tanya. And not missing, just weirder than she's been all summer. Isn't that why you dragged me out here?"

"Believe it or not, I hadn't noticed. About her disappearing, that is. The weirdness…" Libby shook her head. "What happened?"

Phoebe stepped closer, eyes rolling. "Don't know. She brought her kids to breakfast, said everyone was set and asked me to keep an eye on them while she ran to the bathroom. No problem. I figured she meant the dining hall bathrooms, but I saw her sneaking out the back door. That was right after breakfast started, so yeah, it's been almost half an hour."

"Crap, crap, crap." Libby pressed her fingers to her forehead. Her duty was clear: if a staff member was missing, that needed to be her top priority. Anything could have happened to Tanya. Even annoying idiots could have accidents. But the fact that she had misled Phoebe and obviously orchestrated her disappearance left Libby convinced that the only problem facing Tanya was how long Libby would let her live once she tracked the girl down.

The hell with the rule book.

"I'll take a quick look to see if she fell down and knocked herself out or something. If she didn't, she'll wish she had by the time I'm done with her."

"Can I help?"

Who could keep from grinning, if only for a moment? "Only after I get my shot. Now listen. I have a crisis that needs my full attention for a while. Can you handle any problems for the next hour or so?"

Phoebe's eyes went wide. "What's wrong?"

She gave Phoebe the condensed highlights of the morning. But instead of the nod or questions Libby was anticipating in response, Phoebe broke into a smile.

"What?" Libby whirled around to see if Phoebe could see something she couldn't, but the entry to the dining hall remained uncluttered. "What's with the Cheshire-cat thing? There's nothing funny about this."

"Funny? Nah," Phoebe scoffed. "You're just so cute when you're in love."

Denial rose quickly in her mind, but Libby pulled it back just in time. What was the point in lying? Phoebe was right. So instead of snapping, Libby merely rolled her eyes.

"Thanks, smart-ass."

Phoebe jerked her head in the direction of the office. "Go on. Get out of here. You have a man to save."

Libby handed over her clipboard and, finally free, headed up the path to the office. *Hurry, hurry.* The words pounded through her with every step. She tried to slow them down, fought to stay calm. Panic wouldn't help anything. But there were so many things she needed to do and all of them probably needed to be done right this minute. Should she call Dani? Call Brynn and alert her? Try to track down Sam's lawyer and explain what she was pretty sure had happened?

She rounded the corner before the office, emerging from the woods to the clearing and had her Sam-centered thoughts knocked aside for the moment by the sight of Tanya perched on the boulder near the staff parking lot. What the...

"I seriously do not have time for this crap," Libby muttered to herself, but nonetheless she marched over to the boulder. The silly twit had headphones in her ears so didn't realize she was about to be pounced upon until Libby jabbed her on the shoulder. After enduring a summer full of nonsense, Libby found it immensely gratifying to hear Tanya's shriek and see her hands fly into the air as her whole body jerked and practically flew off the boulder.

Libby grabbed the cord leading to the earbuds and yanked them free. "What are you doing? You're supposed to be at breakfast with your kids. And where the hell is your sense, listening to this—" she hoisted the buds in the air

"—when you were all alone near the woods? There are bears up here, you fool. You're lucky it was me who got you."

Tanya had stopped gasping for breath and was recovered enough to assume the look of disdain she'd perfected so well over the past six weeks. She plucked her earbuds from Libby's hand.

"I'm waiting for a delivery," she said in what was probably supposed to be a very haughty and superior voice, but which sounded to Libby like a little girl playing dress-up. "I'm sorry I was away from breakfast for so long but my delivery is late. I didn't mean to impose on Phoebe."

Oh, so imposing on Phoebe was bad, but messing around with Sam and Libby was just fine?

"Back to your group," Libby snapped. "I'll be here for a few minutes. I can pick up whatever it is you're waiting for. Though why you chose to have something delivered here today, of all days, when you know everything is…" She stopped and peered at Tanya, who met her gaze for a moment, then slid her focus somewhere off into the distance.

"This was deliberate, wasn't it?" Libby parceled the words out carefully as she put pieces together. "You knew things would be crazy with the Tour de Camp, and you chose it on purpose. What are you hiding, Tanya? Is there more fake skunk scent on the way? Though Sam's not here, so you can't use this to try to get into his house this— Oh!"

The pieces tumbled together in her mind. Tanya's tendency toward drama. The sudden, intense nature of her infatuation with Sam. The way she had disappeared when Sam walked down the hill with Casey that first day, right before Libby found the files open. The skunk and the disappearing medical file and the fact that Dani would have needed someone here at the camp to feed her information and Dani used to work at Tanya's uncle's hunting supply store and—

Holy crap, she was going to kill the girl.

"This delivery isn't coming from FedEx, is it?" Libby knotted her hands together to keep them from committing a felony. "It's coming from Dani Cooper."

CHAPTER NINETEEN

TANYA MIGHT HAVE BEEN about to deny the accusation, but it didn't matter. For at that moment, a car pulled into the staff lot—a car that Libby knew well, having seen it parked in the driveway next to hers for so many years.

A moment later, Dani slammed her way out of the car, which spilled over with her kids. She looked thinner and even more tired than she had after Aidan's tonsillectomy, and Libby's first fleeting thought was to drag her down to the dining hall and force-feed her before she passed out behind the wheel of her car.

Then she remembered the article.

"Dani, what the hell do you think you're doing?"

Dani smiled as if nothing in the world could possibly be wrong. "Hey, Libby. How's it going?"

Dear God in heaven, she was surrounded.

Dani pulled an envelope from her pocket and handed it to Tanya. "Here you go. Cash, just like you asked. Thanks for your help."

Tanya opened the envelope and smiled at the contents. "Pleasure doing business with you," she said to Dani, and then to Libby, "I'll go back to my kids now."

"You'll do no such thing," Libby snapped. "You'll get your stuff and get out of here within twenty minutes. Or I'll have Cosmo help you."

Tanya shrugged. "Suit yourself." She sauntered down the hill.

Libby turned back to Dani, who was headed toward the car. "Hey!" Dani's head snapped around. "Get back here!"

Dani waved toward the kids in the backseat, who had rolled down the windows and were now doing their level best to outshriek each other. "I have to go. I promised the boys I'd take them out for a special treat brunch."

"With the money you made selling Sam to the freakin' wolves?"

Dani rolled her eyes. "Oh, please, Libby. It's not like anybody actually reads those rags."

"That didn't stop you from selling your so-called journalism to them, did it?"

"Hey! My kid was sick and I lost my job! I'm broke, okay? I had no choice."

Damn, but she was tired of hearing people say that. As though it excused anything or everything they ever did.

"There's always a choice," she said sharply as she followed Dani into the parking lot, but Dani just shook her head.

"Get real. Anyway, it's over and done with. There's no changing it now. And he's had worse than that written about him."

"But he's never been in the middle of a custody fight before this!"

Dani stopped with her hand on the handle of the car door.

"What custody fight?"

The words were so low that Libby could scarcely hear them over the squealing of the kids in the car. She started to explain, but was cut off by a loud "Mom! He's hitting me!"

"Hey!" Libby yanked the rear door open and glared at the three suddenly silent boys, giving each of them the ultimate Glare of Death. "I need to talk to your mother. You three can either sit down and be quiet, or be prepared to scrub latrines for the rest of the day. Got it?"

Three heads nodded in unison. She drew a very deep breath and turned back to Dani.

"Tanya told you Sam has a little boy, right?" At Dani's nod, she continued. "Mom is dead. Mom's sister is fighting for custody. It's being decided today, the very day your little slander-fest hit the newsstands."

To her credit, Dani seemed genuinely distressed. "Okay, look. I never met the guy, and all I know of him is what other people have written and what you and Tanya told me. But I— Damn. Is he a good father?"

Libby crossed her arms over her chest and gave a sharp nod.

Dani bit her lip. "Libby, I'm sorry. I never meant for anything to happen because of this, you know?"

Libby knew. What Dani lacked in judgment, she made up for in heart.

"I believe you," she said heavily. "But there's a judge somewhere in Nova Scotia who might not."

Aidan picked that moment to poke his head out of the rear window. "Mommy, I hafta go potty."

Dani rolled her eyes. "Is there a bathroom he can use? He just started potty training. It's kind of a big thing."

Did she want Dani and her kids in her office, Sam's office? No. But she couldn't refuse a wiggling toddler.

"Come with me. But don't touch anything," she said to the boys as they piled out of the car. "If any of you so much as breathes on anything in there, you'll be doing chores for me until school starts. Understood?"

They nodded and made their silent way to the office. As they climbed the steps, Dani whispered, "Can you teach me how to make them listen to me the way they listen to you?"

Libby's hands curled into tight fists as she clamped her lips together.

As soon as they were inside and Aidan had been dispatched to the bathroom with his brothers, Libby turned back to Dani.

"We have to fix this. With Sam."

"Look, Libby, I feel bad for the guy, but even if the paper retracted everything—which they won't—no one will see it in time to make a difference."

Unfortunately, in this case at least, Dani was one hundred percent correct. "There has to be something we can do. I could call his sister. Or try to track down what court it will be. I guess the one who really needs to know is his lawyer, but I have no idea who that is."

Dani sent her a sharp look. "Did you two spend any time talking at all?"

"Excuse me?"

She shrugged. "Oh, come on. There's no way you would be this upset over the guy and his kid if you weren't head over heels for him. Besides, Tanya told me about the raft and the skunk night and all that. Why pretend?"

It was a sad day when she started taking advice from Dani. On the other hand, she had known how to tweak the résumé that helped Libby get that interview, so…

"Do you have any ideas?"

Dani seated herself in the chair across from Libby. "I'll swear that I wrote the article and twisted things out of shape. We type it up and get folks to witness it. Then you fly to wherever he is and show up at family court in time to give it to his lawyer before they have to go in."

"I can't go there! I have to be here!"

"Why?"

"Because that's my job, remember? To keep things running. With Sam gone, I have to stay."

Dani stretched and hooked an arm over the back of her chair. "You mean there's nobody here who could look after the place for a day while you're gone?"

A burst of applause came from the bathroom. Dani grinned. "Yay, Aidan!"

Turning back to Libby, she said, "What if, say, your appendix decided to go wild on you? You'd have to go to the hospital, right?"

"Right, but that would be life or death."

"You think that keeping his kid isn't life or death for Sam?"

"Of course it is. But I—"

Dani shook her head. "Work with me, Libby. I know you. You do things right. I bet you have at least three people on staff right now who could fill in for you if there was an emergency."

Aidan burst out of the bathroom, followed by his brothers. Libby pointed to the battered sofa in the corner. They seated themselves quietly. Dani watched them in wonder then turned back to Libby and whistled.

"See what I mean? You do things right."

Libby shook her head as she dropped into her own chair. "I don't know, Dani. Phoebe agreed to be assistant next year, but she—"

"She was trained by you, right? She's been working beside you all summer?"

"Five summers."

"And you trust her?"

"Totally. So does Sam. But the parents—"

Dani bolted upright and waved to the boys. "See them? I'm a parent. And if I, as a parent, heard that there was an emergency that made you and Sam leave, but you put a trained, experienced staff member in charge, well, I'd say if I trusted you enough to leave my kid here, then I trust you enough to pick your temporary replacement."

"But— Can't I just call, or fax them something?"

"Court stuff usually has to be originals or certified copies." Dani sighed. "Look, Libby. If there's one thing I've learned, it's that a job is a job, and no one is irreplaceable. Unfortunately. But if you really have it for this guy…"

"I do," Libby admitted.

"Then maybe it's time for you to walk away from the job and go where you're really needed."

Doubts swirled in Libby's mind. Could she? Did she dare?

But there was Phoebe. And Cosmo, and the nurse and all the other folks she had trained herself.

She could put one of them on a plane to carry the documents to Sam. That would work. It would keep everything running according to the regulations. It would be the responsible thing to do and it would keep her here, where she belonged.

Except…*did* she belong here?

Last night, she had told Sam that she had let the camp become her destination. But it was more than that. She had let it become her whole life because she had nothing else. But now she had more. She had a shot at the future she had always planned. She had her love for Casey. She had her love for Sam.

She needed to be with Sam. She needed to tell him what had happened and help make things right. The judge might have questions, which only she could answer. Phoebe could look after the camp, but who else could help Sam?

Dani was right. There was only one place Libby needed to be this afternoon. And it was definitely not at camp.

"Get ready to sign," she said as she opened a blank document on the computer. "I'm going for it."

SAM WALKED OFF the longest flight of his life and made a beeline for the rental car. Casey and Brynn would be with

Sharon for another couple of hours. He needed to get to the hotel and start making some calls.

Sure enough, when he let himself into his suite he saw that it was deserted. Good. It was going to be bad enough getting through this on his own. He didn't need to add to the mix by trying to talk in a roundabout manner so Casey wouldn't pick up on the fact that Daddy was ready to rip some throats out.

He reached into his pocket for his phone but came up empty.

"What the…"

He patted all his pockets and grabbed for his overnight bag. But as he unzipped it, he vividly remembered tossing the damned phone into the seat pouch when the flight attendant started threatening him. He'd left it on the plane.

He groaned and did the head-palm thing. Just what he needed.

"This had better be the end of the lousy turns for today," he growled to anyone who might be listening. Then he grabbed the tiny hotel notepad and the phone book.

An hour later, he'd managed to touch base with both his lawyer and his manager. Joe still insisted that everything would be fine, that Sam's priority should be in staying calm so he would present the right kind of appearance when they came before the judge. Joe was working on a couple of different repairs and would take care of everything.

Taylor, his manager, wasn't as complacent. Even though Sam was no longer playing, he was still associated with different companies and charities, not to mention the commercials. Taylor had spent her morning talking down folks who had developed a sudden case of the jitters over their involvement with him. It would all work out, Taylor said. But it was going to be more complicated, that was for sure.

By the time he hung up, Sam's ear ached and his feet

were itchy from pacing the floor. He needed to get out of the room. He needed some fresh air and some calm, but most of all he needed to talk to Libby. He needed to feel all the messed-up pieces inside him slide into place at the sound of her voice.

Joe and Taylor had both dropped not-so-subtle hints that she might have been involved in the article, but he refused to believe that for a second. He knew her. He knew who she was, and that the biggest mistake he'd made in ages was not trusting her with the truth about Casey right from the start. It would have changed so much for them....

He dropped back onto the bed, and sank into the pillow, ready to call the camp. That line he was straddling was pretty damned skinny now. More like a thread, he figured. But he had this restless feeling...as if there was something he needed to do before the thread could snap. Something he had to take care of.

Or, he realized, some*one*.

He'd used up the hotel notepad so he had to rip a page from Casey's coloring book to scribble a note for Brynn, who should be back anytime. Then he raced from the room to the car. There was one last person he had to talk to before he could move forward—with Libby, with Casey, with the rest of his life. And he knew exactly where to find her.

LIBBY LEANED BACK against the seat and gripped the seat rest as the plane lifted into the air. What was it Sam had said—that hockey sometimes felt like he was flying? With the engines thundering and the plane vibrating and the world sliding away beneath her, Libby couldn't help but be amazed.

She still could barely believe it was true. Getting her here had taken a team effort, with Phoebe booking the flight while Cosmo escorted Tanya off the grounds and Dani used

Sam's emergency contact form to call Brynn and get the details of where and when. All the while, Libby had run around making last-minute arrangements, because even though the manual she'd compiled for Sam was thick enough to strain arm muscles, there was always the possibility that she could have forgotten something.

But Cosmo and Phoebe assured her they could handle anything. As she accepted a minuscule glass of ginger ale from the flight attendant, she had to admit that her staff was right. Hadn't she trusted them already, when she opened up to them about the problem and asked them for help?

But there was no backing out now. In an hour she would be in Halifax, with a rental car waiting for her and turn-by-turn directions to the hotel in Lunenburg and the courthouse in Bridgewater. The one thing she didn't have was a way to contact Sam. No, correction: there was one other thing she wished she had—the confidence that this bombshell hadn't impacted the outcome of the custody case. And that Sam wouldn't blame her for leading Dani to him in the first place.

Because if anything went wrong now...

She shook her head and sat higher in her seat. She couldn't think that way. She had to be strong and confident, certain it would all work out. It could happen. After all, stranger things happened all the time.

Like the fact that she, Libby Kovak, was finally flying.

SAM FOUND THE CEMETERY easily enough—the desk clerk had given him excellent directions, and Mahone Bay, where Robin was buried, wasn't that big—but he surprised himself by locating her grave with very little trouble. He'd been too numb at her funeral to register much except a few details he thought he might want to share with Casey someday. By the time spring arrived and they were able to have the graveside service, he'd thought he had it together, but

that was just after Sharon had dropped her custody bombshell. He'd spent the entire service watching the woman like
a hawk in case she decided to simply grab Casey and run.

Maybe that was part of the problem, he thought as he bent
to check out the flowers around the grave. Maybe he'd been
so focused on Casey that he'd never really said goodbye.

"Hey, Robin. It's me." He glanced around on the off
chance someone might be within listening distance, but he
was alone save for the stones and the trees and a couple of
squirrels playing hide-and-seek among the leaves. "Sorry
I haven't been back. Sharon's been taking care of things
here, and it looks great. Don't know if you can see it, but
she planted those little flowers you always liked, the purple
ones. The stone turned out good, too."

He ran a finger over the lines carving out her birth, death
and the all-too-short dash that separated them. Then he flattened his palm over the word that had meant so much to
her, the one that tied him to her forever.

Mother.

"You were a great mom. You amazed me, the way you
looked after him so easily and were so dedicated to him but
still made sure I was part of his life. I know I said it all the
time, but thanks for that." His mouth quirked up in a grin.
"And I know you're still keeping an eye on him, because
there's no other way that he could smack that dog around
so much and have nothing to show for it without your kind
of help."

His grin faded. He squatted in front of the stone and
lowered his head.

"Babe, I want you to know, you were right to say no.
When I asked you to marry me, I mean. I was asking for
good reasons, but they were wrong. It was all about me.
About me wanting to be the kind of dad I always planned
to be, proving that I was a better father than my old man.

But it should have been about you. It… I'm just figuring
that out now. Because there's someone who…well…yeah. I
think she's the one. And when I'm with her, it *is* about her.
Making her smile, making things right for her…not that I
didn't want to do those things for you. You know how much
I wanted to take care of you and Casey. But it wasn't the
same as it is with her."

He drew in a deep breath.

"I shouldn't have asked because of me. Or Casey. Or
anything else but you. I'm glad you were smart enough to
know that."

He pulled up a weed that had dared to intrude on Sharon's
flowers and rubbed it between his fingers. "But just because
it didn't work the way I would have liked for me and you,
well, that didn't mean you weren't pretty damned special.
You gave me the most amazing gift anyone has ever given
me, Rob. You gave me Casey. He's… God, I hope you can
see him from where you are, because he's so damned funny.
He makes me laugh every night at bath time. He's got your
giggle, you know? And that dimple when he knows he's
being bad but he thinks if he's cute enough he won't get in
trouble—yeah. That came straight from you."

He tossed the weed into the grass. "Rob, I need your help.
Sharon… I know she's your sister and I know she misses you
even more than I do, and you know I want Casey to have
time with her. But she's his aunt. I'm his dad. I want to keep
it that way, you know? And even though the lawyers keep
saying there's no way anything could happen, that I won't
lose him, I can't help being scared. So, Rob, babe, if you
can, could you maybe make things work for us? You and
me and Casey—we might not have been a regular family
the way I wanted, but we were still a family. And we were
making it work. It's not the same without you and it never
will be, but if you can wiggle your nose or something and

make sure Casey and I stay together, I promise you, I'll do everything I can to make sure he has the kind of life you wanted for him. With lots of family and friends and love."

He'd done all he could. There was nothing left to say. He straightened, easing himself up, and rested his hand on the stone that felt warmed now, as if it had been kissed by the sun.

Or, maybe, by someone else.

"I miss you, Robin. But I promise to do right by our little boy. He'll always know about you and love you, I promise, even if Libby and I—"

"Da Da Da Da Da!"

Sam grinned at the headstone. "Here he is. Guess I have to work on the proper kind of manners for when he comes to visit his mom, huh?" He turned and headed for the path, arms already outstretched to pick up his boy, his Casey, when he stopped and took in the sight before him. There was Casey in his little denim shorts and his favorite Camp Overlook T-shirt. That must have gone over well with Sharon. His hair bounced in rhythm with his steps as he half walked, half sort of ran up the path, tugging on the hand of—

Sam squinted, sure he wasn't seeing things right.

"Libby?"

Sure enough, even though she was too far to have heard him say her name, she looked straight at him and gave a tentative kind of wave. She was—here?

She was here. Still in her camp clothes, frantically trying to keep up with Casey, and here. With him.

Somewhere deep in whatever corner of the body controlled emotion, Sam could swear he felt a thread snap in half.

Joy and disbelief and wonder shot through him in a surge of something that couldn't be anything but love. He wanted to run to them, to pull his kid and his Libby into his arms and hold them tighter than tight against him, but he forced himself to stand perfectly still and let the feelings wash over him. It was magic. The kind of thing that happens only once in a lifetime. He was going to make sure he felt every bit of it so he could come back to it whenever he needed to remember a moment when he was perfectly, amazingly, astoundingly happy.

Libby and Casey were half jogging toward him. It must have been too slow a pace for her because she suddenly bent, scooped Casey into her arms and increased her speed.

Imagine that. Libby Kovak, in a hurry.

He couldn't stand it any longer. He took one step toward them, then two, then stopped and turned back to Robin's grave.

"If this was supposed to be a sign, I gotta tell you, kid—you do damned fine work."

Then, unable to wait another moment, he hit the path and ran to Libby and Casey, practically running them over in his joy, gathering them close and closing his eyes and filling himself with the sound of Casey's giggles and Libby's choking half sobs and the feel of them both against him, soft and warm and everything he ever needed.

At last he pulled back and took Casey from Libby, so he had his son in his left arm while his right circled her shoulders.

"I know you didn't do anything," he said to her. "At least not on purpose."

Her eyes filled with tears, but she pulled in a deep breath and said, all in a rush as if she'd been rehearsing, "The night I found out you were buying the camp, I went home and spouted to my neighbor, and I knew she sometimes wrote stuff for tabloids but she said you were too boring, and I believed her, but then her kid needed a tonsillectomy and she lost her job and she needed money so she paid Tanya to spy on you and—"

"Wait." He pressed a finger over her lips. "Tanya wasn't really hot for me?"

She laughed through her tears. "Come on, Catalano. How many women do you need to fall in love with you in one summer?"

The words were no sooner out of her mouth than she stopped, her eyes wide. He let Casey slide down to the ground in a bundle of wriggles and squeals so he could frame her face with his hands.

"Really, Lib?"

She took a deep breath and nodded. The tiniest of nods at first, then more emphatic, as if she had given herself permission.

"Yeah," she whispered. "I know it sounds crazy but—"

"Crazy? Are you kidding? It's the best thing I've heard in forever." He moved to kiss her but she did a quick step backward, dancing just beyond his reach.

"Wait," she said.

He glanced at Casey, who was gathering stones from the path and stacking them on top of each other. No problem there.

"What's wrong?"

"Nothing. But I want you to be clear…I didn't mean for that article to happen."

"I know that," he said, reaching for her, but she shied away and pulled a file from her shoulder bag.

"This is a statement from my neighbor, the one who wrote it, admitting that it's a pack of lies. She signed it, Phoebe witnessed it, I notarized it."

He took the papers and leafed through them. "Holy crap, Lib, how did you pull this off?"

"It was a busy morning. I'll give you the details later. But do you think it will help?"

"It sure as hell can't hurt." This time when he reached for her, she took his hands and let him draw her close enough to nuzzle his cheek.

"I love you, Sam," she whispered. "I think maybe I never stopped. I want you to go in there and win this thing. I want you and Casey to come back to camp tonight. I want to sit down on the sofa with you and tell Casey a story, and I want to wash the dishes while you give him a bath and put him to sleep in his own bed. And then I want to have last night with you all over again."

He nodded into her palm, then grabbed it and pressed a kiss into it. "Me, too. All of it. Except tonight, I want a bed. I'm getting too old for air mattresses."

Her eyes closed and she breathed in deeply, as if something heavy had been lifted from her chest. When she smiled at him it was like seeing everything he felt for her shining back at him.

He pulled her close and kissed her at last, burying one hand in her hair while the other slid down her back, molding her to him, affirming for himself that this was real and she was actually here and she wasn't going to disappear.

He kissed her lips, then her cheek, then her forehead before coming back to her mouth. This time he didn't stop until he felt a sharp tug on his pants leg.

"Casey?" He blinked down at Libby, then at his son without letting her go. "What's up, bud?"

"Some."

"Some what?"

Casey raised his arms into the air. With a laugh, Sam caught him close and hoisted the squirming little body between him and Libby. Casey promptly wound his fingers through Libby's hair, let his head drop to Sam's shoulder, popped his thumb into his mouth and gave a wriggle of sheer delight.

Sam kissed the downy cheek resting on his shoulder. "Love you, bud."

Then he tilted his head to claim Libby's lips once more. Slowly this time. Lingering. Letting himself savor her touch and her taste and the rightness of her within his arms.

"In case you didn't figure it out," he whispered against her cheek, "I love you, too."

Libby inhaled, short and fast before launching herself upright and kissing him as best as was possible with a toddler in the middle.

They stood wrapped up in each other, a knot of grins and kisses and wiggles and whispers. But all too soon, Libby asked, "Is it almost time?"

The warmth he'd been basking in raced away. Though, he realized, not completely. There was a flicker of Libby-love deep inside him even when he pulled back.

It would stay. He knew that. What he felt for Libby, what she felt for him, was the real thing. With that inside him, he was ready to face down anything.

"Let's go." He took her hand in one of his, and Casey's in the other. "We have some formalities to get out of the way."

Libby laughed and snuggled against his side. "For once," she said, "I'm in as much of a hurry as you are."

He squeezed her tight. "Just one more thing." He turned so the three of them were facing Robin's grave. Libby made a small sound and reached to stroke Casey's arm.

"Say bye-bye, Casey," Sam whispered. "Blow Mommy a kiss."

And while his son said his farewells, Sam closed his eyes and offered one of his own.

Goodbye, Robin. And thanks—with everything I have.

CHAPTER TWENTY

BY THE TIME THEY GOT BACK to the hotel, Casey was long overdue for a nap. Brynn took one look at Sam's arm around Libby's waist and said that she would stay with Casey. Then she broke into a giant grin, pulled Libby into an even more giant hug and whispered, "It's about time that idiot brother of mine woke up and saw the light."

They were on Highway 3 out of Lunenburg, well on their way to Bridgewater and the courthouse, when Sam gave a little start at the wheel.

"You can't come in with me."

"Oh." She glanced down at her shorts and Overlook shirt. Just as well she hadn't bothered making time to change clothes. "That's right. Family court is closed, isn't it? I guess there will be a waiting room or someplace I can hang out."

"No. I mean, you can't come in the building. I don't want Sharon to see you."

"Because you don't want her to know you and I are…"

He slowed to make a turn, taking a second to glance her direction. "I kind of glossed over this the other night, but you do look like Robin. I don't want Sharon to see you and get freaked. Not today."

"It's that strong a resemblance?"

"No one would ever think you were twins. But the hair, the build—it's enough that it could send her for a loop. I can't do that to her."

He was about to face down the woman who was fighting

him for his own child, and he was worried about playing fair? "But what about you? She'll have her husband with her. You're going in there alone."

"You'll be waiting outside for me. That'll be enough."

She would have protested more, but when she asked herself how she would feel if their roles were reversed, she knew he was right. Having Sam beside her in a battle would strengthen her immeasurably, but just knowing he was nearby, rooting for her, could get her through almost anything.

She patted his arm. "I'll be wherever I can help the most. You just say the word."

He shot her a quick and grateful smile before focusing on the road once more. She thought he was simply concentrating on the directions until he said, very carefully, "If things don't go my way—"

"They will. They have to."

He drew a deep breath. "But just in case, I want you to know. If Sharon— If Casey— I'll have to give up the camp. Move down here. I can't be that far from him again."

"I know." She also knew what he wasn't saying. If he moved, the camp would revert back to Myra. This time, with her finances secured and her focus on her own new life, Myra would undoubtedly offer it to Libby. Everything she had once wanted.

No more.

"My offer still stands." She gripped his hand. "To go wherever."

Surprise mingled with joy in his face. "Are you sure? What about—"

"Nothing else matters, really. Nothing would be right without you and Casey. The camp, my house—they're not my home anymore." She squeezed his arm again. "You are. You and Casey."

He drove in silence for a second, his fingers tight on the wheel, staring straight ahead. Not long. Just long enough for the rules and fears from her past to form a giant lump in her throat.

A moment later he flicked his turn signal, hit the brake and steered the car into the turnoff for a park. She was still reeling from the sudden shift when he was out of his seat belt and reaching across the space between them, gathering her as close as her belt would allow.

"I love you," he whispered against her hair.

"Me, too. So very much." She buried her head in his chest and felt the lump in her throat slowly dissipate, replaced by warmth and happiness and the knowledge that she was finally exactly where she was meant to be. Then she pulled back enough to drop a fast kiss on his lips and push him toward the steering wheel.

"Over there and drive, Catalano. We have a court case to win."

SAM PULLED INTO a parking spot in the lot behind the courthouse and pried his fingers from the wheel. He took a deep breath and stared at the modern pink-and-cream building. Funny. He'd thought it would be…bigger. Older. More imposing. How could such a modest building hold the balance of the rest of his life?

Libby stirred in the seat beside him. "How can I help?"

"Be here."

"No question about that."

"Pray."

"Constantly."

He tore his gaze from the door to look at her. "God, I wish I could see the future."

She searched his face, then placed a hand on his cheek. One of the knots in his stomach slipped loose.

"I can see it."

"You can?"

"It's one of my many talents." Her words were light but certain enough to fill him with confidence. "I see you walking out of the door right there. Faster than either of us expected. You're running, maybe even jumping from that bottom step. You're probably going so fast that I'm worried you'll fall, but you're an athlete, so you manage just fine."

"I like that picture."

"Me, too."

He sat for a second, soaking up her strength, her faith in him, her love. She pulled him close and kissed him, long and hard, then pushed him away with a grin.

"Go." Her voice was thick and her eyes were too bright, but she was smiling. "The sooner you get in there, the sooner we can make that picture come true."

He nodded and fumbled for the handle. No sooner had he pushed the door open than she placed a hand on his arm.

"Wait. You need these." She shoved the folder at him. "And I brought you a good luck charm." She pressed something small and hard into his hand. He looked down and saw a tiny rock, smooth and oval, striped with a black band that snaked across the speckled gray surface.

"It's from camp," she said, almost shyly. "From that pile Casey keeps in the office. I thought, maybe, it would be a good thing to hold."

Unable to speak, he nodded, leaned over for another fast kiss and launched himself out of the car, hoping the momentum would carry him where his heart didn't want to go.

Live the goal.

The next few minutes passed in a blur of handshakes and low-pitched conversations with Joe, who was waiting for Sam as promised. Libby's documents were reviewed and pronounced excellent as they walked down the echoing halls to the waiting room. Joe made small talk. Sam nodded and grunted and kept his hand in his pocket, curled tight around the stone that was still warm from Libby's hand.

A door opened. A uniformed bailiff motioned them forward.

Sam squeezed the rock, sent up a swift prayer for strength and followed Joe into the hearing room.

He'd expected something more ornate. This room was simple and, again, smaller than he'd anticipated—a raised bench for the judge, a couple of tables near the front, a few rows of seats. Queen Elizabeth looked down serenely from her portrait on the wall. Sam found her picture oddly comforting as he seated himself beside Joe. The queen was a mother, a grandmother, a family woman. Surely she would want this court to do the right thing and keep his little boy with him.

Movement from the back of the room told him that Sharon had arrived. She walked between her husband, who nodded at Sam, and another man who he assumed was the lawyer. Sharon met his gaze for a second before quickly looking away. Sam took in the tight grip she had on her husband, the stark whiteness of her face, and even though he was still more scared than he had ever been in his life, another knot loosened a little. Sharon loved Casey. Maybe not as much as Sam did, but enough that she had mounted what almost everyone had considered a hopeless campaign to keep him. In a perverse way, that knowledge comforted Sam. No matter what happened with the judge, Casey would land with someone who loved him enough to fight for him. He would always be okay.

The judge entered. They rose. Sam forced his feet to stay put when they itched to flee.

As expected, Sharon's lawyer immediately raised the issue of the tabloid article, which Joe shot down just as fast. The judge examined Dani's statement and grunted, but gave no indication as to whether or not she was impacted by any of it.

Sharon's lawyer presented his case, emphasizing the huge role Sharon had played in Casey's life until Sam took him. Joe countered with DNA tests, proof of flights documenting Sam's many visits to Casey throughout his life, and the report from the social worker, which stated that Casey was happy, healthy and adjusting well to the changes in his life.

Sam held tight to the rock deep in his pocket, turning it over and over in his grasp and longing to do something, anything. This was his son they were discussing. To have to sit, silent and impotent while the legal eagles tried to out-talk each other, was the worst kind of torture. All he could do was rub his thumb over his good-luck charm and make himself replay Libby's words when she assured him that anyone who would turn his life inside out the way Sam had, was, without a doubt, the best parent for Casey. Something about hearing her say it, even just in memory, made it impossible for him to believe anything else.

Then, abruptly, it was over.

The judge rose, nodded as Sam and the others pushed to their feet, and disappeared into her chambers. Sam looked across at Sharon and saw what he was pretty sure was a mirror of everything he was feeling, all there in her face. For a moment he held her gaze. Not out of anger, or resentment, but because, as twisted as it seemed, she was the only one in the room who knew.

And in that moment, he promised himself that if— *when*—the judge ruled in his favor, he would block off time each and every month to bring Casey to Nova Scotia. Because anyone who loved his son the way Sharon so obviously did deserved no less.

He lowered himself gratefully into the solid support of the chair, then let his head drop into his hands and prayed.

He was on what felt like his twenty-fifth hour on the rack when the judge returned. Joe clapped him on the shoulder as they rose. Sam had the wild thought that if he hadn't spent decades pushing his body to perform through whatever he threw at it, there would be no way his legs could hold him now.

Everything he had ever been, everything he had ever done, was all for this moment.

"I've reached my decision," the judge announced, and Sam reached into his pocket and gripped Libby's stone with everything he had.

LIBBY WALKED BACK AND FORTH in front of the courthouse and looked at her watch yet again.

She had lasted in the tiny rental car for all of two minutes before she admitted she was going to go bonkers if she stayed there, so she scribbled a note for Sam and went to the back of the lot. Far enough away that it was unlikely Sharon would spot her by mistake, close enough that she would see Sam the moment he came out the door.

And there, she paced.

Her wait was interrupted twice. First came a call from Phoebe letting her know that everything was fine, the Tour de Camp had gone off without a problem and Dani had actually been amazingly helpful. Oh, and everyone on staff was waiting for either Sam or Libby to call and report that the hearing was over and Sam had won.

Libby could scarcely speak when she hung up. With so many people pulling for Sam, he had to win. Didn't he?

Her second call was from a number she didn't recognize. She made sure she blew her nose before taking it, and was immediately glad she'd given herself that moment.

It wouldn't have sounded very encouraging if she'd been talking through tears when she received the offer of the teaching job.

She was still stuck in a half joyous, half frantic daze when the courthouse door flew open and Sam barreled down the steps, taking them two at a time, exactly as she'd pictured.

"We did it!" he shouted from halfway across the lot, then raced the rest of the way to catch her up against him. She jumped up and down as best as she could while he held her so close she could scarcely breathe.

"Tell me," she said when she finally stopped laughing and kissing him.

"It was hell." He pushed her hair back from her eyes. "We got through all the presentations, then the judge disappeared for a while and I basically died a thousand deaths, waiting. Then she came back and said Sharon's lawyer had no grounds for trying to take Casey from me. She said she understood Sharon was hurting, and she was sorry, but doing this wouldn't bring Robin back and the best thing now would be to make sure Sharon built a good relationship with me so Casey wouldn't feel like he had to choose sides. And then she said she didn't need any time to think this over, it was clearly in my favor, and Casey is, was and always will be mine."

"I'm so, so happy," she said, and buried her face into his shoulder.

"Wanna be even happier?" He kissed her lightly.

Warmth poured through her. "I don't think that's possible in public."

His chuckle sent heat straight down her spine to where it mattered most. "Maybe not," he agreed. "But if we hustle, we can get the last flight back to Ottawa and be back home tonight."

"You're right. Let me text Brynn and Phoebe with the good news and— Oh!" She stopped in the middle of the sidewalk. "I got the job!"

"No way. Really?" He swept her into another hug. "Damn, Lib, if life with you is always this exciting, I'm gonna need a pacemaker!"

She laughed, free and easy, until he cupped her chin.

"Are you sure?" he asked. "About the job, I mean. Because you know—"

"I know. And I… Yeah. I'm sure. I need—no, I want to do this. I want to try something new and test myself. I want to be in a classroom. At least for a while."

"And maybe would you like to come home to me and Casey every night?"

She wound her arms around his neck and pressed her forehead to his, blocking out the street and the court and everything but the sound and the smell and the feel of Sam. "That," she whispered just before she kissed him, "is what I want more than anything else."

ON A BRILLIANTLY BLUE-SKY Labor Day Saturday, Libby walked down the path to the waterfront, inspected the pavilion and the crowd gathered around it, and heaved a sigh of exhausted relief.

"You nervous?" asked Phoebe, almost unrecognizable in a kicky fuchsia sheath that was a perfect match to the beads in her hair.

"Not in the least. I took care of all the details myself. It's going to go perfectly."

Phoebe rolled her eyes. "Of course. How could I think anything else? I mean, you got Cosmo into a suit. Anyone who can do that wouldn't have any trouble pulling a major celebration together in two weeks."

"It was a bit insane. I can't argue that one." Libby waved

her handful of daisies to indicate that Phoebe should precede her to the pavilion. "But Sam and I agreed this was the perfect time. And since it worked out for Myra and Cosmo, too, well—it was worth a few late nights."

"Oh, is *that* what's been keeping you awake lately?" Phoebe waved at Alex, who looked ready to burst out of the tux he had donned to perform with his string quartet. He winked at Phoebe over the top of his viola. "Silly me. I thought there might have been other reasons you've been walking around with bags under your eyes and a grin that could light up half the continent."

Libby was still searching for the appropriate comeback when Myra let go of Cosmo's hand to meet them at the edge of the pavilion.

"Everything is beautiful, dear," Myra whispered. "Especially you."

"You, too." Libby smoothed the front of her full-skirted dress, brushing over the beading at the waist, then pinned the daisy corsage she'd been carrying to the front of Myra's crisp white jacket. "Are you ready?"

"Anytime, dear."

Libby caught Brynn's eye and pointed to the podium that had been set up in front of the massive stone fireplace. Brynn got the message, took Casey's hand and moved toward a group at the far side of the pavilion, where Sam was undoubtedly deep in a discussion of either hockey or *Sesame Street.* Confident that Brynn would get Sam where he needed to be, Libby scanned the building—the tables of refreshments, the flowers in every corner, the flags on their poles just outside the structure—before turning back to Phoebe with a smile.

"Showtime."

They moved to their places near the podium. Myra and Cosmo followed, Cosmo muttering something about monkey suits and damned fools beneath his breath. Libby grinned and took her seat as the assembled parents, civic leaders and local media began to quiet. She caught a glimpse of Dani scurrying for a better position and smothered a giggle at the way she slipped through the crowd. Dani had promised to give up her tabloid ways and was now aiming for a job in public relations. Libby wasn't sure who she should wish luck upon—Dani, or any future potential employers.

Thoughts of Dani were knocked from her head as Sam vaulted the step to the podium. He flashed a wicked grin at her and her insides went a little squishy at the heated promise in that swift look.

Phoebe let out a soft whistle. "Damn, if I wasn't already attached…"

Libby shushed her as Sam took his place at the podium, looking tall, dark and ever so gallant in his suit and the green-striped tie that had brought him back to her—the tie that matched the green in the emeralds flanking the diamond ring he had placed on her finger just the night before.

He spoke into the microphone. "Thank you, one and all, for joining us at this dedication of the Myra MacLean Pavilion."

Libby's heart filled to overflowing as she took in the beloved faces around her. Myra and Cosmo. Phoebe and Alex. Brynn and a squirming Casey. And Sam, always Sam, her one-and-only Sam.

Her family. Her future.

Her forever home.

* * * * *

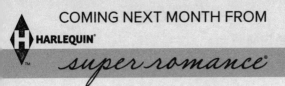

Where It May Lead
By **Janice Kay Johnson**

Being the police liaison for the local college's alumni event should be straightforward for Detective John "Troy" Troyer. That is, until he meets Madison Laclaire! Read on for an exciting excerpt from the upcoming book *WHERE IT MAY LEAD* by Janice Kay Johnson.

"I doubt we'll have any problems this weekend," Troy said, glancing through the schedule. "I think my role is going to be an exciting one. I'll hang around. Maybe even play golf."

Madison tilted her head in interest—and he liked being the object of her interest. "Do you play golf?"

"Poorly," he admitted. "I've got a hell of a slice. But from a security standpoint, having me lurking in the rough probably isn't a bad plan."

Her laugh was contagious…and unintentionally erotic. "I'll look for you there."

"You'll be playing?"

"No. Actually, I'll be frantically arranging the luncheon." She rose gracefully to her feet. "Thank you for coming, Detective Troyer."

"Troy." He stood, too.

A smart man would bide his time, not make any move until after the weekend. He didn't want her to be uncomfortable with him when they had to work together. Troy had always thought of himself as a pretty smart guy.

Turned out he wasn't as smart as he'd thought.

"So. I was wondering." *Slick. Really slick.* "Any chance I could talk you into having dinner with me?"

Madison blinked. "Tonight?"

Tonight, tomorrow night, every night. Startled by the thought, he cleared his throat. "Tonight would be good. Or tomorrow." He hesitated. "Unless you're too busy."

Her expression melted into a sunbeam of a smile. "I would love to have dinner with you tonight, Troy."

Down, boy, he cautioned himself when his enthusiastic response threatened to overflow.

They agreed on a restaurant, then he left before he did something stupid. Like kiss her.

He grinned as he exited her office. She'd said yes. He *felt* young. Half-aroused, too.

He would definitely be kissing her tonight.

**The weekend may hold even more surprises
for Madison and Troy. Find out what happens in
WHERE IT MAY LEAD by Janice Kay Johnson,
available May 2013 from Harlequin® Superromance®.**

REQUEST YOUR FREE BOOKS!
2 FREE NOVELS PLUS 2 FREE GIFTS!

HARLEQUIN
super romance

Exciting, emotional, unexpected!

YES! Please send me 2 FREE Harlequin® Superromance® novels and my 2 FREE gifts (gifts are worth about $10). After receiving them, if I don't wish to receive any more books, I can return the shipping statement marked "cancel." If I don't cancel, I will receive 6 brand-new novels every month and be billed just $4.69 per book in the U.S. or $5.24 per book in Canada. That's a savings of at least 15% off the cover price! It's quite a bargain! Shipping and handling is just 50¢ per book in the U.S. and 75¢ per book in Canada.* I understand that accepting the 2 free books and gifts places me under no obligation to buy anything. I can always return a shipment and cancel at any time. Even if I never buy another book, the two free books and gifts are mine to keep forever.

135/336 HDN FVS7

Name	(PLEASE PRINT)
Address	Apt. #
City	State/Prov.	Zip/Postal Code

Signature (if under 18, a parent or guardian must sign)

Mail to the Harlequin® Reader Service:
IN U.S.A.: P.O. Box 1867, Buffalo, NY 14240-1867
IN CANADA: P.O. Box 609, Fort Erie, Ontario L2A 5X3

**Are you a current subscriber to Harlequin Superromance books
and want to receive the larger-print edition?
Call 1-800-873-8635 or visit www.ReaderService.com.**

* Terms and prices subject to change without notice. Prices do not include applicable taxes. Sales tax applicable in N.Y. Canadian residents will be charged applicable taxes. Offer not valid in Quebec. This offer is limited to one order per household. Not valid for current subscribers to Harlequin Superromance books. All orders subject to credit approval. Credit or debit balances in a customer's account(s) may be offset by any other outstanding balance owed by or to the customer. Please allow 4 to 6 weeks for delivery. Offer available while quantities last.

Your Privacy—The Harlequin® Reader Service is committed to protecting your privacy. Our Privacy Policy is available online at www.ReaderService.com or upon request from the Harlequin Reader Service.

We make a portion of our mailing list available to reputable third parties that offer products we believe may interest you. If you prefer that we not exchange your name with third parties, or if you wish to clarify or modify your communication preferences, please visit us at www.ReaderService.com/consumerschoice or write to us at Harlequin Reader Service Preference Service, P.O. Box 9062, Buffalo, NY 14269. Include your complete name and address.

HSR13